Twisted Li(v)es

Arnie Arnstein

First published in 2020

© 2020 Arnie Arnstein

The right of Arnie Arnstein to be identified as the author of the work has been asserted by him in accordance with the Copyright, Designs and Patents Act 1988.

About the author

Dr Arnie Arnstein enjoyed a varied medical career, working as a British anaesthetist at home and abroad. Civilian contact with the UK defence services and aeromedical transfer experience inspired this story.

Acknowledgements

I would like to thank my editor Mary-Jay Spraut and everyone at Heliprint for their support and endless patience, without whom my attempt at literary excellence would have been unintelligible.

By the same author

Alternative Li(v)es
Published 2018

Available as a paperback or ebook
through Kindle Direct Publishing at
https://amzn.to/2TdfNz7

Author's note: This is a work of fiction. Any resemblance of any characters to anyone living or dead is purely coincidental. Please accept my apologies.

Cover illustration by Tom Arnstein

For those whose freedoms are suppressed

Chapter 1

'To dare is to lose one's footing momentarily.
To not dare is to lose oneself.'
Søren Kierkegaard

If my mobile had tumbled into the toilet rather than just beside it, life might have taken a very different course. But it didn't. Dressed in theatre greens and taking a piss, the ringtone of an incoming call startled me mid-flow. Fumbling to retrieve the device from my pocket, I swore as it slipped from my grasp and watched helplessly as it caught the edge of the bowl before hitting the floor. For a few moments the phone lay on the lino broadcasting a lament, falling silent as I scrabbled around the back of the loo to recover it. Screen cracked. I cursed again, but it still worked: the caller's number unfamiliar, definitely not from within the hospital. *Who would pester me at this hour? A cold caller? Surely not. Every bloody boiler salesman would be asleep - lucky bastards.*

3am Sunday morning, slaving away in a major London hospital's Accident and Emergency department. Knackered and yet to see my bed. Clubs and pubs disgorging their youthful clientele onto the grey streets; sozzled, staggering and vulnerable. Doors bolted behind them. Ours wedged wide open for all, as the drunken hordes, victims of accidents or violence, hobble in or are dragged by their friends into the gleaming sanctuary of the unit.

1

A garage for humans; a place to diagnose and patch-up. But sometimes, depressingly, they are beyond repair. The effects of alcohol and drugs instigating hilarity, bizarre behaviour and transient ecstasy too often ending in a fight or collapse. The evening's joy cut short by the thrust of a knife or the aspiration of putrid vomit where deep in the lungs its acid burns the delicate tissues, drowning the victim despite the desperate efforts of terrified friends and passers-by to save the limp blue corpse.

Here I am, thirty-three years old and already jaded. Sympathy limited, empathy tanks regularly run on red; any reserve earmarked for the worthy. Military life in Camp Bastion had taken its toll: The endless stream of casualties – theirs and ours. You never forget the innocent Afghani child who bleeds to death, a victim of a concealed IED intended for us. And now I am required to utter "there, there" to London's legless revelling in a weekend binge. The public demand care with smiles while deep inside you wonder whether your actions are worthwhile. I washed my hands, splashed cold water on my face and wiped down my phone. Just as I opened the cubicle, it rang again. Same number. I tapped the screen.

'Dr Wright? Dr Paul Wright?'

'Yes. Who is this?' I asked, yawning, fighting the urge to end the call and close my eyes.

The man who spoke sounded official, and suddenly I felt a tinge of anxiety. There were issues in my life to be resolved which I had hidden from my employer. This job, any job, was helping me back onto the straight and narrow. *Had they discovered my past and all my efforts were about to come to nothing?* But it was three in the morning. Surely even the General

2

Medical Council's great and good slept. And debt collectors, experience had shown, chose to ruin someone's day early on a Sunday just as they tucked into breakfast, and usually in person.

'Dr Wright. Let me apologise for the intrusion at this ungodly hour. Your contact details were provided by the locum agency. You see, I understand you requested to be notified immediately of any highly paid work, and they advised us your skill-set fits exactly with my organisation's requirements. Our remuneration is exceptional, which I'm sure would be most helpful.'

'And what is the name and purpose of your outfit?' I asked, annoyed the agency hadn't had the courtesy to inform me of a potential job, and that this man seemed aware of my desperate need for cash.

'I represent a medical assistance company. Our role is to help British subjects, and sometimes other nationals, who have fallen ill or been injured overseas. We ensure they receive appropriate care and arrange repatriation to the UK or another country by whatever means necessary; all paid for by the travel insurance industry or the government. As an experienced anaesthetist and emergency medicine doctor, coupled with an albeit "brief" military career, you are the ideal candidate to support our work.'

'I see. But why phone in the middle of the night? What did you say your name was?' My irritation was growing and something alarmed me about his familiarity with my past. I hadn't been completely open with the agency, omitting to tell them about my stint with the forces. A dishonourable discharge doesn't impress on any job application, but the caller clearly knew more than I had revealed.

3

'Oh, apologies on both fronts. My name's Sandy Driffield, senior director. Currently we are caring for a patient stuck in East Africa; Kenya, to be precise. Although the medical facilities are adequate, it's not the best place to fall ill, and he is very poorly. Most likely malaria, or at least that's the local doctor's opinion. Nevertheless, experience tells us to be wary of any reports that originate from that part of the world. While it sounds as if his current condition is stable, he is sick and needs to be brought home as soon as possible.'

I interrupted. 'But why me? Surely you employ other staff. I'm booked to work another two shifts here; tomorrow and Tuesday — I can't let this hospital down. And to be frank, I'm dog-tired. The NHS never fails to deliver on that front.'

'Of course, understood. Please think it over though when you've a moment. You have my number. As I say, the pay is very good but if the offer is of no interest, sorry to have disturbed you. I hope the rest of the night passes peacefully. London never sleeps, does it?' He rang off.

I arrived back in the department hoping to grab a quick coffee before suturing the next arm, leg or face but was met by the sister in charge, clearly agitated.

'Where have you been?' she demanded. 'I've been looking for you everywhere. We've a major coming in. The paramedics say it's a young woman hit by a night-bus and trapped underneath for at least ten minutes. Might well be a DOA, but let's prepare, anyway. Why they aren't taking her elsewhere, I don't know. They've been told our trauma team is already tied up in theatre. The consultant is on his way from home but won't arrive before the casualty, so we need you.'

4

I followed her through to the Resus room. Staff were definitely thin on the ground. Sister, one nurse and a junior medic looking like a startled rabbit, standing wide-eyed, nose twitching, gloved hands clasped tightly in front.

Dressed in a clean apron and fresh gloves, I took charge. 'OK. Listen. I'll be the team leader. When the casualty arrives, resuscitation first and then we'll carry out a primary survey. It's likely she'll have suffered significant blunt trauma; internal injuries as well as fractured limbs and a possible head injury. And don't forget her spine. When she's moved, work together, alright? If we can save her, it would be disastrous if she was left paralysed. And the paramedics mustn't leave until we've got the whole story. Understood so far?' I glanced around. Everyone nodded as the sound of a siren approached.

'Graham.' I said, turning to the frightened junior. 'Place a couple of big lines. Don't bother with the peripheral veins, they'll be empty. Try at the elbows and once I've secured her airway, stick a central line in her neck, OK?'

'Dr Wright,' he mumbled, 'I have never done one in this situation before. Not sure I'll manage it.'

'Bugger,' I thought. 'A real new boy. I suppose we were all there once.'

'Hey, don't worry. I'll supervise and take over if necessary. At worst, there's always the external jugular if it's still visible. Anyway, call me Paul.' I said with a smile, in an attempt to reassure him. There were plenty of reasons why my hair had already turned grey. Graham's might soon go the same way.

'Sister and staff; you two, cut off her clothes, then make sure the Level One infuser is switched on and warm. Cold fluids won't do much good. She needs enough fluid to keep her brain

5

alive but don't overdo it. If we push her blood pressure up too high, everything that's pumped in will simply leak out and her clotting fail. And check the O negative blood is in date. Finally Sister, is the trauma team on its way?'

She shook her head. 'I've phoned theatres but doubt anyone is free to join us before the ambulance arrives.'

'Well, we'll just have to do our best then, won't we?'

Memories of Camp Bastion flooded back. Too many bloodied casualties. A blur of death and destruction. Sweat started to pool inside my gloves as I struggled to focus on the here and now, desperately pushing the gory images from my mind. *Forget the past, what is done is done. This next patient needs me.*

The clatter of a trolley being rushed into the department dragged me back to the present. The black plastic flip-flap doors banged open, and the paramedics wheeled in the young victim. She lay comatose, strapped on a scoop stretcher, her neck and head wedged between foam blocks secured with Velcro. The crew lifted her slender body across to the hospital trolley. While one paramedic continued to force air into her lungs with a facemask, the other told her story.

'Hit by a number 73 bus about half an hour ago. Speed between twenty and thirty. Driver braked but casualty trapped under a front wheel for more than ten minutes. Fire service released her. Unconscious throughout. I'm sorry; we couldn't manage intravenous access, but she had a faint pulse palpable at the groin as we left the scene. Apparently the idiot had been flitting back and forth across the road like a butterfly, her pissed female friends giggling and cajoling as they played chicken. But

6

no-one was laughing when we arrived – the girls were sat on the kerb howling hysterically.'

The team released her arms from the bindings and set to work, cutting her party dress from her limp body before attaching monitors. Blood oozed from her mouth and nose making the facemask slip, her once blond hair matted, patchily dyed red. I took over from the paramedic working at the top.

'Thanks guys. Do we have a name?'

'Yes. Samantha Greenwood, eighteen. It was her birthday night out.'

'Greenwood, how innocent and apt,' I thought as I removed the mask and picked up a laryngoscope. With this in her throat, I sucked out vomit from her airway before inserting a tube into her windpipe and connecting it to oxygen. Her skin, naturally pale, was now snow-white, almost translucent as her blood and life seeped away.

'Graham. Any luck? Found a vein?' I asked, more in hope than expectation.

'Think so. A size sixteen in her upper arm. Fluids started,' he replied gleefully.

'Well done. Now Sister, can you feel a pulse, any pulse?' A quick review of the monitors showed it was unlikely. The numbers were bad: rapid regular heartbeat, blood pressure too low and the pulse oximeter which should have shown her oxygen levels failed to register. We were losing her. The image of the young Afghani boy missing his legs abruptly overwhelmed me and I froze. Someone was calling. I heard the team at Camp Bastion barking orders in the desperate fight to save the child. The shouting grew louder...

'Dr Wright, Dr Wright. I think she's arrested. Are you alright?' Sister shook my arm. In an instant I was transported back from one hell to another.

'Yes, yes, I'm fine. Nurse, connect the pressure infuser. We must give her blood. Graham start cardiac compressions.' I glanced down at her abdomen, the skin grazed and raw. Moment by moment, it swelled as if she was pregnant; nine months compressed into a few minutes. The problem was obvious.

'Guys, she's bleeding out from within. Could be her spleen or liver. We need the trauma team now or... Sister, prepare an abdo set. We have to open her up and stem the blood loss. It's her only chance.'

'Dr Wright. I don't wish to be rude, but can you do that? I mean, have you done it before? Normally, the vascular or general surgeons would operate.'

'Too many times, Sister, far too many. Get that pack and a spot lamp,' I replied with a grimace. I turned to the staff nurse. 'Keep squeezing that bag while I put on a fresh gown and gloves. You are her lungs. And somebody pour a bucket-load of antiseptic over her tummy. It's not going to be a sterile field, but it's all we can do.'

For a moment my scalpel hovered over her exposed abdomen, my attention caught by the sparkle of a green navel piercing, and then I sliced her skin from sternum to pelvis, working on autopilot. Deeper and deeper I carved through layer after layer of tissue until I was able to insert a retractor with which I pulled apart the muscles of her abdominal wall. Blood welled up from inside.

'Suction, suction now,' I demanded, as I entered her abdomen. Clots spilled from the open cavity, raced into the suction bottle and spilt over onto the floor. I thrust my fingers deep inside, pushed aside tangles of gut and extracted handfuls of congealed blood. Her liver looked and felt intact, but the spleen was mashed.

'The biggest pack you've got, please. I'll hold it in place until the trauma team come. Keep the fluids going in, Sister. She must be losing a unit every few minutes.' I checked the monitors; her cardiac rhythm irregular. Was it interference from Graham's efforts at compressing her chest or her heart failing? Blood pressure unrecordable, the cuff on her arm inflating repeatedly, as the machine desperately searched for signs of life. 'Nurse, check her eyes. How are the pupils?'

She waved a pen-torch across the girl's face 'Dilated, not reacting, Dr Wright. Definitely fixed,' she said quietly.

'Damn it. We need help, or she's had it. Where are those bloody surgeons?'

Suddenly the monitor alarmed, a piercing continuous monotone. Blood pressure zero, no heart activity, battle lost. Another young life snuffed out by momentary madness. My stomach tightened and the sweat from my forehead and nose dripped onto the floor where it mixed with the pools of sticky blood smeared by our boots. No-one wants to give in, but I knew it was pointless continuing. Enough was enough. I relaxed my grip on the swab. 'Sorry team. I think she's gone. I propose we stop. Anybody object?' The nurses nodded in agreement but Graham, his face taut, continued to compress the poor girl's chest, her pale breasts rising and falling in time with his efforts.

I withdrew my bloodied hands from inside her body and gently pulled his arms away. 'It's OK Graham, you did your best. We can't do anymore.'

9

The distraught young doctor kicked the trolley. 'Stupid bitch,' he muttered. 'What a fucking awful end to a birthday.'

'We've all done crazy things,' I said. 'But sometimes the cards don't fall in your favour. I'll see if anyone who knows her has arrived in the department. There's no choice but to tell them although, as ever, it's not a conversation I relish. Do your best to make her look decent but remember to leave our kit in place; it's definitely a coroner's case. After that, I could murder a cup of tea. Bet you all could too.'

I peeled off my gloves and gown then dropped them on top of the dead girl's ripped clothes, already stuffed into the orange waste-bag lying at her feet. At the Resus bay door, I slipped off my blood-spattered boots and padded out into the corridor in my socks. The department seemed quiet and peaceful, almost serene. In reception, the waiting area was virtually empty. A filthy bearded drunk lay along three chairs in the corner, snoring and grunting. In the middle of the room, two young women dressed in short skirts and high heels sat together holding hands, their heads bowed. As I padded over to them, they looked up and it was obvious both had been crying, their make-up streaked by tears. 'Are you Sam's friends?' I asked gently.

One of the two started sobbing again, and the other tried to comfort her by putting an arm around her shoulder. 'We're her sisters,' she whimpered. Suddenly I saw the likeness — three peas from a pod.

'I'm so sorry,' I said, clutching the little green jewel tightly in my hand. 'You had better come with me. I have something to tell you and it is not good news, I'm afraid.'

10

Both women started to wail, their cries echoing through the empty room, the sound almost matching the despair of the little boy's father in Afghanistan. Universal loss, but with causes poles apart. Tragedies so horrific they would always lay etched in my brain. I fought to control my emotions.

'Please follow me,' I said, beckoning to the distraught women.

Chapter 2

Forty-eight hours earlier.

Something bothered Gathii Kwambia about the two guests to whom he served dinner on the terrace that overlooked Shela beach on Lamu Island. As the Peponi Hotel's senior waiter, he had looked after many rich and famous visitors with most guests welcoming his and the other staff's discretion. It was, perhaps, the main reason why the secluded boutique hotel built up such a loyal clientele. Millionaires with secret affairs, carnal or financial, knew they could enjoy the first-class facilities undisturbed. The distraction presented by the excellent cuisine, fine wines, beautiful suites and manicured gardens, often a side-show to the primary purpose of their stay. So what was it that perturbed the waiter? Both gentlemen had stayed before to discuss business, usually in good humour and generous with their tips, sending their aides or bodyguards away to frequent the tourist bars. Reth Chebet, a slight younger African of athletic build, immaculately dressed in his kanzu and jacket, ostensibly from the Northern Territories. And Jeffrey Cheboi, the man with whom he shared the expensive imported vintage French Bordeaux? Quite different: middle-aged, overweight, chain-smoking, western style suit too tight, always sweating, with dyed hair and a scar from his upper lip to his nose that disrupted his smile. Both used Kenyan passports but Kwambia, who was himself a Turkana, suspected Chebet's was false and that Mr

Cheboi worked for the government. This, coupled with the obvious disagreement between them, made him uneasy.

Although the men dined in their own alcove, on this occasion their voices could be easily heard above the roar of the Indian Ocean as it crashed onto the distant reef. The waiter realised, with growing anxiety, that the exquisite gold watch being offered by Mr Chebet, which he surmised was a bribe, wasn't enough to satisfy the businessman's dining companion who was clearly threatening severe consequences if a larger offer wasn't forthcoming. He worried that the evolving dispute might disturb the honeymoon couple at the next table. But perhaps his concern was misplaced as the pretty black girl in the silk floral dress with her Pokot tribal scars and pink coral earrings gazing at her handsome husband appeared oblivious. Despite the commotion, the newlyweds appeared to be enjoying their only night at the hotel.

However, as a faithful employee, Kwambia was increasingly concerned the argument could end in violence, and this risked tarnishing the hotel's reputation. He decided it would be appropriate to calm the situation with the offer of another bottle of Bordeaux; on the house. But when he returned with it, open and set in ice as the climate demanded, both sets of diners had disappeared, their main courses untouched and the gentlemen's chairs upturned.

Gathii Kwambia would never know that by the time he had cleared the evening's tables and tasted the untouched wine, naturally for quality control reasons, the toxic vapour, abruptly released from the mosquito coil that had been burning on the table between the two men had, after inducing stupor, dispersed. While Mr Cheboi snored heavily in his room, his so-called business partner lay unconscious in the hold of a dhow as it plied its way through the waves to Mokowe; the port linking the mainland to Lamu. Ordinarily, a drugged and intoxicated person is vulnerable. Yet two people accompanied Mr Chebet, both qualified to prevent him from choking should he vomit and trained to supplement the initial sedative to sustain coma — the honeymooners had departed early.

Chapter 3

Even though it was almost summer, London's sky was overcast and a chilling drizzle penetrated as I walked the short distance home after that terrible night shift. The tube would have been quicker, but I needed the fresh air. I was shattered, and the vision of the cold, dusky corpse lying in Casualty tripped unwanted memories that would prevent sleep coming easily. Passing a row of shops, I paused outside a bookies. A few quid lost or maybe a few won, it would be a welcome distraction. Temptation lured me, and I struggled to resist the urge to enter and play the odds. This dank day, however, it was as if someone or something restrained me, forcing me to see sense. I hurried back to my bedsit, desperate for coffee.

While the kettle boiled, I checked my phone. There was a text from my mother and another one from Sandy Driffield, repeating his offer. I poured myself a mug of the strong black stuff and stared out of the window. Cold, grey London. What a contrast from the Middle East. Such diverse lives. Such varied cultures. But, I reminded myself, everyone bleeds the same way whoever they are; it's simply the cause that is so often different. I pictured the girl with blond hair lying naked on the trolley and the boy with shredded limbs, his partug stained and in tatters. Both innocent. Both dead. Both too young. A sense of despair crept up on me. Medicine was my chosen path and in the beginning, I had been full of optimism, brimming with altruism, but time and events had taken their toll. My hands began to shake, and hot coffee splashed over the brim, burning. As I bent down to wipe the floor, my mobile rang.

'Dr Wright?'

Instantly I recognised the voice and was tempted to cut the call. Instead, I said nothing and waited. It continued, threatening.

'You need to pay. You know that. We've been very patient up to now. Perhaps too kind. I appreciate no-one plans to gamble away all they have, but debts are debts and must be settled, with interest. You, in particular, are a responsible member of society. As a doctor, surely you can access some cash. Let me reiterate; my clients are becoming impatient. It pains me to say this, and it sounds like a cliché, but believe you me, we have ways of making you pay. This is my final warning. I will allow you two days to find the money or you can expect a visit.'

I tapped the cracked screen, and the lecture ended. 'Bastards,' I murmured between sips of coffee. 'Let me sleep and when I wake, perhaps I'll have to call Sandy Driffield.' Depressed, I sank into the only chair in the room, feeling the springs poke through the grubby velour, and looked around the cramped bedsit. Tatty furniture, clothes scattered across the floor hiding a thread-bare carpet, boxes piled up against the faded chipped painted wall. *There had to be more to life than this. At least flying again would get me out of this place and might, just might, solve my other problem.*

Chapter 4

Sandy Driffield didn't sound surprised. 'I expected you to call Dr Wright. You see, in my humble opinion, your aeromedical evacuation experience is wasted in the NHS.'

'Is that so?'

'Yes. A man of your calibre should do so much better; that is self-evident from your CV. Even if there have been hiccups along the way; we're all allowed to trip up occasionally. When would it be convenient to meet so that I can explain our organisation to you?'

He seemed assertive but friendly and enthusiastic; his tone warmer than before though for some reason I found his words disconcerting. Mr Driffield, whoever he was, clearly knew more about me than my CV revealed. It seemed he had delved deep into my past, but why bother to dig so deep when all he wanted was someone to escort an ill patient across continents? Yes, it required specialist skills, but any doctor who had been involved in transporting wounded soldiers back home could do it. In that respect I was a rare bird, though not unique. However, he was right: toiling in the Capital's hospitals, day and night, was grinding me down and despite my best efforts I couldn't see how my debts were ever to be repaid. Was this an opportunity to change direction and turn my life around?

'Well, I'm due back on duty this evening at eight. Any chance of getting together before then?' I asked.

'Of course. As I've said, there is some urgency in extracting our patient from Kenya. The locum agency has essentially carried out all necessary checks, so I simply need to show you our kit and systems, and I want you to meet our team. We're based in Croydon, top tier of a tower block just off the main London to Brighton road. I'll text you the address. When you arrive, look for IMS Limited on the entry phone and I'll come down to collect you. It's two-thirty now. Shall we aim for five? That should give you time to get back for work.'

'OK. I'll manage that. Perfect. Oh, what does IMS stand for?'

'Nothing clever. International Medical Services. States the obvious.'

After a shave and shower, I searched for clean clothes amongst the piles scattered across the room, and with relief found a new shirt still wrapped in cellophane, ideal for the interview. In service accommodation, I would have been reprimanded long ago for living in such a tip but my civvy life had become chaotic and I was paying the penalty. As I dressed, I surveyed the mess and determined the moment had come to sort myself out. I grabbed my coat. 'Sandy Driffield, please be my lucky break,' I thought, and headed out.

I arrived in good time. The concrete tower, set back one street from the main road, was grey, anonymous and ugly, the building's top floor immersed in low cloud. A monument to 1970s architecture that no doubt would soon be listed for preservation. Being the weekend, the small surrounding pedestrianised plaza was almost empty. Youths skateboarded, crashing along ledges and across the loose cracked paving while a lone council worker chased litter with his broom. Otherwise, in the damp dusk, it looked forlorn and dead. I walked up to the entrance. At the top of a list of residents, a discreet plastic plaque advertised the presence of IMS. I pressed the buzzer.

'Hello,' said a crackly voice. 'Can I help you?'

'Dr Wright for Mr Driffield, please.'

'Ah, Dr Wright, I'll tell him you've arrived. Please wait, he'll be down shortly.'

I stood patiently watching the opaque glazed door, waiting for the shadow to appear behind it that might herald a new start. A few minutes passed before the door opened. A slight, tanned, balding man, and to my astonishment, wearing shorts held out his hand.

'Welcome Dr Wright,' he said, beaming. 'Delighted you decided to come.' He shook my hand, his grip surprisingly vigorous, and I followed him inside. 'Sorry to have kept you. The entry-phone is broken, as is the lift I'm afraid; we'll have to take the stairs.'

As we ascended the bare fire escape, I guessed Sandy Driffield to be in his late forties. But, despite his bandy legs, he bounded up two steps at a time, chatting without becoming breathless as we climbed. It was a struggle to keep pace, so I was grateful he didn't ask questions.

'So you'll be interested to learn a little about IMS. We were established a few years ago with a small team based here; admin personnel, linguists and travel specialists. Then there's a pool of experienced doctors and nurses we can call upon to evaluate cases and core staff who repatriate our clients or should I say patients. Most have a background in intensive care or

19

emergency medicine. It is moderately busy at the moment, and we have one or two challenging situations. Hence my call to you. Generally, we find medics with past military service to be particularly suited to our work.'

'Are all your usual staff unavailable?' I asked.

'Yes, precisely. People come and go. And we've lost an experienced team member recently.'

'Lost?'

'He no longer works for IMS. As you will be aware aeromedical transfers are arduous. Antisocial hours, time zone changes, a challenging environment in which to work and little notice. It's all disruptive and tiring. Not good for family life. Though that shouldn't bother you too much, should it?'

It was a rhetorical question. Tina had left less than a year ago, unable to tolerate my gambling any longer. Naturally I had been upset, but understood her misgivings. I had fouled up, and she had lost faith in me. Too many false promises. But how did Sandy Driffield know?

At last we reached the top floor. Although I was out of breath, he had barely broken sweat. He turned to me, still smiling.

'Excellent exercise, this stair climbing. Saves going to the gym. Never understood the desire to be a human hamster. Normal life can be so monotonous, a miserable treadmill. That's why I stepped off it years ago. Work should be enjoyable and adventurous, ideally more like play, don't you think?'

I didn't reply but thought back to my time in the RAF medical branch. Without doubt there had been lots of laughs, but much of the frivolity was based on black humour; the serious side had been grim. War guaranteed that. Too many service men and

20

women left to fight their demons in their own way when the physical battle's over. Drugs, alcohol, or in my case, gambling, taking their toll.

Sandy Driffield slotted a plastic pass into a box fixed to the wall and keyed in a code. The anonymous steel door to the offices of IMS clicked open.

'After you, Dr Wright. I'll introduce you to our duty ops-coordinator first and after we've had a chat, she'll take you on a tour of our facilities.'

In what appeared to be the reception area within an open plan office, a young pretty woman wearing cat's eye spectacles sat at a desk tapping on a keyboard. She looked up as we approached.

'Patricia, this is Doctor Paul Wright. Perhaps you could show him around once I've outlined our business.'

'Hi,' she said, smiling, and flicked her dark hair from her forehead. 'Welcome. Certainly, Sandy. Just say when you're ready.'

The room wasn't busy: a few people sat at desks typing or making notes in paper files while others, wearing headphones, chatted to far-off places; the sound of their conversations deadened by thick carpet. On one wall, a line of clocks gave the time in various prestigious capitals, the remaining adorned with large whiteboards that detailed ongoing cases, coded with tasks to be done. Sandy guided me to a coffee machine.

'Double espresso?' he asked. 'That's how you like it, isn't it?'

I nodded, surprised. *How did he know that?* Another tiny part of my persona exposed.

He handed me a mug and pressed buttons again for his own choice.

'We survive on this stuff here; it's our lifeblood. If this machine fails, Trish has to make a panic call to the service company, otherwise the whole organisation risks collapse.' He laughed. 'Everyone has at least one addiction, don't they? Some less harmful than others.' He raised his drink, took a sip and eyed me knowingly. 'OK. Let's go to my office. On a clear day, there's a magnificent view of South London to enjoy from there, but I suspect we're out of luck this afternoon.' He opened a solid door and ushered me into a modest space furnished with a basic desk and chair, the desktop computer positioned to enjoy the picture window. There were two further functional armchairs casually placed either side of a low glass table. He indicated for me to sit.

'We can talk here without being disturbed. Let me tell you what we do and I'm sure you'll have questions.' He took another mouthful from his mug and gently laid it down. 'You're acquainted, of course, with military aeromedical transport: Primary retrieval from the battlefield to a forward first aid post or if necessary directly to a major field hospital. And once the casualty's stabilised, he or she is flown home to Blighty or sometimes an intermediate facility in an Allied country.'

I sat impassively. Mr Driffield didn't need to explain; I had done two tours doing just that.

'IMS is the civilian equivalent of the secondary phase. We're a modest outfit but pride ourselves on our specialist skills and past successes. We operate on behalf of clients who are mostly insurance companies but occasionally private concerns or government departments. Once we receive a call that someone somewhere in the world has fallen ill or been injured, we do

22

everything to ensure the patient receives good care. Our team liaises with agents overseas, foreign clinics, hospitals and medical staff, gathering information. We need to be satisfied that our patients are safe and their treatment is appropriate. Any doubt demands further action. Maybe send a person, like yourself, to verify or arrange an urgent repatriation by whatever means; usually by air.'

'Do you have your own aircraft?' I asked.

Sandy laughed. 'As I said, we're a low key participant but even the bigger players can't afford to run their own planes. They would lie idle too often. No, we lease what is required when needed at the best price we can negotiate. It's a competitive market.'

'Typically what aircraft types do you use?'

'Whatever's necessary to achieve our goal: Range, capacity and country of registration. Not every machine is welcome everywhere. And when possible, we fly on scheduled services — much more room and toilets! Many of the smaller air-ambulances lack the most basic facilities. It's the military equivalent of a C17 compared to a Chinook.'

He was right. Managing a casualty on the floor of a helicopter, even a large one, had been a constant challenge. Noise, dust, rotor vibration and a tilting platform; the pilot flying low-level, dodging obstacles and incoming fire as he raced to escape the frontline back to a place of relative safety. A secondary transfer from Cyprus to Brize Norton by long range fixed-wing transport was always a picnic in comparison.

'You must have had many stimulating moments during your military career, Doctor Wright?'

It was more of an understatement than a question. I looked at him, trying to figure out who he really was and how he had discovered so much about my past. It was perturbing; he had done his homework, but I hoped he hadn't delved too far. I shifted uneasily in my seat.

'It was frequently an interesting and rewarding experience,' I replied, unwilling to admit the utter terror I had so often experienced. 'Of course, there were times I would prefer to forget. You see so many terrible things. It's hard to imagine what human beings are capable of doing to each other.' I wasn't going to admit to suffering from flashbacks or reveal my coping mechanism. 'But that's enough about me. Tell me about the patient you want rescued.'

'Yes, of course. An unusual case. An African employed by a multi-national company as a senior security manager based in the north of the country at a place called Eldoret. They run a major mining operation there which has suffered from terrorist incursions from Somalia. There have been several killings over recent years and terrified workers were leaving the organisation in droves: the mine almost brought to a standstill. Our Mr Mbuto's role was to stop the rot, but unfortunately he fell ill after taking leave at the coast. Apparently multi-resistant strains of malaria plague Lamu and its environs. The poor man has deteriorated, and the firm wants to help him the best they can so they approached us. It's a private job.'

'Sounds straightforward though surely the Kenyans have adequate facilities in Nairobi with medics who are very proficient in the treatment of severe malaria?'

Sandy Driffield swirled the dregs of his coffee in his mug before finishing it.

'Ah. Perhaps not quite so simple as we had first hoped. You see our Mr Mbuto, who has an intriguing background, was taken on because of his reputation as a bit of a tough guy. It appears the Kenyan authorities would be interested in asking him a few questions, although our client is adamant that they should not be afforded the opportunity. Hence he hasn't been moved to Nairobi and remains in a small rural clinic attached to the mine.'

My life was complex enough without becoming embroiled in the movement of a dodgy security man wanted by his own government. I peeled myself from the moulded plastic chair and stood up. Sandy Driffield looked at me in surprise.

'I'm a doctor,' I said. 'My job is to preserve life and limb, always bound by a code of ethics and within the law. Your proposal seems to go beyond that so I'm sorry, I can't help.'

Sandy remained seated, his mug in one hand, and waved dismissively with the other. 'Ethics Dr Wright, an interesting and controversial subject. So much debate between right and wrong. To my mind, a quagmire. But, even if you are a believer, are you sure you've always worked within such a code?' He cocked his head to one side and tugged his chin. 'Then there is the minor matter of your debts. Naturally, everyone makes mistakes in life. What matters though, is how you manage the consequences, wouldn't you agree?' His voice was calm but also threatening. He inverted his mug and sighed. 'When the coffers are empty, problems just seem to multiply, don't they? And I understand, failure to pay may prove quite detrimental...' He tailed off, his smile still present though transformed, almost sinister.

Anger and frustration rose inside me. Again I wondered how the man opposite knew so much and why he seemed so intent to employ me to undertake this mission. I hesitated, but he held all the cards.

'Are you blackmailing me, Mr Driffield? And how is it you know so much about me?' I asked, barely able to conceal my rage as I slumped back down into the chair.

Sandy Driffield placed his mug gently onto the glass table between us.

'It's my job to know everyone and everything. And if, on the off-chance, I don't have the answer to a particular question, then usually I can call on someone who does.' His voice softened. 'Look, I'm offering you a way out, Paul. I want to assist an ex-serviceman to make good as long…' He paused briefly. 'As long as he is willing to help me in return. I need someone with excellent credentials who can act with complete discretion for our mutual benefit. You save a dying man and IMS wipes out your debts: no more hassle from creditors; that's guaranteed. A gentleman's agreement and no-one else needs to know.' He pushed back his chair. 'Would you like more coffee? I could murder another.' Without waiting for an answer, he got up, taking both mugs with him. 'I'll leave you here for a minute to consider my offer.' The door closed behind him and there was silence, the soundproofing of the office absolute.

I looked around the room. It was devoid of anything that gave any clue as to the character and true identity of its resident; bare and benign. 'Sandy Driffield,' I muttered, 'You little so and so. You've got me by the short and curlies.' I played the options over in my head. Return to A & E, locum shift after shift, nibbling away at my financial crisis or escape but risk resuming a life where standards are eroded and morals bent. If I didn't act decisively soon, the knock would come and I would lose every last possession to the bailiffs. And the possibility of a beating remained. I could defend myself up to a point but never relished a fight: working in casualty made it obvious that such behaviour often came with serious unintended consequences. I checked my watch. Quarter past six. Next shift due to start in less than two hours. Another night patching up the rough and ready, dealing with the dross, holding the hands of the distressed. Sandy had suggested work should be fun and an adventure — not simply a means to an end. 'Sod it,' I said to myself, 'One job and I've a chance to start afresh. If I'm lucky, Tina might even consider taking me back.' The idea prompted the memory of her beautiful face, wisps of black hair blowing across her lips, catching in her open mouth. That joyful expression had faded years ago. I had tried to reinvigorate our relationship with small gifts and weekends away, but the spark had died and sex become a routine ritual.

My thoughts were interrupted as Sandy Driffield returned.

'Have I given you long enough to change your mind?' he asked, holding out a fresh mug of coffee.

I took it from him and nodded. 'Quite possibly. Tell me precisely what you are offering.'

'Certainly. Our client is willing to pay handsomely for the successful completion of this task. It's likely to prove challenging; that's why I considered you to be the right man for the job. But tell me, how much do you expect to be paid?'

'Well Mr Driffield, somehow you seem to have an inkling into my current situation so anything that helps me financially would be welcome. Suggest a figure and I'll tell you if it's enough.'

Sandy Driffield sat there tapping his mug.

'Would an upfront payment of five thousand pounds keep the wolf from the door? There's more, lots more, when the job is done. It's a promise.'

His offer appeared outrageously generous. A few days away collecting some sorry soul from the tropics and it would be goodbye to the bailiffs. It seemed almost too good to be true, but his warning "It might prove challenging" repeated in my head.

'How much more?' I asked.

'I believe you are short of nigh on fifty grand. That sort of money doesn't come often in this line of work, but it's on offer now and I imagine it might solve your pressing problem.'

Sandy Driffield stared at me, gauging my reaction.

Of course, he was almost spot on. It was very disconcerting how he knew me so well; from the way I drank coffee to the huge gambling debt I had run up. I had little choice.

'OK,' I said, 'I'll do it.'

'Good man, I'm delighted you've decided to join us. I'll make sure Trish organises everything for you. Now drink up and I'll accompany you back to the reception desk and she can show you around.'

Sandy Driffield stood, walked to the door and opened it.

'I probably won't see you again until you've returned from Africa. I wish you a safe and successful trip.' He smiled. 'Work with us and you won't regret it.'

Back at reception, the pretty woman with the spectacles looked up from her computer.

'Trish, please show Dr Wright around and explain how everything works. I'll be in my office briefly and then I'm away. You know how to contact me if necessary.'

'Certainly Sandy.'

She stepped out from behind her desk. I noted she was wearing an elegant flowery short skirt. I struggled to stop myself glancing at her long slender legs, somewhat ruined by a pair of white trainers, suppressing any ubiquitous male urge with the memory of Tina. It was too early to be unfaithful, and I still longed for a reconciliation. A bead of sweat formed on my forehead and I swiped it away.

'Follow me, Dr Wright. I'll show you the equipment store first: it's cooler in there. I'm sorry it is so hot in this office, always roasting. That's why Sandy wears shorts all the time, even in winter.' She spoke with confidence, her voice hypnotic.

As we walked past the line of desks, some staff nodded in our direction, barely pausing as they spoke quietly into headsets; a few languages familiar, others incomprehensible. I paused at the Africa board.

'Patricia, I assume that's my case there,' I said, pointing. Mr Mbuto's life threatening illness summarised in a few pen strokes. In the column marked 'Repat Team', I saw my initials and below 'SA'.

'Isn't that a little presumptuous?' I suggested, somewhat irked.

'What is?' she asked.

'Adding my name before I've signed a contract. I assume PW's me. Who's SA?'

She offered a cheeky, knowing smile, revealing perfect teeth.

'Don't be cross,' she said, gently taking hold of my forearm. 'Sandy was sure you would agree to his offer. He's persuasive and generous in equal measure, providing...'

'Providing what, Patricia?' I asked, calming down.

'Providing staff do their job and avoid asking too many questions. Anyway, you're lucky. You'll be flying with Stella. That's SA. She's one of our most experienced nurses. We always send her with a fresh recruit. With her at your side you can relax as she knows all the ropes. But please call me Trish. Everyone else does; we're a close team here.'

'OK, of course. Trish it is. And you better drop the formal "Doctor" too.'

She laughed and then glanced up at the London clock.

'Come on, Paul. To the equipment store. There's lots to show you and you've the NHS to save this evening. Mustn't hold you back.' She opened a door and flicked the light-switch.

Inside was an Aladdin's cave of kit. One wall was covered in shelves neatly stacked with monitors, infusion pumps, defibrillators and battery packs attached to chargers. Rucksacks labelled doctor or nurse below and on the floor vacuum mattresses, splints and stretchers. On the opposite side, linen and sundry supplies. Trish waved her arm around.

'I expect this is all familiar,' she said.

'It's impressive. There's enough here to run a small field hospital.'

'Good, I can tell you like what you see,' she said with a seductive air.

She was right. The equipment impressed me, but her suggestive comment appeared rather more personal. It was impossible to ignore her beauty, but I pushed to the back of my mind the idea of physical adventures in the linen cupboard. That was the stuff of historical NHS legend when doctors and nurses rarely left their posts and lascivious satisfaction was fleetingly grasped between clinical duties. I noticed the time.

'I'd better head off. Lives to be saved and all that.'

'Yes, of course. Don't worry, Stella will sort everything. She's super-efficient, an ideal companion for anyone's first deployment. Let me show you out.'

As we passed the reception area once more, Trish leant over her desk, retrieved a small fat brown envelope, and handed it to me.

'Here,' she said. 'From Sandy. Open it when you're outside.'

I fingered the package and looked at her quizzically. She laughed again.

'I told you. Sandy's generous but don't cross him. Everything comes at a price. Oh, you'd better sign this for me.' She held out a sheet of paper and a pen. 'Your contract.'

I scanned the document. It looked harmless, so I scrawled my initials at the bottom and handed it back.

'Thank you,' she said, and opened the door.

'Look forward to seeing you on Tuesday,' I replied, wondering if I should suggest a drink together after my return from the mission.

'Sorry, day off. Have a safe trip, Dr Wright.'

As I descended in the lift, I wondered about Trish. She was attractive, intelligent and seductive, almost over-friendly. *Did she really find me good-looking too, or was her game simply to draw me into the clutches of IMS?*

Out on the street, I opened the envelope carefully. Inside, a wad of fifty-pound notes secured with a rubber band and nothing else. It wasn't necessary to count them. Trish had told me Sandy was true to his word. Five thousand pounds should stave off the bailiffs for a while. They were demanding settlement in full, but maybe an interim payment would pacify them. A sense of relief and calm swept over me. IMS might just be the answer to all my problems. Striding away from the grey damp square, I imagined Tina welcoming me home: financially solvent, back on the straight and narrow. Was there now a chance we could rewind the clock and rekindle our relationship?

Chapter 5

It was about a mile to the railway station and I had time to spare. As I walked past a parade of shops, my attention was caught by the window poster of a gleeful young man clutching a fistful of cash; his broad grin and the oversized banknotes alluring. Today had been good, I surmised, and there was no reason my luck wouldn't continue. If I converted at least part of the advance into a small fortune, anything earned in Africa would prove a bonus. On impulse, I entered the betting shop. It was empty apart from the attendant who sat behind a counter chatting to an old gent wearing outdated and faded clothes. Neither looked up as I moved along the bank of slot-machines. I would only gamble for a few minutes and risk no more than half of the money, but which game to play? I stopped in front of a machine, its screen adorned with enticing symbols and bright, garish colours. My heart thumped as I extracted the envelope from my pocket. *Just half, remember. You need the rest. Fortune favours the bold.*

As I fed a single note into the machine, it lit up and began to play an abstract electronic tune. From that moment, focused on the game, the world around me dissolved into a haze. My head buzzed with excitement. Roulette — I knew I would win. There could be only one result. First bet on red. Something or someone told me where the ball would fall. Red again, followed by black three times. Lights flashed, and bells sounded. I was winning and elated. The machine displayed an ever larger balance in my favour. Red, black, red, black. I glanced at my watch. Less than half an hour left to play. I upped my stakes to £100 and noticed my hands tremble as I pressed the 'bet now' button again and again, delirious and euphoric in equal measure. Ecstatic, unable to see or reason, I was out of control and couldn't resist. But the odds seemed to be in my favour, so why stop? Red, black and red again. Faster and faster, the colour of the bets mirroring my finances since my discharge from the Air Force. I checked the time. Only ten minutes before I had to leave. Then it happened. My losses mounted. I thrust in note after note, thumped the button and gripped the sides of the machine as fear swept over me. Not a single win. I prayed as I posted my last fifty pounds into the slot, feeling it slip from my grasp as the bastard box sucked it from my fingers. Sweat poured down my temples. The little ball danced around the screen, hopping from black to red and back again. Green. I slumped to the floor. 'Fuck, fuck, fuck,' I shouted, oblivious to my surroundings.

Someone touched my sleeve. 'You Okay? Are you feeling alright? You look like you've seen a ghost. Let me help you.' He tugged at my arm.

A kindly, understanding face looked down at me. The shop owner had witnessed it all before. I nodded, struggled upright and staggered to the door.

'Thank you for your custom, better luck next time,' he called after me.

I shuffled along the pavement, cursing my stupidity, trying to justify my behaviour with cold clinical reasoning. It wasn't my fault I was an addict, but the sun that had dawned seemed to have set again. 'At least,' I told myself, 'Sandy

Driffield has promised lots more.' I had to try harder. I screwed up the envelope and flicked it into a nearby bin. 'Bugger, what an idiot,' I muttered, scuffing my shoes like a truculent teenager.

The staff entrance to A & E was hidden down a short alleyway at the side of the ambulance ramp. As I approached, I noticed two workmen beavering by the door. One tall, the other much shorter but built as heavily as a shot putter; both in brand-new overalls.

'Excuse me,' I said, holding up my pass, ready to press it against the security pad, 'I need to go in, I'm late.'

As I reached forwards, the short man grasped my forearm from behind, pulled me away from the doorway, spun me round, grabbed my other arm and shoved me against the wall. His taller colleague stepped forward, waved a long screwdriver in front of my face then leant towards me, so close the smell of his aftershave was nauseating.

'Our boss says you're somewhat reluctant to settle your debts,' he hissed in my ear,

'I will pay, I've told him. I'm a doctor, for Christ's sake. You can trust me.' I tried to wrench my arms free, but my assailant was too strong.

'Yeah, yeah,' whispered the tall man. 'Have you any cash with you now? If not, let us escort you to a hole in the wall.'

What to do? I had only a little loose change left in my pocket, certainly not enough money to satisfy their demands and if they abducted me, god knows what might happen. Better to fight it out here. In the military, I had learnt the one guaranteed technique to deal with an assailant. I kicked out as hard as possible at the tall man's groin, my shoe finding its target. But as

35

he fell to the ground groaning, I felt a sharp pain in the front of my outstretched leg. Shocked, I shouted out in anger and glanced down. The screwdriver had penetrated my trousers and stuck in my thigh, twitching like an arrow. Enraged, I swung my head backwards, smashing my skull into the shorter man's face. There was a crack as the bones in his nose disintegrated. Instinctively, he released his grip and raised his hands to protect himself. I turned to them, fists raised.

'Fuck off,' I said. 'Unless you want more.'

The two men backed away.

'We'll be back. And you'll be repaying it all with interest.'

Hands shaking, I slapped my pass against the entry pad and the door opened. The casualty department was quiet, the evening mayhem yet to begin. Steadying the screwdriver, still stuck in my thigh, with one hand, I hobbled to an empty examination cubicle and searched for a dressing pack. A familiar face poked her head around the corner.

'Dr Wright, it's you! I thought we had missed a patient at this end. What are you doing? May I help?'

'I'm OK. Just a little DIY accident, Jane.'

The nurse stepped inside, closed the curtains behind her and then spotted the cause of my injury. 'Blimey! How did you manage to do that?' She patted the examination trolley. 'Hop up if you can and let me look.'

I levered myself up and lay down. Jane raised the head of the bed. The screwdriver had pierced my outer thigh and a trickle of blood ran down to the back of my leg, soaking my chinos and the protective paper under-sheet.

'Unless you're able to wriggle out of them, I'll have to cut your trousers off,' she said, wielding a large pair of scissors.

'Go for it,' I replied, 'I've always wanted to be stripped by a nurse like you and anyway never liked the colour.'

She giggled. 'Well, it's better than yours currently.'

With the wound exposed, it was clear the weapon hadn't penetrated far.

'Jane, please open a suture pack. I'll pull the thing out and stitch the hole myself.'

I sensed her hesitation. 'Might be sensible if the vascular surgeons took a peek, just in case the tip lies in a major vessel?'

'Trust me, it's nothing. A mere flesh wound, as they say. You can help me by passing me things but do me a special favour.'

'And what would that be?'

'Please don't tell anyone. I've made a real arse of myself this time and would prefer it remained just between the two of us.'

'OK,' she said, 'but you really shouldn't work tonight.'

'With local anaesthetic and a clean set of theatre greens, I'll be fine.'

I yanked the screwdriver out and immediately applied pressure with a dressing. After a minute, I cautiously peeled away the swab and was relieved to see little further blood. Jane cleaned the wound and passed me a syringe loaded with local. It stung as I injected but within seconds the tissues numbed and it took only a single silk suture to close the hole.

'Wait here,' she said. 'I'll be back with some clean scrubs, although it will be a shame to cover up those lovely legs.' She pointed to the screwdriver lying on the dressing trolley.

'Shall I throw away your dangerous tool? Can't trust you with DIY.'

'No, no. I might need it again.'

'I'm not sure you should be allowed to keep it,' she said with a frown. 'Do you want it washed?'

'Don't bother, thanks. I'll do it later. Just seal the thing in a plastic bag for me, please.' I thought about Sandy Driffield, who had boasted that he knew everybody. Perhaps I had met the person who could use the screwdriver to help me track down the bastards who had assaulted me. He had certainly demonstrated his ability to unearth someone's past.

Chapter 6

Two days later, back in Croydon, I dropped my flight bag on the pavement and pressed the intercom at IMS's office. The door buzzed open, and I hobbled across the foyer, relieved to discover the lift had been repaired. I could have climbed the stairs, but my leg throbbed. As the lift door opened, a short woman wearing a smart dark blue suit waited to greet me.

'Dr Wright? Hi, I'm Stella Atkinson. You're in good time. I hope your last casualty shift went OK.'

'Glad to meet you Stella,' I replied and followed her into the office, noting she too walked with a limp. I looked around hoping to spot Trish as I had planned to give her a little parcel for Sandy, but she wasn't there.

At the reception area, Stella collected a thin file and a manila folder. She offered the file to me. 'These are the case-notes. You might want to have a peek before we leave.' She pointed to a pile of medical bags lay in the middle of the floor. I've sorted out all the kit I think we might need. We can check it together just in case there's something missing. As you know, once we're in the air, we can't nip back for anything we've forgotten.' She tapped her finger against the folder and then passed it to me. 'That contains our visas, various currencies including a float of Kenyan shillings and most importantly the shopping list.'

'Shopping?' I asked, surprised.

She looked at me as if I was stupid. 'Duty free requests from office staff. It's important to keep everyone happy, a minor reward for all those who never have the chance to fly. We'll be joining our aircraft at Biggin Hill where the booze is dirt cheap although you have to rouse the guy who sorts out your order. Too often he's been on the bottle.'

'Why Biggin Hill, surely not just for bargain alcohol and fags?'

'No, of course not. We're using a French plane and crew tonight. It's only a quick hop across the channel for them so doesn't eat into their flying hours much, and all formalities are dealt with discretely. Apparently aviation fuel is also cheaper compared to the big airports. So it suits them and us.'

I considered her words. *"Discretely" — strange; what did she mean by that? It was an air-ambulance flight, surely nothing more.*

Stella glanced at the London wall clock. 'Our transport should be here in a few minutes. Suggest you check the paperwork while I collect the drugs box from the fridge. Back shortly.'

I sat down and opened the medical file. Mr Mbuto had been taken to hospital a week earlier and IMS contacted three days after his admission. The few notes, which were surprisingly short on detail, recorded daily summaries: a diagnosis of falciparum malaria, the need for intensive care and a request for repatriation. The decision to fly halfway across the world without knowing more seemed strange. In the Air Force, we had always kept meticulous records with a clear discussion of the pros and cons of moving a patient, a manoeuvre potentially fraught with

40

difficulty. I closed the file and turned to the folder. Inside there were transfer forms to be completed during the return flight, wads of cash, a scribbled list looking like a bar order, and two sheets of headed notepaper from the Kenyan embassy granting Stella and me temporary visas. I noted the accuracy of my personal details.

Stella returned carrying an insulated white plastic container. 'This will keep our drugs safe for hours. When we board the aircraft, remind me to plug it in to maintain the temperature. Shall we go through the rest of the equipment?'

We knelt on the carpet and studied the checklist: Ventilator, monitor, infusion pumps, defibrillator, emergency kit, bedding and mattress, oxygen concentrator and cylinders. Nothing missing. Trish had been right, Stella was clearly very good at her job. She got to her feet, using an arm to push against her weak leg.

'Can I help you?' I asked.

She looked at me, slightly offended. 'Absolutely not. I've learnt to manage since childhood. Trish probably told you I suffered Polio, but I was lucky, it only left me weakened on one side. I don't consider myself an invalid. I noticed your limp though. At first I thought you were making fun of me, but then you were wincing. Are you in pain?'

'No, I'm fine thanks. I managed to bash myself, that's all, but glad the lift's working to take this lot down,' I replied, pointing to the heap.

'Are you happy we've got everything?' she asked.

'Looks good but tell me, how did IMS obtain my visa when I have my passport here?' I asked, tapping my pocket.

'I expect Sandy will have arranged it. If there's ever a problem, he seems to be able to sort it. Come on, let's go.'

Around the corner from the IMS tower, a glossy black Mercedes estate waited. 'Is that for us, Stella?' I enquired, somewhat incredulously.

'Of course, we're not expected to struggle onto a bus with this lot!'

As we approached, the chauffeur leapt out, doffed his cap and raised the car's tailgate ready to receive our equipment. Stella gave the driver a smile. 'Evening, Arthur, you're looking well.'

'Good evening, ma'am. You too, if I may say so. Biggin Hill, I presume?'

'Yes please. We're due to take off at nine, so hopefully there won't be any hold-ups. This is our new doctor; Dr Wright.' She turned to me. 'I hope your shoes are clean. Arthur's very proud of his car.'

A few minutes later and the Mercedes glided through the South London suburbs. Inside, the driver and passengers conversed little, even though evidently Stella and Arthur knew each other well. I was exhausted after recent events but also exhilarated by the prospect of flying again. Although there were moments in the RAF which had proved petrifying, generally, once in the air, I experienced a sense of peace and tranquillity, life's problems left far below.

Biggin Hill airport lies no more than twelve miles from Croydon, so despite the evening rush-hour traffic, the Mercedes arrived at the entrance to the General Aviation Terminal before the sun had set. Arthur helped locate trolleys and together we emptied the vehicle.

42

'Have a good flight.' He doffed his cap again, climbed back into the estate and drove silently away.

The waiting area was quiet. Stella walked over to a small desk and rang a bell. An immigration officer, who doubled up as the customs official appeared, checked our passports and Home Office drugs license.

'Are you collecting any duty free? If so, I'll stamp your list for Paddy. You can collect it just before take-off but remember no sampling en route. The seals need to be intact on your return. Oh, and your flight-crew are sitting over there,' he said, gesticulating with his thumb. 'And they're drinking all our coffee; typical French,' he grumbled.

The two men, both dressed in immaculate dark blue suits adorned with excessive silver braid, finished their drinks and ambled over. The older man held out his hand.

'Captain Montpellier at your service. This is my co-pilot, Andre Delaroux. If you are ready, we can load. I expect refuelling has been completed and in-flight catering delivered. Let us help with your equipment. Fortunately, the aircraft is less than fifty metres from here. Take-off slot is in thirty minutes.'

Armed with only schoolboy French, I was grateful his English was excellent. If on the return journey it became necessary to change altitude or divert for medical reasons, I didn't want a language barrier to cause problems.

The Falcon 20 stood gleaming on the apron. Its gold paint polished and lit by the fading rays of the sun. Compared to the military transports I was more used to, it was pure bling. A celebrity plaything rather than an air-ambulance. Stella noticed me gawping.

43

'Wait till you see the inside, it's all leather armchairs and teak,' she said.

'And a bar?' I asked.

'Undoubtedly, but not for us, I'm afraid. It's going to be a long haul and you certainly should get some sleep; you look shattered. I'm sure you know as well as I do once we've collected our patient there will be little opportunity to rest. Let's load and we mustn't forget to collect the duty free.'

With the equipment on board and while the flight-crew circled the aircraft, visually checking for faults, we walked over to Paddy's store. The duty free facility lacked the glamour familiar to most travellers; a rusting steel shed positioned conveniently close to the terminal. Stella hammered on the door. 'If he's been drinking, let's hope we can wake him,' she said.

After a minute or two it creaked open and a bleary-eyed unshaven man dressed in overalls stood blinking, swaying slightly. The distinctive smell of alcohol mixed with cheap perfume wafted out.

'Here again?' he said to Stella, his speech slurred. 'You must be downing the stuff faster than me!' He peered at me then turned back to Stella and winked.

'A new partner? Another exotic trip. Where are you taking him? Thought the last one was your favourite,' he teased.

Stella ignored the comment and handed over the customs declaration.

Paddy took the slip. 'Wait here, won't be long. I'll collect your loot,' he said, and slammed the door shut.

'He seems to know you well? You're obviously a regular, Stella,' I said. 'And who was the other guy, anyway?'

'As I've told you before, we favour Biggin Hill. It's conveniently close to the office and as you have seen, everyone is helpful and friendly. If there's an urgent case we can be airborne within a few hours of a call. It's ideal.'

I noticed she hadn't answered my question and was about to repeat it when the shed door swung open again. Paddy held out two bulging carrier bags.

'Thanks, Paddy,' Stella said as she took them and passed them to me.

'You're welcome. Now remember, drink responsibly,' he said, stifling a burp, before disappearing back inside and bolting the door behind him.

'OK,' said Stella. 'That's the most important bit done. If we returned to the office empty-handed, we'd never hear the end of it.'

I followed her to the aircraft. Despite her limp, she walked quickly and with confidence. I remembered visiting friends recovering at the Tri-service Rehabilitation Centre at Headley Court, feeling their way with new artificial limbs. Men who had been at their physical peak reduced to shadows, heaving themselves along parallel bars as they learnt to control their shiny new titanium legs. IEDs had destroyed them and, for different reasons, my career within the Force too. It had been a bloody awful conflict. As I watched Stella climb the aircraft's steps with ease, I wondered how long it had taken her to learn to cope after her illness. But then she had been a child, and perhaps that had helped.

Inside the Falcon, two seats had been replaced by a stretcher platform. Across the aisle, the remaining two leather armchairs faced each other, separated by a polished table. To the rear of the cabin, opposite the toilet, was the space where we had stored the medical equipment and personal bags. Stella pressed a button beside the doorway, and the aircraft's steps retracted smoothly. We sat facing each other and secured our seatbelts.

'Ready, Paul?'

I nodded. She twisted round and gave a thumbs up to the flight crew.

The Falcon's twin jet turbines whirred and the aircraft slowly taxied to the end of the runway. I peered through the small dome of Perspex that separated our cosseted luxury from the outside world. Dusk had fallen and the multi-coloured guidance lights scattered across the airfield glowed brightly like jewels. A sense of optimism rose within me. It felt good to be back doing what I had been trained to do. I may have been forced out of the Air Force, and suffered the consequences, but was determined to make amends. This was a chance for a fresh start, an opportunity to move on from my failures. Thoughts turned to Tina: *I wished she knew how hard I was trying. Would she be willing to get together again?* Anything was possible.

The crew pushed the throttles forwards, and the aircraft accelerated down the runway, forcing me back into my seat. Within seconds the plane took off and climbed steeply before banking south. Below, the orange glow of London faded rapidly. Suddenly, and without warning, brief turbulence displaced my confidence with anxiety. The last time I had a similar experience I was belted up in the rear of a C17. Standard procedure had been to climb as fast as possible, the lumbering giant discharging

46

white-hot magnesium flares in an attempt to confuse Taleban missiles. But during that flight, the enemy had pointed their AKs to the sky and struck lucky. Lead had punctured the aircraft's outer skin and rattled through the fuselage, forcing the pilot to return to base immediately, weaving sluggishly from side to side. As the aircraft dived to earth, a brief terrifying roar told us a rocket had flashed by, missing its target by inches. We had landed safely with a cheer, but everyone on board was shaken and knew that after repairs we had to face the journey again.

As the aircraft breached the clouds England disappeared, and the setting sun lit the cabin. Stella pulled down the blinds. 'Why don't you climb onto the stretcher and get some shut-eye?' she said, handing me a blanket. 'We'll be refuelling in Malta so you've more than four hours. After that it's non-stop to Kenya.'

'What about you?' I asked.

'I'm fine. I've a good book to finish and no doubt Captain Montpellier will soon demand more coffee. You have to remember we are not just the medical team but the cabin crew too.'

I climbed onto the stretcher. 'I've never considered a career as a trolley-dolly before but if it comes with this luxury, I might apply for a full-time position.' Dog-tired, I closed my eyes. Everything seemed surreal. Not long before I had been labouring in a London hospital, but now I was dozing in an aluminium canister as it hurtled through thin air at forty-five thousand feet with a mere millimetre or two of precision engineering protecting its occupants from the elements.

Chapter 7

Suddenly I was aware of someone restraining my arm. I thrashed out with my free hand, clumsily swiping until my fist thumped the low ceiling. The debt collectors were back, stabbing me with screwdrivers and chisels, slicing open my body until all my internal organs were exposed. A high-pitched voice called urgently.

'Paul, Paul, are you alright? Wake up.'

I rubbed my eyes, smearing tears across my cheeks. Stella relaxed her grip as I turned to face her.

'Sorry,' I said. 'A nightmare. Didn't mean to frighten you.'

She looked concerned and then smiled. 'It's OK. I wasn't afraid. It takes a lot more than someone else's bad dream to scare me. But you seemed so distressed. Can I make you a drink? I've just boiled a brew for the boys in the cockpit.'

I slid off the stretcher and returned to my chair. 'Yes, please. How long have I been asleep?'

Stella passed me a gold-rimmed mug full of steaming coffee and picked up her own. I sipped, waiting for the caffeine to kick in.

'For ages. We've less than an hour before we start our descent.'

Stella placed her drink back on the table. 'So what was it about then?'

'About?'

'Yes, your dream. People often say that when you first wake if you recall the details it helps you understand what caused the nightmare and stops it recurring.'

I snorted. 'I remember every nightmare in detail, and they plague me most nights.'

'Oh, I see. Why not tell me about it? Does it involve work? I know you've had a challenging career, Sandy told me.'

I couldn't decide whether to be angry or not. Sandy Driffield had clearly dug deep, but why? And if he had discovered the real me, was it really his place to inform others?

'It's rather personal. I'm not sure I wish to burden you with my problems.'

Stella nodded but didn't give in, her gentle voice persuasive.

'Paul, we're going to be sharing the next few days and hopefully, if this job goes well, many future trips together. If you don't want to talk, that's fine, but a problem shared is a problem halved. And I can't have you waking me in the middle of the night, shrieking.' She smiled encouragingly and reached across to squeeze my hand.

She was right and, anyway, I didn't consider my premature discharge from the RAF dishonourable. The board had made that decision a thousand miles from the frontline. They were not the ones fighting with their bare hands, but wielded pens in the corridors of Whitehall instead. By anyone's standards they couldn't be considered true combatants. The circumstances of my fall from grace had been hushed up, and I was cast out, damaged and addicted, my marriage destroyed. I swallowed another mouthful of coffee and began.

'Are you aware of the Swiss cheese model of consequences?'

She looked bemused. 'No, explain.'

'It's when at a particular moment, the holes of fate line up and the result, whatever it is, becomes inevitable. Some believe everything's written in the stars, but I view it more scientifically.'

Stella's expression changed to one of confusion. She laughed. 'Don't talk in tongues, Paul. Remember I am but a simple nurse.'

It was my turn to laugh. 'That I doubt,' I said. 'Simple, I mean. Anyhow, I never judge people that way. Hierarchies are essential but everyone has a purpose, holds their rightful place in the grand scheme. That's doubtless the cause of my downfall.'

I glanced out of the window. The aircraft flew so high, it seemed we had almost reached space. The sky was full of stars, and a new moon shone. Below it was pitch black, a void.

'Go on, Paul,' said Stella, softly.

I nodded. 'If you've never been to war, it's probably hard to understand. And, if like me you have, it's difficult to explain. There's no doubt I found it exciting, but as my time in Afghanistan dragged on, fatigue set in. You are promised leave, then it's cancelled, and you keep going. The soldiers and civilians, men, women and children, shot and blasted, won't wait. And eventually, one incident cracks you, sets off a train of events over which you have no control. For me that incident involved a young Afghani boy who had stepped on a mine and arrived missing both legs, his partug bloody and shredded. There was no screaming, not a whimper. He lay on the stretcher, his face full of terror and pleading in equal measure. Despite our best efforts,

I knew there was no way to save him. The explosive had, in an instant, vaporised his legs and much of his pelvis. The little blood still inside him drained from tatty vessels, hanging like pulsing worms in the morass of his guts and genitals. The severity of his injuries was an all too common sight, so I held his hand as his eyes rolled skywards and his eyelids closed. I guess he wasn't even twelve years old. Soon after, there was a commotion in the receiving area. The boy's father had heard his son had been whisked away in our helicopter and had rushed to the hospital. He demanded to see the boy, accusing us of kidnapping him. Through an interpreter, I tried to calm the distraught man, gently explaining we were there for everyone but despite all our efforts the lad had died. The poor man, dressed in frayed clothes, his skin sun-wrinkled and face covered with a dense black beard, collapsed to the floor, beating the bare concrete with his fists. I remember bending down to help him to his feet, but he shoved me away and spat.'

Stella sat listening intently. 'You did your best,' she whispered.

'Oh I can rationalise that bit. He wasn't the first we had lost in similar circumstances by any means. Traumatic death was a daily occurrence, but that's not the whole story. The following evening a call went out for a medic to join a MERT.'

'Mert?' asked Stella.

'Medical Emergency Response Team. You know, typically a doc and a pair of army paramedics airlifted by Chinook to the frontline when someone's down. Get there quickly, stop the bleeding and fly them back low and fast. Then straight into theatre to give them the best chance: it's all about time. Well everyone was knackered so muggins here volunteered.

Should have been a short hop in and out. We landed close to the action in a small village called Washir. The marines were taking a lot of incoming and as we approached bullets were pinging off the ground and surrounding stone walls. A suspected IED had gone off while a patrol passed, killing three of our guys and injuring others, including a local. As the marines gave covering fire, we rushed forward keeping our heads down until we reached the crater in the road. Dead bodies lay to each side, limbs missing or bent, helmets nowhere to be seen. The two medics sprinted to the injured soldiers who were screaming while I helped the civilian. He sat propped up against the boundary wall, clutching something. A length of cable ran from his fist to a mound of earth. I cocked my Browning, terrified he was about to detonate another device. Then I recognised him, the black beard distinctive. It was the dead boy's father. As I neared, he opened his hands and turned them palm upwards as if in prayer. I yanked the wire from him and kicked away the switch. He looked at me in despair and then stared to the heavens. Blood oozed through his torn clothes as he fought to breathe. With one hand, I gently lifted his stained shirt, at all times my weapon ready in the other. With disgust I watched his guts slide out and blood spurt from multiple hissing chest wounds. The man started murmuring, his voice almost imperceptible, Pashtun and a few simple English words. "Please, please, my son," was all I could make out. He pointed to my gun, and then raised his hands again. I knew instantly what he craved. With my mind oblivious to the mayhem going on around me, I cocked my pistol and shot him twice in the head. No hesitation. As he slumped, I turned and caught one of the army medics grinning. I can recall his exact words. "Well done, sir, the cunt deserved it" he had shouted gleefully, showing me the wire. "He must have been the shit that triggered the bomb." I felt and said nothing. Instead, I reverted to automatic and helped the marines load the wounded onto the Chinook. And that would have been that, except the bastard sergeant couldn't keep his mouth shut. So there was a board of enquiry and the miserable medic's helmet cam footage did for me. It was obvious I was in for it even though I tried to explain. To this day I remain convinced the poor guy wanted to join his God and his son. And who was I to deny his wish? Anyway, the whole affair was brushed under the carpet and I was quietly sent home, relieved from my duties with an early discharge arranged. However, they didn't hang me out to dry. The war was still going on and who would benefit from the bad publicity? Though it left me fighting my own demons. In the heat of battle I had ignored the Geneva convention and changed from being a caring professional to a killer. That's why I have nightmares. It usually starts with the young boy and ends with the scattered brains of his father.'

'I'm really sorry,' said Stella quietly. 'It's not your fault.'

I sighed. 'It is, you know, it is.'

'It's post-traumatic stress. Surely, you can get help for that,' said Stella.

'Oh yeah, it's PTSD alright but I've tried everything and nothing seems to work. The RAF wouldn't speak to me, of course, and my family doctor was next to useless, so I found my own way to deal with it. It never goes away, but I'm able to control it. The trouble is my solution has led me to where I am now.'

'Meaning?'

'Let me explain. During my war work I lived in a state of never-ending tension. Strangely, it was uniquely stimulating, but unfortunately death and despair was everywhere and those grim memories pervade. Well, the way I've found to inhibit those dark memories is to rediscover the excitement of war without the risks. So now when the chemistry inside my head goes awry, I try to distract myself, create a buzz which can make the bad stuff disappear.'

'So how do you achieve that?'

I was in two minds whether to answer. I had only just met Stella, but somehow it felt good to unburden. 'It's embarrassing but gambling helps and I admit, I gamble a lot. Predictably, that's created its own problems. You see, when you gamble no-one loses their life, but something else dies inside. You lose perspective, emotions flatten and you end up completely ignoring those you love and treasure. So I've not really escaped, not yet anyway. In essence, I've fucked up.' I looked at Stella, trying to ascertain if she felt sympathy or disdain, but she gave nothing away. 'Anyway,' I said, lightening up. 'That's enough of my background. Tell me your story.'

Stella hesitated for a moment. 'Compared to your drama, my steps to this point have been pretty straightforward. Happy childhood interrupted by Polio, although on reflection I realise I was lucky. Six months in hospital left with one weak leg and a wizened arm, but I avoided the iron lung. Perhaps it turned me into a rather determined individual. The nurses were wonderful, and I knew I wanted to follow in their footsteps despite my physical limitations, so I studied hard and secured a place at St Bartholomews. Over the next few years my career was my life, and it blossomed. Eventually, I became the sister in charge of Intensive Care. But I suppose, a bit like you, though for different reasons, I always yearned for more. I craved excitement and the job at Barts had become routine.'

'Surely, you were too young to have caught Polio? The vaccine's been around for decades.'

'Ah, everyone assumes their parents are wise and do anything and everything for their children. Mine did not believe in vaccines. In fact, both of them were convinced they were dangerous. Sadly today, too many ignorant people embrace the same view. So when my father's work took us to India, I was exposed to a wonderful culture but dirty water. The disease caught me less than a month after our arrival.'

'Every parent will do anything for the sake of their children – or their memory,' I thought, as the image of the Afghani boy's father flipped into my mind again. A few moments passed before I could continue.

'So, how did this line of work come about then?' I asked.

'Well, one day we had an admission from overseas. A poor woman who had been knocked off a motorbike in Bali. Multiple injuries complicated by sepsis. The team who delivered her were professional and enthusiastic. Once they had handed over their patient to us, I offered them a cup of tea and we got talking. One thing led to another and soon I was introduced to Sandy Driffield. That was more than ten years ago and the rest is history as they say.'

'No partner then? No-one to return to?'

Stella snorted. 'Come on,' she said. 'Look at me. Forty two, crippled and no oil painting, am I? No, I'm a traditional nurse, a spinster. Anyway, it means nothing interferes with my work and I prefer it that way.'

Our conversation was interrupted by Captain Montpellier announcing that we would soon begin our descent into Malta. We tidied, then strapped in as the aircraft dipped earthwards. Through the cockpit door it was possible to make out the tiny island, a beacon of light in a sea of darkness.

'We'll have a chance to stretch our legs,' said Stella. 'The crew won't let us stay on board during refuelling unless we have a patient.'

A few minutes later the Falcon touched down with a brief squeal as its tyres burnt the warm tarmac. The aircraft taxied past the main terminal building and came to a stop at the end of the apron by a small hangar. The engines fell silent and Captain Montpellier waved to Stella.

'It's safe to open the door and step out. But please be careful and don't wander far, there'll be a tanker on its way. It won't take long to refuel and we need to be airborne again as soon as possible.'

Having unbuckled, we moved to the rear of the aircraft where Stella pulled a lever to initiate the automatic opening of the door. Warm moist night air flooded into the cabin carrying the delicious scent of wild Mediterranean herbs. I breathed in deeply as I followed Stella down the steps. She stood stretching, using her good arm to manipulate its weaker partner, then arched her back. 'Look at the stars,' she said. 'Magnificent, aren't they? We might have a serious job to do, but it's moments like this that I cherish.'

I looked up. She was right. The cloudless sky bristled with light; the milky way formed a glowing river stretched between the horizons. It was beautiful, awe-inspiring, and it made my existence seem totally insignificant. I glanced back to Stella. She was trying to touch her toes.

'It's all madness really, isn't it Stella?'

She stood upright again. 'Madness? What is?'

'I mean, here we are flying halfway round the world just to save one man. Think of all the resources being consumed. You look up and see infinity, but down here we're gobbling up everything our planet has. And in the time it takes us to reach Kenya, God knows how many others will have died from malaria or another perfectly preventable disease for want of a simple pill.'

A rusty refuelling tanker trundled up and parked by the Falcon's starboard wing.

'See, this plane will burn more fuel than most Africans consume in a life-time. Bonkers.'

Stella laughed. 'You philosopher. But maybe it's more complicated than you assume. As you say, every person has a role to play, good or bad: a tiny but critical part of the jigsaw. My father, who is sadly long gone, once told me that if you abandon the individual, then all hope for humankind is lost.'

'Now who's the thinker?' I quipped. 'I'm going for a stroll. My sore leg needs a stretch. Back in a mo.'

'OK, but remember, don't go far. The Falcon will be ready soon and we mustn't annoy our French colleagues.'

I strode around the corner of the hangar and spotted a group of grey dome-shaped shelters, standing like giant pigsties. A brief walk to them and back would suffice. As I neared, the moonlight revealed the shape of an American stealth bomber. I padded towards the awesome machine and then heard a click.

Startled, I spun round to see two USAAF guards, their weapons raised.

'What ya doin' bud?' demanded the larger man, the voice gravelly with a southern drawl.

'Nothing. Just having some fresh air. My aircraft is over there,' I replied, gesticulating with my thumb.

'Keep yer hands where I can see 'em,'

'He sounds like a limey,' commented the other.

'Gentlemen,' I said slowly, 'I am British and my air-ambulance is being refuelled. Rest assured, all I craved was fresh air, so I'm sorry if wandered somewhere where I shouldn't have.'

'Are yer carrying anything dangerous?' the first guard asked. He lowered his automatic and patted my body from head to foot, the smell of stale sweat and strong aftershave replacing the sweet aroma of the herbs.

'Air-ambulance? Where from? You say you're British, but that's a French registered aircraft. You'd better come with us and show the boss some ID. No-one is allowed to roam around this part of the airfield, even if they are allies. Keep yer hands raised and walk slowly to that building on the right.'

'Damn it,' I thought, 'Stella is going to be pretty pissed off if I don't talk myself out of this quickly.'

Inside the guardroom the air-conditioning worked overtime and the bulkhead fluorescent lights bathed everything in pure white. The cold made me shiver. An overweight sergeant looking tired, pale and grumpy, his uniform barely constraining the fat, slid a metal stool towards me. He slumped into a chair opposite. The sound of a baseball game blared from a TV in the

58

next room. One of the armed men stood on guard at the exit while the other hovered behind.

'OK, the guys say they found you nosing around our aircraft.' He waggled his finger at me and repeated the mantra. 'Nobody is permitted to walk unescorted without authorisation in this area. Better come up with a good reason why you're here and fast. I'm missing the game.'

'As I explained, I flew in on the French Falcon. We're only here to re-fuel. Undoubtedly the crew were directed to this zone by ground control. I simply wanted some exercise. Look, I was in the Royal Air Force once and understand you have to do your job but, believe me, I wasn't trying to cause any hassle.'

The sergeant sighed. He had spent too long cooped up on this tiny island with little leave and, despite the climate, not enough sun.

'Give me your passport.' he demanded.

I reached into my pocket and flipped it across the table. I was starting to feel annoyed but also anxious. He slowly flicked through the pages.

'Dr Paul Jonathan Wright. Bet you always think you're just that – "right". He chortled at his own joke, his grotesque belly wobbling up and down. The others sniggered. 'Wait here, I'll need to run you through the computer.' As he rose a cheer went up from the TV.

'Good timing. That's your exercise done for the day,' I thought as I watched him waddle through to another room. I looked to my guards. 'How long have you been stationed here?' I asked in an attempt to warm the atmosphere.

'Too long,' answered the one by the door. 'And with all that is going on in Afghanistan, Syria, Yemen and God knows where else, can't see we'll be leavin' anytime soon. What did you do in your military?'

'I was a medic. Spent two hot holidays in Afghan, rescuing casualties from the battlefield, and the repatriation of our men and women home. That's why I work in the air-ambulance business now. It's my specialist field.'

The sergeant returned, looking baffled but also pleased. 'I'm not sure who or what you are about,' he said, 'but your details check out and the system's telling me to allow you free passage. Some sort of higher clearance, I guess. Must be somethin' to do with your RAF tale. Anyway, you're allowed to go and I can return to the baseball which is the main thing; the game's nearly over. Soldiers, take Wally back to his aircraft and don't let him near any of our planes.'

The guardroom door opened, and I stepped back out into the warm Maltese air followed by my escorts.

'I'm surprised to see B2s stationed here,' I said, endeavouring to make conversation. 'I didn't know you Americans operated out of Malta. I would have thought we would have given you space in Cyprus, at Akrotiri.'

Neither man answered my question.

'See yer limp,' said the larger airman, 'war wound?'

'Something like that,' I replied, not willing to offer more than I received.

As we reached the Falcon, there was Stella standing on the tarmac beside it with Captain Montpellier leaning out from the cabin.

'What a relief,' she said. 'Where were you? I was getting worried.'

60

'Belongs to you Ma'am? Please don't lose him again,' said the senior airman. 'Have a safe flight, Mr Always Wright.'

Stella waited while I climbed the steps and then followed me inside. We strapped in without a word being spoken as the jet's engines fired up again. Moments later the aircraft sped down the runway, lifted into the air and banked south.

Stella sat frowning. I caught her eye.

'Sorry,' I said.

Her serious expression broke. 'Mr Always Right. Obvious, though I love it,' she said, grinning. She unbuckled. 'Want some nosh? There's a delightful selection of plastic-wrapped sandwiches in the fridge.'

'Where's the haute cuisine? Thought this was meant to be a luxury flight,' I retorted. 'Anyway, yes please, I'm famished. And more coffee if it's on offer.'

Stella rummaged at the front of the cabin and returned with the food and coffee. 'Don't say I don't spoil you,' she said as she handed me a tray. 'See, a chocolate mousse for dessert.'

As we sat chewing, Stella piped up. 'So, how did you convince those Americans to let you go?'

'Well, that was the strange thing. I simply told them the truth about the air-ambulance and showed my passport. The guy who checked it muttered about releasing me because of higher clearance or something. I suspect he bull-shitted because he wanted to get back to watching TV. Anyway, they didn't hold me long which was a relief as I was more frightened of your reaction than theirs.'

'Quite right,' said Stella. 'If that had been the end of our rescue attempt, I wouldn't have been best pleased. No patient, no payday and a very disappointed Sandy. Be warned, he's Mr Nice until someone fowls up.'

'Warning noted, thanks,' I replied, dipping a plastic spoon into the dark chocolate goo and wondering why Stella had referred to the mission as a 'rescue attempt'.

The Falcon levelled off at altitude as it crossed the Libyan coast, heading for the Sudan, then South Sudan and finally Kenya. I thought of all the misery below. One armed faction fighting another, control of territory gained and lost, alliances made and broken. And as always, the common man eking out an existence in the mayhem, desperately craving peace. Once again, it seemed surreal to be cooped up and cosseted within the plane, isolated from the world's realities.

'Another place where our meddling didn't achieve much good,' I said to Stella, who had returned to her book.

She laid it down. 'Sorry, what did you say?'

'We're overflying Libya. I was considering how we failed to resolve the Libyans' problems by removing Gaddafi. The Arab Spring could have worked but somehow it all fell apart and our interventions have left a terrible legacy.'

'You are philosophising again although, yes, you're right. The West stirred up a hornets nest and we've been stung repeatedly ever since: terrorist attacks across Europe from multiple groups with no end in sight. It makes you feel helpless but remember the jigsaw. All we can do is play our little part when it's our turn.'

Sunshine flooded into the cabin from the East. Stella squinted as she watched the dawn through the oval window. 'You see,' she continued, 'another glorious day. Don't let the World's problems weigh you down. We only have to do our bit to the best of our ability; no-one should expect or demand more.'

Chapter 8

As the Falcon crossed over the border between the two Sudans, Captain Montpellier called for us to join him in the cockpit. 'Look straight ahead. Most unusual at this latitude and for this time of year. Must be a once in a decade event.' In front, immense cumulonimbus clouds rose in towers like giant mushrooms, their flat tops spreading across the horizon. Frequent lightning flashes lit the clouds from inside, turning the dense vapours blindingly white. 'They almost reach the stratosphere, way beyond where this machine can go. I'll fly her between their stems, but it's going to be a rough ride. Please make sure everything in the cabin is secured. And I'm afraid there's more. Nairobi Air Traffic says the whole of Northern Kenya is off-limits due to the weather, so we must overshoot our intended destination and proceed all the way to the capital. They're insisting we land at Wilson rather than the Kenyatta International where the sky is crowded with many larger aircraft diverting because of the storms.'

'OK,' said Stella. 'How long do you think we will remain grounded before we can fly north again?'

'That's the problem. The weather has to settle and the extra time to Nairobi means we will run out of flying hours. Realistically, with the required rest period, I can't see us being airborne again for at least a day.'

Back in the main cabin we checked everything was correctly stowed

'Damn it,' muttered Stella. 'Let's hope our patient is still there when we eventually reach him.'

'You mean alive?' I said.

'Yes, yes, of course, alive and kicking,' she replied quickly, but something in the tone of her voice made me think she was worried. Why, I couldn't fathom. The medical notes suggested the man was poorly but not critical. There was no reason to suspect he would deteriorate much further by waiting an extra day. And anyway, if his condition worsened significantly, it wouldn't be sensible to move him at all. No-one wanted an unstable patient for such a long return journey; it might prove fatal.

We buckled ourselves in just as the aircraft banked around the first column of cloud. The sun disappeared and outside it fell dark, as if night had fallen. The Falcon began to toss and turn, flipped by the turbulent air like a leaf in an autumn gale. Flashes of light lit the cabin. Suddenly the plane plunged, and I felt my insides float as my body lightened, grateful that the seatbelt held. I watched Stella. She was grasping the table with her good hand and grinning crazily.

'It's the best funfair ride in the world,' she shouted, 'Don't you just love it?'

My stomach churned, and I swallowed hard as my food tried to make a reappearance. The Falcon rose and fell as if on a big-dipper accompanied by incessant flashes and thunder. It took me back to rough rides in a Chinook, ordnance exploding all around, scaring everyone on board shitless. It was during those times I wished I had been sedated like my patients. Sweat poured off me, soaking my shirt. Unable to hold on any longer, I grabbed a sick bag and retched.

'Poor you,' Stella called out, 'didn't realise you were going to be ill, not with your background and experience.'

I wiped my mouth with a tissue. 'It's the memories not the turbulence,' I said, trying to smile.

'Sorry,' replied Stella, her exuberance gone.

'Don't be. Logically I know this aircraft can take it and we're safe, but I can't readily control my emotions. I call it my Icarus's curse. Even when I took my wife away for a short break, the slightest unexpected lurch on the flight could catch me out and set in train an almost Pavlovian response. Tina became quite irritated by it, saying my behaviour embarrassed her. If it happened on the outbound leg, I could expect to be dammed for the whole weekend with every meal eaten in stony silence.'

Stella butted in. 'I'm no expert on relationships, but it seems unreasonable to walk out on you because of that. Tina's lovely, I'm sure, but where's the compassion, the empathy? Are you certain there was nothing else?'

I ignored the question. There was no doubt my behaviour had taken its toll on our relationship. Tina knew I suffered from post-traumatic stress, but what she couldn't accept was how I handled it. Being unpredictable and irritable was bad enough, but self-induced financial meltdown brought the stresses between us to another level. Stella sat waiting for an answer.

'Tina was wonderful. To be frank, I still adore her. I would give anything and everything for us to get back together. But I made the mistakes and pay heavily for them now, although I haven't given up hope. No-one can do my work or live my life without being an optimist.'

66

Stella nodded. 'You're right, Paul. Medicine is a strange game. Everyone must die but we, as professionals, continually fight the inevitable. Our glass has to be half-full at all times.'

'That's exactly my problem though. My glass has cracked and as fast as I try to top it up, the contents leach out uncontrollably. What I seek, and hope I've found in IMS, is a new way forward. Maybe with a little tincture of time my troubles will fade and lady luck shine on me.'

Stella burst out laughing. 'Now, you're being a poet. Oh, I'm sorry, I didn't mean to laugh. Don't trust to providence, Paul. That's the folly of a gambler. Use your skills and drive to carve a better path.'

I turned and looked out of the window. The clouds thinned, the turbulence settling, the aircraft back on a steady heading. "*The folly of a gambler.*" *She had got that right.*

Stella changed the subject. 'Look down. See those dark lines far below meandering across the landscape. What do think they are?'

'We must be above the Rift Valley and those are probably migrating Wildebeest. They will welcome the rain. Although inevitably some drown attempting to cross the swollen rivers, the majority will reach fresh pastures. So every challenge offers a reward: for those four-legged creatures down there and for us who walk upright, watching them.'

Captain Montpellier shouted from the cockpit. 'Anticipate landing within the hour. Soon be flying over Lakes Navaisha and Bogoria. If we're lucky, there will be ribbons of pink lining the banks. In English, what do you call those pink swans?'

It was my turn to laugh. 'Flamingos, Captain. There are millions of them in Kenya.'

'Flamingo. Ah yes. And I thought that was a Spanish dance.'

Whether he was being serious or not I wasn't sure, but it didn't matter. We had escaped the storm and would soon land at Wilson. An unexpected stopover in the capital, even if only for one night, would be fun.

'Stella, where will we sleep in Nairobi? Is anything booked?'

'No. We'll sort something out. London won't be aware of our diversion yet.'

'Well, providing IMS is willing to pay, may I recommend the New Stanley Hotel. It's quite modern and situated right in the centre. Hopefully nothing much has changed since I last stayed.'

'You've been there before? You kept that quiet, Paul. Enlighten me.'

'Oh, I enjoyed a brief secondment with the Kenya Air Force. We were stationed at their main airbase at Nanyuki. Although we had little free time and spent most of our R&R sunbathing on the coast, some of us managed a few trips to Nairobi. We probably downed a few too many beers in the Stanley. Hopefully the management have forgiven or forgotten our antics.'

The Falcon swept in a tight curve across the periphery of the Nairobi Game Reserve, dropping height rapidly. The wild residents of the park, startled by the jet's engines, briefly scattered then resumed grazing as the plane crossed the Langata

Road and touched down leaving time enough for them to fill their stomachs before the next twenty-first century interruption shattered their peace once more.

The aircraft came to a halt a few metres from the main terminal building. As soon as Stella released the door, the familiar smells and noises of Africa poured in replacing the stale air. I paused on the steps, squinting in the bright afternoon sunshine, listening to the endless traffic interspersed by the occasional complaint made by a wild animal across the road. It felt good to be back.

'Right Paul,' said Stella, 'let's take our luggage and head into town. You know this patch better than me, so lead on. I'd love a shower and a gin and tonic: we're not officially on duty yet.' She tucked her long dark hair under a large straw hat and slid on a pair of horn-rimmed sunglasses.

'What about the crew? Where will they stay?' I asked.

'They said they'll follow on later. No doubt flight plans to be rearranged and so forth. We'll get going – I need that drink.'

As we walked across the tarmac and into the terminal, an onlooker might have wondered: who were the celebrities that had arrived in their shiny gold plane? And unbeknownst to us, we were being observed…

Chapter 9

At border control, the immigration officer was gruff and direct. 'You're only staying for a few days? What business do you have in our country?' He stood, a towering figure, looking down on us like a teacher about to admonish a miscreant.

Stella removed her sunglasses and fluttering her eyelashes explained the role of the air-ambulance and described the violent storm that had caused the diversion. 'Unfortunately,' she said, continuing with her flattery, 'we will only manage only one night here in lovely Nairobi before we have to fly north to collect our patient.'

The officer checked our passports against the records on his computer screen. He frowned.

'And who is your patient?' he asked.

'Just an unlucky tourist who has contracted malaria,' she answered politely, winking at me. 'In a clinic at Eldoret,' I added, trying to be helpful. The immigration officer hesitated, raised his eyebrows and then stamped our documents. 'Welcome to Kenya. Enjoy your stay,' he said. Taking the passports, Stella gave a cursory smile and thanked the official. As we walked towards the customs desk, she thrust my passport into my hand.

'Unlucky tourist!' I said. 'You've got a nerve but surely you're setting us up for problems if he checks?' Stella glanced across. 'They'll be checking alright. Eldoret; why did you have to mention that? Did you not notice the other two men in plain clothes slip into the room with the mirrored glass as we approached Border Control? Let's hope we will be gone from this place before they discover who we are really here for. And pray Customs prove to be a formality.'

Striding past worn wooden tables a rotund customs officer with greased hair gesticulated towards me. 'A moment, sir. A quick check of your luggage, please?'

Whether it was my demeanour or part of his routine to boost a modest government salary wasn't clear, but he made great play in pulling out all my belongings, holding them up one by one as if at an auction. Stella stood back, amused.

Finally, he extracted a plastic bag containing the bloodied screwdriver. He dangled it in front of me, raised his eyebrows, patiently anticipating an explanation.

'An unfortunate accident while I was fixing something at home,' I muttered with little conviction.

The officer looked baffled. 'So why do you have it here? It could be considered an offensive weapon. I'm not sure I can allow you to import such an item?' He swung his hand over a large bin next to the table and held the bag above it between his thumb and forefinger. 'Do you really need it?'

I cursed myself for not leaving the tool behind at IMS with a note for Sandy Driffield.

An arm brushed past me and pushed something across the table.

'Will this do, sir?' said Stella. 'It should cover the cost of the requisite permit, shouldn't it?'

The officer nodded, snatched the money and simultaneously dropped the screwdriver back into my bag.

'You can re-pack your things. I suggest you take extra care next time.'

Walking out to the taxi rank, I noticed Stella looked cross.

'Why did you bring it with you?' she grumbled. 'That guy could have made life very awkward. And, yuk, it's covered in dried blood. Whose?'

'Sorry. The screwdriver doesn't belong to me, but the blood does. Unfinished business.'

'Well I hope you don't come up with any more surprises which could derail our mission. We almost fell at the first hurdle.'

'Tourist, DIY injury,' I retorted. 'Half-truths both. Perhaps I'm just learning the ropes?'

Stella's anger faded. 'Possibly Paul. Now let's get a taxi and that drink. I'm gasping.'

The taxi lurched along the Langata Road towards the city centre, swerving to avoid potholes, other traffic and the youngsters who dashed into the highway bearing newspapers or armfuls of brightly coloured plastic goods for sale to the occupants of vehicles that queued. To each side, corrugated tin roofed hovels stretched from the roadside into the distance, an endless shanty town that merged with the city boundary. People sat outside on chairs peddling their wares or simply chatted while others pushed heavily laden barrows made with car wheels. And everywhere happy children; shouting, screaming, laughing - mostly dressed in spotless school uniforms. I stared through the open window in disbelief. Kenya had changed a lot, but then so had I.

As we turned into Kimathi Street, it was reassuring to see the New Stanley Hotel remained as I had remembered it; a not unattractive concrete tower, occupying the corner between that

72

road and the Kenyatta Avenue, with an elegant entrance shaded by a glass canopy. Stella tipped the driver, and we stepped out onto the dusty street, inhaling the hot air rising from the pavement as we walked the few steps to the hotel entrance. A security guard, wielding a club in one hand, opened the door with the other and bowed. Stella swept in like a film star and I followed, laden with our bags. The receptionist was polite, welcoming but apologetic; explaining they only had two rooms available. One smaller on the first floor, facing onto the street, the other at the top of the hotel; their Panorama Suite, luxurious but three hundred and fifty US dollars per night. Stella handed over a credit card.

'Excellent, we'll take both. I'm sure you'll be quite comfortable down here, Paul. Don't want you having to cope with the climb, not with your sore leg.'

'Oh no,' interrupted the receptionist, 'We have a lift.'

Stella made a face. 'But does it always work?' she quipped. 'No, the suite's for me. Anyway, I'm sure Dr Wright doesn't require a Jacuzzi.'

Even though a long soak would have been welcome, I decided not to object. I was familiar with Nairobi and had recommended the hotel, but it was clear Stella was the boss.

'Suggest we brush up and then meet in the outside bar. See you in ten,' I said.

'It might take me a little longer, but if you're there first, I'd like a triple of gin, with a soupçon of tonic and lots of ice. But don't mix it until I arrive. There's nothing worse than a weak tepid cocktail.'

'Certainly Ma'am,' I replied. It was my turn to bow.

73

Stella laughed. 'Even though we aren't honoured with a professional title, glad you appreciate us nurses are in charge.'

It was nearly ten years since I last sat in the Thorn Tree Cafe, the hotel's famous outside bar, listening to the sounds of the city and sipping a glass of Tusker. The beer tasted the same, but the famous tree with its thick trunk onto which travellers pinned notes had long gone. In its place, a young delicate sapling encircled by wooden notice-boards. I tipped the waiter and asked him what had happened to it.

He lowered his voice and glanced around before whispering. 'The ancient tree was a bit like our government, sir: rotten to the core; endemic corruption and no justice. Sometimes the old needs to be cut down, swept aside, to make space for the new.' He pointed to the sapling. 'It will grow and be strong. Until then, you are welcome to leave a note on the boards.' He pointed to a biro and a small pad on the table.

Legend had it that your message would eventually be read by the person to whom it was addressed because it was said that everyone would visit the Thorn Tree Cafe at some point in their lives. I thought of Tina, then picked up the pen and hesitated, the tip poised over the paper. *Was it all over? I didn't want it to be. I still loved her but had failed to show it. Could she forgive me, brush away the past and make a fresh start?* I scribbled a few words and rose from the table just as Stella appeared.

'Where are you going? Is that my drink?' she asked, pointing.

I clutched the note to my chest. 'Yes, your ice is in the bucket. Won't be a moment.'

The notice-boards were crammed with messages; some explicit, others in code, but the themes familiar and predictable. Expressions of affection and hope interspersed with the occasional request to arrange a rendezvous. Finding a small space, I fixed my little slip of paper to the cork and re-joined Stella.

'An innocent declaration of love or something else?' she asked. 'I read about the tree business in the hotel brochure in my room.'

I didn't answer. 'How's the gin and tonic? We could eat here if you wish. The menu looks better than I remember.' It had been hours since we had devoured the rubbery inflight sandwiches, and I was ravenous.

Stella sipped her drink. 'It's excellent Paul, thank you. You've clearly followed my instructions to the letter. Some food would be good, I'm starving.'

I waved to the waiter.

'Bugger,' said Stella suddenly. 'Shows how short of calories I am, I forgot to phone London to explain the delay. They'll have been expecting a call confirming our pick up. Won't be long; I'll nip up to my suite. Order something for me. Anything except game. I prefer to see those wild animals running free rather than on my plate.' She took a large swig of gin and departed.

The waiter ambled over and handed me a menu. 'I can recommend the Nile perch. It's fresh today, but before you order there are two men waiting at reception who wish to have a word. They say they know you.'

'Strange,' I thought, 'who could it be?' I laid the menu on the table, downed the rest of my beer and headed back inside.

As I stood at the reception desk, two burly Kenyans dressed in grey suits sidled up to me. I turned to face them, but had no idea who they were; one tall with polished black shoes, the other quite short, heavily built, almost fat, his jacket and trousers bulging. They didn't look friendly.

'Hello. How can I help you?' I asked, feeling uneasy.

'Flight Lieutenant Wright? Please come with us.' The man flashed an official looking card. 'I'm Detective Njenga. If you wouldn't mind, sir, we would like a few words. Our car is outside.'

'I'm sorry. What is this about? How do you know my name and rank?'

'All will be made clear at the police station. And please don't be difficult. We prefer our guests to come voluntarily rather than making an arrest.' He pulled his jacket to one side to reveal an automatic pistol secured in a leather holster. 'After you, Flight Lieutenant.'

I glanced back, hoping to see Stella returning to the foyer, but without luck. She would wonder where I had gone.

'Could I leave a message for my colleague? She'll be here shortly and won't know why I have left.'

The other grey suit nudged me towards the door. 'Sorry, the car's waiting. We have to go,' he said.

Outside, I tried to catch the doorman's eye, hoping to ask him to speak to Stella, but as we passed, he lowered his head and turned away. It was as if he recognised the policemen and didn't want to get involved.

The police car was unmarked, an old black BMW with tinted windows. Detective Njenga opened the rear door; the other policeman shoved me in and climbed in beside me. Njenga went to the other side of the vehicle and joined us, squashing me between them, my knees bent over the transmission housing. The driver glanced at me in his mirror, his eyes wide and excited.

'Go,' ordered Njenga and with a squeal of worn rubber on hot tarmac the BMW lurched forwards and merged into the heavy evening traffic.

As the car weaved through the queues, I spotted familiar landmarks: the National Bank, Parliament buildings and the Central Post Office. I remembered how, all those years ago, I had posted cards from there to Tina on which I always wrote how much I missed her.

After leaving the Central District, we headed south on Uhuru Highway, red taillights stretching into the distance. 'Where are you taking me?' I asked, aware we had bypassed the Central Police Headquarters. Inebriation and exuberance had resulted in too many of my RAF colleagues spending an uncomfortable night in the cells courtesy of Kenyan law enforcement. But the BMW sped on, breaking the speed limit, barely slowing at intersections. No-one replied, silence within only interrupted by the clunk of worn shock-absorbers as they bore the brunt of endless potholes accompanied by the sound of my head thumping against the roof. As the temperature and my apprehension rose, sweat oozed from every part of my clammy body, soaking my shirt and trousers. My companions barely seemed to notice the odour or dampness; only the skin on their faces glistened. Despite my repeated requests, the BMW's windows remained firmly shut.

Shortly after passing the junction with the Langata Road, we turned off the main highway. We sped along a dark road, the blackness broken by the occasional streetlamp, before stopping abruptly outside a nondescript office block. The armed guard at the security barrier, recognising the vehicle, saluted, and without further ado, raised the barrier. The BMW inched forward until it was wedged between the metal bar that had dropped behind and another reinforced gate in front. A second guard, his weapon at the ready, approached. Our driver lowered his window and showed his pass. The guard stuck his head inside the vehicle, ignored me, but acknowledged the men sitting to either side. He stood back as the next gate clanked open and the car rolled down a ramp into an underground carpark.

With the engine switched off, the driver climbed out and opened the rear door. It was a relief to clamber out. I rubbed my sore leg and stretched. The air in the basement was hot and stale; contaminated with diesel fumes and the stench of leaking drains. My sweaty clothes clung to me, crumpled and grubby. Njenga's sidekick lifted my arms, kicked my legs apart and then patted me all over. He nodded to his boss.

'Nothing, Bwana, he's clean,' he said.

'Excellent. Flight Lieutenant, please come this way,' said Njenga, smiling. 'I'm sure if you can answer a few questions, we will deliver you back to the New Stanley before dinner service has ended.'

My stomach ached, but I wasn't sure if it was as a consequence of hunger or anxiety. I followed the detective, his partner so close behind I could hear him wheeze. At the far end of the car-park, Njenga held open a door to a stairwell.

'I see you have a limp. Our interview rooms are on the next level. I hope you can manage the stairs.' He seemed to show genuine concern.

'No I'll be fine, thank you, it's nothing,' I replied.

On the ground floor, a series of grey painted doors led off a long corridor lit by a line of bare fluorescent strip-lights. There were no signs or notice-boards, in fact nothing suggesting this was a police station. 'Perhaps,' I thought, 'this is the cell block.'

Njenga stopped, fumbled in his pocket, withdrew a key and unlocked a door. 'After you, please take a seat,' he said, waving me inside.

This was definitely a cell; bare, hot and dank, with minimal ventilation. A tiny window high on one wall allowed a little air from outside to enter, as did the hum of air conditioners that serviced rooms elsewhere. It brought back memories of my military escape and evasion course, which had involved long periods of exercise and sleep deprivation before finally being snatched by members of the Special Forces who took me to a secret location. During the subsequent incarceration, in cells like these, I underwent regular interrogations interspersed with hours of squatting in stress positions until my ligaments ached as if they had been torn. No food, minimal water and no visits to the toilet. Hooded, I pissed where I stood, exposed to the white noise generated by a detuned radio. But I had learnt to cope and, with instruction, mastered the survival techniques necessary: give the interrogators just enough information to buy time and inhibit them from hurting me. A smidgen of truth and nothing more.

I sat down on a hard steel chair as the door banged shut. Detective Njenga slipped off his jacket, pulled out a pen and notebook from an inside pocket and sat opposite me behind a bare desk. He held the pen ready, his delicate fingers twitching.

'So tell us why you've come to Kenya?' he asked.

I thought for a moment. My job was an innocent one. Collect a poorly man and deliver him to where he would receive the best medical care available. Sandy Driffield had indicated there was more at stake but hadn't expanded further. My captors were probably already aware of the air-ambulance; the French crew would have filed a new flight plan revealing the aircraft's destination. There was no reason not to be helpful and, anyway, my military career was over. It would be better to tell them as much as possible. After all, if I failed to satisfy them, they might arrest Stella, and I didn't want that responsibility.

'I've come to collect a sick patient. That's my job as an employee of a British company that flies patients across the world, moving them to facilities in their home country where they will receive the best care. Most of our work is paid for by the travel insurance industry.'

Njenga, his pen poised, nodded, encouraging me to continue.

'You called me Flight Lieutenant Wright. I have to tell you, I am no longer in the Royal Air Force. Now I work as a civilian doctor and aeromedical retrieval is my new career. In fact, this is my first mission.'

'Oh, I see,' said Njenga. 'I apologise for any inconvenience. Hopefully our intervention won't deter you from working in such a worthwhile field. But please be so kind as to tell me who you plan to collect and from where?'

'It's a man suffering from malaria, based in the north of the country.'

Njenga twirled his pen in his hand. 'Yes…' He paused.

Sandy Driffield's words came back to me. *'It appears the Kenyan authorities would be interested in asking him a few questions although our client is adamant that they should not be afforded the opportunity.'* 'I'm sorry,' I said. 'Medical confidentiality. I'm not allowed to give away patients details. But I don't understand why you want to know. Maybe you could explain what all this is about?'

'Flight Lieutenant, I appreciate you believe it is important to abide by your Hippocratic Oath but sometimes perhaps, one's community should take priority. If your patient is a criminal or is an enemy of the state, then surely you recognise the need to set aside any ethical guidelines, even temporarily.'

I was weary and irritated. 'Look I'm tired, thirsty, need a piss and haven't slept properly for days. Give me more background and I guarantee to do my utmost to help.'

Njenga stared at me. 'OK. Here's the deal. It's simple. All you have to do is tell us where your patient is and we will return you to your hotel… but don't say Eldoret.'

So they knew. Mr Mbuto should have been waiting there, tucked up in bed at the mine's clinic. But if they already had that information, why ask me? They could have gone and arrested him without all this fuss unless… unless someone had moved him. But who and why? I had to play their game, be on their side, otherwise it was going to prove difficult to extract myself.

The muscles in Njenga's thick forearms twitched as he sat tapping his pen on the desk; 'Made a decision, Flight Lieutenant? Remember; don't annoy me by saying Eldoret.'

'That's exactly where I was expecting to go. You are probably aware that we were forced to divert because of bad weather. Anyway, it gave me a chance to enjoy your capital once more.'

Njenga looked unimpressed. The tempo of tapping increased. 'So where is he now? You must know; otherwise your journey will have been wasted.'

I shook my head. 'Sorry, your guess is as good as mine. It sounds as if we've burnt a ton of aviation fuel for nothing.'

Njenga stood up, put on his jacket and returned the unused pen and the notebook to his pocket. He sighed. 'Dr Wright, would you care for something to drink? You British adore your tea and are famous for your integrity. But sometimes I wonder whether it's all a façade? You're as crooked and corrupt as the rest of us. We have a word in Swahili "uaminifu"- it means honesty. Every language has a word with that definition, but it doesn't seem to be an absolute. There are degrees of honesty, and I'm not convinced you are being totally open with me. I'll ask for you to be brought tea. The refreshment might encourage you; improve your memory.' A brief smile passed across his face, but it lacked warmth.

Njenga opened the door and disappeared into the corridor. I heard him speaking to someone in what I assumed was Swahili. The only words I recognised were 'chai tafadhali.' I turned to my guard and smiled meekly with the aim of garnering his support, but he didn't respond, his deadpan expression unchanged.

'Have you worked for the Kenyan Police for long?' I asked in an attempt to break the ice.

The fat man stood motionless, watching me as sweat from his nose regularly dripped to the floor, each slow and laboured breath straining his jacket buttons.

'It is extremely hot in here,' I said. 'This room would benefit from a bigger window.' Just as I pointed to the tiny hole set high in the wall, the cell door opened again. A giant of a man wearing trainers, a white T-shirt and jeans held up by a wide leather belt, entered accompanied by a cloud of smoke; his appearance quite different from Detective Njenga's. Hair thinning, too black and shiny for his age, definitely dyed, a scar from a hair lip repair that interfered with his attempt at a smile. Leaning against the desk, he dropped his cigarette butt on the floor, ground it to a pulp with his shoe, then flipped open a packet and tapped a fresh cigarette against the box before lighting it. He took a long drag, puffed a lung-full of smoke towards the ceiling and then began to speak; his English perfect, the accent almost Etonian.

'Good evening, Dr Wright. Let me introduce myself. My name is Mr Cheboi, but everyone calls me "Chai". My job is to encourage you to cooperate and I can assure you that I'm very persuasive. I overheard you saying that our accommodation is a little warm for your liking. Sorry about that. Of course you haven't had time to acclimatise yet, familiarise yourself with how we live and how we achieve our aims.'

He took another long drag on his cigarette, exhaled in my direction and chortled, a coarse guttural laugh. 'As a doctor, it's obvious you don't approve,' he said, waving the thing in my face. 'But I tell you, the smoke keeps the mosquitoes away and nobody likes to be bitten, do they? That's how malaria is transmitted, isn't it? One whining insect, one bite and so much trouble. Better to die tomorrow from lung cancer than from a nasty disease today.' He snatched at the air and then held his fist in front of me. 'Caught one,' he said grinning, and opened his hand slowly to reveal a small smear in his palm where the bug had met its fate. 'So easy to squash a little creature, but it should only be done with good reason. It's not rational to kill things just for pleasure, wouldn't you agree? Apparently insects can't experience pain, but I'm not so sure. When I catch a cockroach, I rip their legs off one by one, and they always squirm. Why would they do that if they didn't feel pain, Dr Wright? Tell me, as a physician and a scientist, you must have an explanation.' He moved to the empty chair, slumped down and drew repeatedly on his cigarette.

My mind raced back to Afghanistan, to the moment I pulled the trigger and the old man's head disintegrated. There had been brief euphoria, a flash of ultimate power. Since then I had wrestled with the memory, uncertain whether I had been in complete control of my actions, sickened by the strange pleasure I experienced. *Had I really enjoyed killing another human being? Was there a sadist in us all?* I recalled, with disgust, my childhood behaviour one summer. On a particularly hot day, I had squatted in the garden burning ants with a magnifying glass, fascinated by the power of the sun. The tiny insects smoked and shrivelled before bursting like popcorn. Although just a young boy, I still felt uneasy acting that way, but during those long school holidays couldn't stop, justifying my activities as scientific study. The sadist inside me had stirred. As I grew older, I suppressed the urge to hurt and strove to help, but memories of days spent at the anthill never left. I stared at Chai and shrugged my shoulders. He looked disappointed.

'You surprise me. There's me thinking, the good doctor would be a fountain of all knowledge, an oracle, but clearly not.' He took out yet another cigarette, lit it and puffed hard; the smoke filling the room. 'Now, Dr or Flight Lieutenant Wright, you do look hot. May I suggest you make yourself more comfortable by taking your clothes off? Yes, don't be shy, all of them. You see, us black Kenyans, rarely get the chance to see a naked white man. Especially a Brit, someone whose ancestors plagued our people as pests just like the anopheles mosquito.'

'Mr Cheboi,' I said quietly, 'you're not a police officer are you? And this isn't a police station, is it? Let me call the British embassy.'

'Well done, Doctor, an excellent deduction. Quite right. We're not regular police officers and this is an interrogation centre. I'm afraid your wish to speak to someone from your diplomatic service can't be fulfilled at this time. It's much too late at night to disturb anyone.' He rose, flicked the remains of his cigarette across the room and then slammed his fist onto the table. 'Now, stop fucking about and take off your fucking clothes,' he growled menacingly.

I stood and stripped off slowly, feigning embarrassment; interrogation while naked had been standard practice during my military training. This attempt to unnerve me was familiar and anyway, as a doctor, the exposed human body had long since failed to excite or shock me. I had observed every shape and form, but rarely did people look better undressed. I guessed Chai had seen it all before too.

'Good, good,' murmured Chai as he circled me, inspecting my body. he leant down and stroked my leg wound with a forefinger, his smoky breath blowing across my genitals. 'Nasty but neat stitching. How did you hurt yourself? A small gunshot injury, perhaps?' He paused waiting for a reply but as I didn't answer he sighed and pinched my thigh. 'If you leave here,' he said, 'better use plenty of sun cream. Thin pale skin doesn't like our strong African sun. Now sit. The gentleman behind needs to ensure you're comfortable while I persuade you to be rather more forthcoming. And you will speak, that much I learnt from your own intelligence services.'

I noted the "if" rather than when you leave here, but with no choice, sat down.

The fat man shuffled towards me, clutching a pair of handcuffs. He yanked my hands behind the chair and there were two clicks as my wrists were fastened to its steel tubes. I felt him pulling at my fourth finger on the left, twisting off my wedding ring. He held it up for his boss to see.

Chai smirked and put out his hand. The fat man tossed over the ring.

'Ah, good,' said Chai, examining it closely. 'Payment for board and lodging.'

I looked to Chai. 'This is ridiculous,' I began, 'I've not come here to do anything wrong, to break your laws. Listen, I'm a doctor, not a spy or terrorist. I have told you I was expecting to travel to Eldoret, where I understand my patient is staying at a clinic run by a mining company and that's it. I can't see what you want from me or what else I can tell you.' I thought of Stella, wondering whether she was nearby being asked identical questions.

Chai stared at me, smoke from a fresh cigarette curling past each side of his broad nose. He screwed up his face. 'Dr Wright. There is no clinic at the mine.' He paused again, watching my reaction. 'So you can appreciate our problem. We have a great desire to speak to your patient but he can't be found, although we do believe he's still in our country.'

I swallowed hard. I had revealed all I could, but clearly it wasn't enough. I feared for Stella, but perhaps she had a better answer.

'Have you spoken to my nurse?' I asked.

'Ah, we'd love to, but I'm afraid she's disappeared. Our men visited your hotel several times, but she had checked out already even though she had been booked into their best suite. What a missed opportunity. Of course, we searched your room in case she had hidden there or was waiting for you, but no luck.'

Chai sucked on his cigarette until the tip glowed red and reached down. 'Your wound looks inflamed. Do you think an infection has set in, Doctor? They say heat is the simplest and best steriliser.' With that he suddenly stabbed his cigarette into my thigh, burning the stitch and flesh. I gritted my teeth as the pain overwhelmed every other sensation. Instinctively my leg kicked out, catching the desk, propelling me backwards, and there was little I could do to stop my head from smashing against the solid floor. For a moment, my mind went blank as my brain reverberated inside my skull. Then I became aware of someone lifting the chair, tipping me upright. Chai was still there, the cigarette still poised in his hand. I tried to stand, but my ankles had been secured to the chair legs with thick plastic restraints.

'I'll give you three choices,' he said, holding the cigarette so close to my nostrils it singed my nasal hair creating a nauseating aroma of burnt keratin mixed with strong tobacco. 'I can stub this out on your balls or my friend here has a great trick he does with a car battery and some wire. From my perspective either of these first two options would be enjoyable, although I'm forced to recommend a third.'

'And that is?' I whispered, knowing full well what he wanted but aware that I couldn't deliver.

'Tell us who really employs you and where you're hiding our man.'

My leg throbbed, and I had an awful headache. Up to now, I had coped with the pain, but everyone has a breaking point and Chai would find it. If I had the information he desired, I would have told him. There was no need to suffer further. *Damn Mr Mbuto, damn IMS, damn the money.* Any prospect of a successful new life had faded so quickly, tangled in a mysterious business that seemed increasingly dark and threatening. It wasn't worth it, but I struggled to think of a way out. My mind was befuddled, probably as a consequence of the blow to my head.

'Mr Cheboi, I have been honest and told you everything. I don't know what else to do. Please be reasonable and show some mercy. I'm not responsible for this mission, simply a professional medic doing my job.'

Chai looked at his watch, yawned and then nodded to the fat man. 'Oh dear, I'm late for dinner; the wife will be so angry. Let's hope our good doctor will remember a little more – or how do the English say, come up trumps. Otherwise, we'll have to continue our work tomorrow and the next day and maybe the day after that.'

The door opened and the fat man shuffled out, his sandals scuffing the floor. Chai turned to me and leered.

'He won't be long. Needs to collect his equipment. We call him the electrician. He's very knowledgeable when comes to anything requiring repair or attention. To be honest, I'm frightened of the stuff that wings its way along cables. High voltage, current, it is all a mystery to me but to him, it's nothing.'

88

He peeled the cellophane from a new packet of cigarettes, took one out and waved it in the air.

'Everyone has an addiction,' he said. 'Opium, alcohol or worse. Mine's nicotine. Can't live without it. And you, what's yours?'

I didn't answer. It wouldn't help to tell Chai about my compulsive gambling. Chai was clearly a chain smoker, but I believed his real addiction was his need to inflict misery and pain on others. He was, without doubt, in the right job.

Chai lit the cigarette and puffed for a few moments before continuing. 'It is a shame you decided to be so difficult, and I have to say I'm a little surprised. I mean, I've checked your record. You were so helpful with our military when you last visited although, of course, it was your role to be cooperative. Perhaps you were already planning something during that stay? Discretely observing and reconnoitring. Maybe, my good doctor, you think I'm paranoid but it's better to be safe than sorry. Your MI6 taught me that.'

The door opened again and the fat man entered pushing a steel trolley. The wheels squeaked as he manoeuvred it into position.

'Carry on,' ordered Chai. 'This shouldn't take long.' He glanced at his watch again. 'I'm betting on no more than five minutes. Are you a betting man, Dr Wright? I'll make you a wager. Within the time stated, you will tell us everything. If I am right, we'll check what you've said, and then release you. However, if, I'm wrong, your reward will be that we stop for the night and return to our discussions tomorrow. I can't keep Mrs Cheboi waiting forever. Dinner will get cold and she might elope with another man. Who wants to lose their partner?' he said with a knowing grin.

I thought of the little note I had pinned to the board at the Thorn Tree. Njenga's men must have seen me do it. They had probably taken the scrap of paper and were trying to analyse the simple message, looking for clues. But the few words were simply an expression of love and a request for forgiveness. Fleetingly, I saw Tina's sad face the day we separated. She had worn make-up and looked beautiful. It was obvious that neither of us relished the moment, but recognised we had reached the point of no return.

My thoughts were disrupted by the fat man's rubber-gloved hands fiddling in my groin. I winced as he attached crocodile clips to my scrotum, the bare metal teeth biting the soft skin. I looked at him focusing on his features. '*If you hurt me, you bastard, one day I will find you and seek revenge.*' But in my heart I admitted it was an empty threat. If I survived and was deported, there would be little purpose in searching for a single black man amongst the sea of faces that comprised Kenya's rapidly growing population. I was out of my depth.

The fat man stepped back, wound a wire to one of the battery's terminals and held the other a few inches above the second contact.

'Last chance, Wright,' said Chai, puffing on his cigarette.

I didn't know what more to say, and then someone screamed. *Who?* I sensed my whole body spasm as every muscle cramped. The screaming continued, a deafening shriek, interspersed with gasps. I fought the excruciating pain, but this was beyond anything I had ever experienced before. The contents of my scrotum desperately tried to retract as my testicles burnt.

The stench of smouldering hair once again reached my nostrils. Between each howl, I heard laughter, but I didn't know whose it was: I was blind, all vision blocked by the agony. Then suddenly it stopped. Someone whimpered. It was me. My body trembled as if I was cold but I felt hot, so hot. There was damp between my legs and under my backside. I opened my eyes expecting to see the fat man standing there, but he had gone.

Chai grinned at me, his eyes wide with delight, virtually ecstatic. He reached forward and stroked my inner thighs. 'Oh dear, how disgusting, you've wet yourself,' he said. 'Clearly too much excitement.' He withdrew his hand and wiped it on a silk handkerchief from his pocket. 'I would love to hear what you have to say, but the wife's waiting. I'll leave you to think about our conversation overnight and visit first thing tomorrow morning. But don't worry; if you need anything, there are guards you can call on though I can't promise they will deliver everything you want.' He levered himself off the desk and walked around me to the door where he paused. 'Magnificent performance, Flight Lieutenant. Wonderful. Almost better than an orgasm.'

'You pervert,' I muttered.

'Heard that,' he said. 'We all have our likes and dislikes. It's best to be honest with oneself, and with others too, don't you think? Good night.'

He switched off the light and slammed the door shut, plunging the cell into darkness.

I listened as his footsteps drifted away then wriggled on the chair in a desperate attempt to release myself but remained firmly secured. Although I ached all over, the pain in my private parts was the worst and despite my efforts to keep calm, my body

91

shook uncontrollably. Mr Cheboi and his henchman had found my limit. Tomorrow, I needed to give them something to make them stop even if I made it up. But Chai was a sadist: would he accept my explanation or continue using me as his source of satisfaction? I trembled at the thought, but there was no time to waste. A few hours respite, one night to plan a way out, either verbally or physically though neither looked promising.

I sat in the dark waiting for my eyes to adjust. The tiny window glowed like a lantern, letting in the moonlight and the distant sound of traffic. I strained to hear anything from within the building but apart from my own breathing there was silence. At least they didn't bother to hood me, I said to myself, but then a terrible notion dawned. Of course; it wasn't necessary. There would never be a time when I might recognise them. Once they had done with me, I would be murdered. They'd probably concoct a story to explain my demise to the British authorities: an accident or assault with fatal consequences. Nairobi had become a dangerous city, the armed Askari security men posted outside every bank and bar were testament to that decline. No doubt, the Kenyans would be very cooperative but any investigation a forgone conclusion. Listening again, I heard the whining of mosquitoes as they sensed the sweat leaching from my skin. One by one they landed on my face and limbs. I wriggled and shook my body though the more I writhed the more excited they became, enticing further insects to feast on my skin, biting and sucking.

And then it happened. One of the little critters crawled into my ear, its delicate wings still vibrating. I tipped my head to the side and pulled at my restraints as hard as I could but the ties held. The sound drowned out everything else, driving me insane as the bug's feet tap-danced on my eardrum. In desperation, I jiggled the chair only to topple over, banging my face on the solid floor as I went down. 'Fuck, fuck, fuck,' I shouted as I lay on the ground, curled tightly with my steel companion. My nose hurt and was running as if I had the worst cold but I knew it was blood. A continuous warm trickle ran down my cheek and into my mouth. Despite spitting repeatedly I couldn't shift the salty taste. Suddenly the creature dwelling in my ear, satiated, decided to leave the way it came.

Someone must have heard my shouts because soon there were footsteps outside my cell, a key rattled in the lock and the door opened. Light from the corridor flooded in forcing me to squint. A young guard with a full head of frizzy white hair stood over me, staring at the blood, saying nothing. I raised my head, one half of my face covered in congealed clots, a sight worthy of the best Halloween costume. He looked terrified and his expression reminded me of Edvard Munch's 'The Scream', although this man's albino skin was even paler than the man's complexion in the picture.

'Lift me up,' I begged, 'Can't you see I'm bleeding badly? You must help me. The blood loss has to be stopped, otherwise soon I'll fall unconscious. My nose must be packed, and the flow stemmed. Don't let me bleed to death. You don't want to be handing over a corpse in the morning, do you?' Blood continued to drip from my broken nose, catching on my chin before splatting on the floor. I knew it wasn't enough to kill me but he clearly didn't and there was a chance he could be persuaded to release me.

'What's your name? Can I have a drink? I'm so thirsty,' I asked.

'Ashura,' mumbled the youth, 'I'll need to check with my superior.' He stepped back, and the door closed again.

I rested my head in the pool of blood and waited, hoping the guy in charge at night wasn't Chai or Njenga. No doubt both of them would be rather unhappy to be disturbed.

It seemed as if hours passed, but it must have only been a few minutes before I heard more footsteps, the door opened and the light was switched on. Ashura and another man heaved me upright.

'My goodness,' said the second, 'you are in a mess.'

I lifted my head to look at Ashura's boss. There was something familiar about him and from his expression, despite the blood, dirt and insect bites, I guessed he felt the same about me. He turned to Ashura.

'Fetch me a bowl of water, a cloth and some chai, real chai.'

The youth trotted out and once he was out of earshot, the man standing over me exclaimed, 'Jambo, Flight Lieutenant Paul! What the hell are you doing here? They told me an ex-British military officer had been brought in, but I had no idea it was you. It seems our Chai has paid you a visit. So sorry about that.'

Relief. Now I recognised him. His face rounder than I remembered but the smile as broad as ever – Sergeant Okeyo Kamau of the Kenya Air Force. We had trained, played cards and enjoyed beers together at Nanyuki. At this moment, the idea of cold beer was torture in itself.

'Okeyo. Am I pleased to see you! It must be more than ten years, but I could ask you the same question. Why are you here? You look in good shape although maybe carrying a little more weight? You're not with the Air Force anymore?'

Kamau's face changed. 'Paul. I never was.'

His answer baffled me. He had worn the uniform, been a quick learner and spoke all the technical language.

'As Kenyans, we welcome our British friends, especially when they are willing to make our country stronger but history has taught us to be suspicious. That's why I was assigned to your group. Play the role but be forever vigilant.'

'So the beer we enjoyed together was all a pretence?'

He let out a deep roar of laughter. 'No, no. I considered you a great guy, and it was a pleasure to get to know you. Rarely do I feel that way about foreigners but you appeared honest and genuine. It was never necessary to spy on you. So now, I'm confused. Tell me what has brought you to the attention of Mr Njenga?'

I was about to speak when Ashura returned carrying a bucket and a small towel in one hand and a tin mug in the other.

Kamau took them from him. 'Where's the soap, Ashura? Find some.'

The youth was about to complain but thought better of it and trotted back out.

Kamau held the tea to my lips. It was warm, milky and syrupy sweet. As soon as I swallowed, the sugar did its magic, returning strength to my body. Kamau placed the empty mug on the desk and as he cleaned me, I explained what had happened. When I was about to describe my experience within the interrogation centre, Kamau butted in.

'Don't bother,' he said, 'I know precisely what Chai is capable of. You're lucky he hasn't done more damage. Not yet, anyway. Look you must escape before he does.' He stopped wiping and stood for a moment, thinking.

'Can you help me? Are you able to get me out?' I was pleading, one friend to another, but it was the only card I had left to play.

'It's not going to be easy,' began Kamau, 'but listen carefully. No doubt Chai will return tomorrow to resume his questioning. He's quite mad and unfortunately is keen to cause misery but he has a weakness; he detests human excrement. You see, I've noticed when someone's being beaten, frequently they can't prevent themselves pissing or shitting and as soon as that happens, Chai has to stop. Apparently, it is the sight and smell that gets to him. He starts to rant and rave and invariably has the poor bastard dragged out to the showers, hosed down and then…' He tailed off.

'And then?' I asked.

Kamau looked embarrassed.

'Then our furious lunatic of a senior interrogator finishes them off.'

'I'm not sure how this helps me,' I said, despair setting in.

'But that's it,' said Kamau. 'After you've had enough, simply say to him you think you're about to crap. He'll stop and have you escorted to the shithouse. Once there, you'll have to persuade whoever accompanies you to remove your handcuffs, and then this is your chance. First, you will have to deal with the guard, though I'm not sure who's on duty tomorrow. In the floor you'll find a drain cover. If you can lift it, you might be able to escape through the pipes. They lead out into the road.'

'How do you know?' I asked.

'Ah, the centre was renovated last year. The toilets were a priority as they were blocked so often they made the whole building stink. Even Chai considered handing in his resignation.'

'But what do I do once I'm out?'

'Come on Flight Lieutenant Paul, you've done the survival course, remember? Use your imagination. You'll be fine. Ideally, I would help more but I can't let them think I had anything to do with your disappearance. Once we've cleaned you up, we'll get you dressed. Chai won't mind that. He enjoys watching men strip so perhaps you should suggest your bowels need emptying early on.'

He wrung out the cloth then continued to wipe. The water was cool and soothing.

'The bleeding from your nose appears to have slowed. You'll live.'

'So the First Aid I taught wasn't wasted on you then.'

'No, no. You were an excellent teacher and I must apologise for the manner in which you've been treated. If I had my way, we'd gather all our intelligence over a friendly drink. Alcohol loosens tongues more than anything. Friendship's preferable to enmity. You were lucky that Ashura was on duty tonight. Anyone else would have left you to drown in your own blood. He's a good boy but shouldn't be here. Did you know Ashura means "friend"? How does an innocent young man with such a name take a career in this business? I suppose we're a poor nation and a job is a job but we could do better.'

'You will, I'm sure. Kenya's a magnificent country. Hopefully I'll come back sometime for a proper holiday but perhaps with a different passport. I would certainly prefer to stay at the New Stanley rather than this place. And thank you for everything.'

'No problem, Flight Lieutenant Paul, no trouble at all.'

Ashura appeared at the door shaking his head. 'Sorry Bwana, can't find any soap.'

'None? Who stole it all? Well the prisoner looks OK, his bleeding's stopped so we should leave him alone. The day shift can clear up the mess. Lock us in Ashura and I'll call you when he's back in cuffs. Pass me the keys.' Ashura looked confused by the request but being an obedient subordinate decided not to question his boss and threw the bunch towards Kamau. With lightning reflexes, Kamau's hand shot out and caught it.

'You see, I should have been a cricketer, not a security officer.' He released the handcuffs and tossed the keys back. As the key in the lock turned, Kamau reached into his pocket and took out a knife. A single swipe of the blade to each plastic tie freed my legs.

With relief, I slowly stretched my limbs. They were stiff and sore. I gingerly fingered the back of my head and nose. Apart from an egg, my skull felt intact but my nose was definitely broken. A gentle squeeze with finger and thumb resulted in a grating sensation as the detached cartilage slid against the fractured bones. Kamau helped me to my feet.

'Can you manage to dress yourself?'

I nodded.

'Good, good. We can't have a British officer looking in such a state.'

'Ex-officer, Okeyo,' I corrected as I bent to pull up my trousers.

He looked surprised. 'How come, Paul? But you're still with the wife, yes? I know I never met your lady, but you were always talking about her and showing us pictures. A truly beautiful woman.'

My shoulders dropped. 'Life has been rather difficult since I left the Forces but hey ho, first world problems, eh? At least I rarely worry where my next meal will come from. How's your own wife? Any family?'

Kamau beamed. 'We have been blessed with four children and they all love school.' He eyed me up and down. 'Ah, that's better, now your appearance is more becoming of an English gentleman, even if the clothes need laundering.'

Kamau moved towards me, rested his hand on my shoulder and gently pushed me down onto the chair. His smile dissolved, replaced by worry and sadness. 'Sorry to do this, mtu, but I have no choice.'

I put my arms behind the back of the chair. Kamau clicked the cuffs, surreptitiously slid something into my pocket and then whispered in my ear.

'You remember our last game of poker when I won, and you had run out of cash?' He winked mischievously then stood upright. 'And you really don't know the location of our man?'

His eyes penetrated, trying to ascertain whether I was telling the truth or not.

'No,' I replied, staring back at him.

'OK, I believe you. Good luck, Flight Lieutenant Paul. Let's hope we meet again in happier circumstances.'

'Me too Okeyo and thank you. That's all I can say.'

Kamau banged on the steel door and ordered Ashura to open it. 'We'll let this bastard rot!' he shouted as he winked again, extinguished the light and closed the door behind him. The key turned in the lock once more and the footsteps faded leaving me alone with my memories and thoughts but also a plan. Kamau had offered me another throw of the dice and for that I was extremely grateful.

Chapter 10

The tropical dawn arrived accompanied by the sounds of cockerels and the hum of morning traffic. The little window lit up like a tiny fire as the sun rose; its rays piercing the gloom. It must have been about six o'clock and I had barely slept, but years of night work had prepared me. I pushed away the urge to doze and forced my mind to waken. The day shift would arrive shortly and no doubt Chai would be itching to carry on his interrogation. It wasn't a pleasant prospect. I needed to give him something to stop the torture. If I was seriously injured, any chance of escape would be gone. Just as I tried to imagine what fictitious titbit I might offer, my thoughts were interrupted by the rattle of a key in the lock. The door opened, and the cell was instantly bathed in electric light once more.

'Good morning, Flight Lieutenant.' Chai entered followed by a muscular young man with the stretched ears of a Masai warrior, carrying a metal tray. Chai indicated to him to place it on the desk. There was a plate of papaya and lime together with a bowl of a pale sludge, which I assumed was agali. Beside this, a white china cup and matching teapot. Chai sat down, picked up a fork, pierced a slice of papaya and shovelled it into his mouth. 'What is it you British say? Breakfast as a king. Something like that.' He waggled his fork before skewering the next piece of fruit. 'Sorry to tease you with this but I can't start work on an empty stomach. I expect you're hungry and thirsty too. Of course, if you help me, I'm sure Mr Mwangi over there would be willing to rustle up a snack.'

'He doesn't deserve anything,' grumbled the guard.

Chai, his mouth full of papaya, hooted, spraying saliva and orange fibres. 'Come, come, don't be like that Mr Mwangi. We should be welcoming to our guests; you know it's not polite to dine in front of someone.' He slurped his tea. 'So, Flight Lieutenant, I'm sure you've been reflecting on my request. Do you have anything to tell me?' He squeezed lime onto the remaining fruit.

I searched for an answer. What could I say? Apparently, Eldoret lacked a clinic, let alone a Mr Mbuto suffering from malaria.

Chai chewed slowly, staring intently at me, waiting patiently for an answer, his fork suspended in mid-air. Finally, he swallowed and wiped his mouth on his sleeve.

'Your nose looks sore,' he said. 'I heard you had a rough time last night. I'm surprised by Kamau. He's usually so gentle, a real mister nice guy; always tells me his technique for gathering information is more effective than mine. I assume that's why he allowed you to get dressed. But you must have made him very angry for him to mash your face. I'll have to tease him about that.' Chai stabbed a segment of lime with his fork, stood up, walked around the table and leant over me. He held the fruit close to my nose but I couldn't smell a thing as both nostrils were blocked with clotted blood. 'They say lime helps wounds to heal. Something to do with the vitamin C. You British and especially a medical man should know that. What did they call your kind in times past? Limeys, wasn't it? Kept your sailors alive as they crossed oceans to burn, pillage and occupy foreign lands.' He

102

stooped, placed his lips by my ear and hissed. 'Including our country, you bastards,' he growled. 'And now you've returned, poking your noses into our business, interfering.' He rose again, waved the lime in front of my face and twisted his head towards the door. 'Well shall we test the theory, Mr Mwangi? Let's play doctors and nurses. You can be the doctor and me the nurse.'

The strong man sniggered.

'Here,' Chai said, passing him the fork. 'Administer the medicine while I finish my breakfast. If your patient squeals, I'll give you this.' He rummaged in his pocket and pulled out my wedding ring. 'You deserve a little bonus.'

Mwangi moved forward, leered at me, flushed with excitement. He grabbed my hair, wrenching my head back until I was staring up at the blazing fluorescent light and his flared nostrils. I tried to move, but with each twist his grip tightened and it felt as if he could, with a single yank, scalp me. I glanced down just in time to see the lime's advance. Mwangi shoved the fruit into my bloodied nose, making the broken bones grind. My scream was followed by applause as Chai laid down his tea and clapped.

'Excellent operation, Mr Mwangi. I offer you an honorary degree,' said Chai, tossing my ring to his subordinate. 'From now on, you will be called Dr Mwangi. But crucially, is the patient cured?' He turned his attention to the agali. 'Well, Flight Lieutenant, are you?' he demanded between swallows.

I was in agony, hardly able to speak, and tears streamed down my face. The bastards had only just begun, and I had reached my limit again with nothing to offer. If I concocted something, and they checked, the consequences of lying might accelerate my demise.

'Come come, don't mumble, Flight Lieutenant.' He jabbed his spoon towards Mwangi and held up his plate. 'My good Dr Mwangi. The operation is only half complete. Here, another slice of lime.'

Mwangi sniggered again, clearly enjoying the opportunity to impress his boss. He reached forward and pierced the fruit. I shook my head violently and snorted, but the acid pack in my nose wouldn't shift.

'Stop, stop,' I shouted.

Mwangi looked at Chai, fork poised, waiting for direction.

'I'm going to shit myself,' I blurted out.

Chai dropped his spoon into the agali, horrified.

'You filthy bastard. No-one empties their bowels during my breakfast. Mr Mwangi, the doctor game is over. Take him to the shithouse and when you bring him back, I will be ready to administer a more effective cure. May I suggest, Flight Lieutenant, while your trousers are around your ankles, you consider your position carefully. You don't want this to be your last shit. Although, correct me if I'm wrong, isn't it true that sphincters relax when people die?'

Mwangi took out a key, released the handcuffs and ordered me to stand. He tugged at my hands, secured the cuffs again then dragged me to the door and into the corridor. I hobbled past closed doors, each cell either empty or its occupant silent, Mwangi never letting go of my arms. At the far end he opened another door, shoved me forwards and followed me inside. In the middle, I spotted a drain cover, precisely as Kamau had indicated. The windowless room was bare apart from a single small steel sink and a cubicle. Mwangi kicked the toilet door open and nodded to the filthy bowl. I held up my wrists.

'I can't crap wearing these,' I insisted, 'Might make a mess and what would your boss say?'

Mwangi grunted, took out his key and unlocked the cuffs. He withdrew a club suspended from his belt and waved me in.

'Thank you,' I said, entered the cubicle and closed the door. Delicately, I extracted the lime from my nose, desperately suppressing the impulse to call out with the pain, dropped the clot-coated fruit in the toilet, then bent my ear to the door listening as Mwangi paced the room. *What to do?* The manhole cover was only a metre or so away, but the presence of my Masai guard eliminated any possibility of escape. In desperation, I looked around for something, anything, to use as a weapon but there wasn't even a loo seat, only a steel bowl fixed to the ground. Despondent, I concluded even if I could have armed myself, Mwangi was a giant and no doubt proficient with his club.

But as I slumped to the floor in despair something hard in my trouser pocket dug into my thigh. I pulled it out and recognised it at once: my old army flick-knife, wrapped in a few Kenyan shillings. Not standard issue, but an antique I had purchased in a flea-market a month after signing up, and lost to Kamau over a game of cards. Perhaps my unlucky hand had just been flipped an ace. I opened the knife and shaved a fingernail against the blade. He had obviously taken great care of it. It was as sharp as ever, though not long enough to ensure it would incapacitate a man of Mwangi's proportions with a single stab. But the handle also concealed a vicious spike designed to pierce the thick tin cans of corned beef that had been the soldier's staple during the Second World War. I pressed the tip gently against my thumb and revised my anatomy. Mwangi banged on the door.

'You done in there?' he growled.

I flushed the toilet, pulled the door open and adjusted my trousers.

'That's better,' I said. 'I'll just wash myself.'

I hobbled to the sink and turned on the tap. As a trickle of brown water splashed into the bowl, I let the knife slip from my sleeve into the palm of my hand. Mwangi watched me from behind as I carried on slowly washing, hands hidden in the basin.

'Come on, hurry,' demanded Mwangi. 'Mr Cheboi will be getting impatient.'

I ignored him and bent over as if to wash my face. Mwangi shook the handcuffs and then his fingers gripped my shoulder, pulled me upright and around. In an instant, I lunged at him, driving the metal spike into his Adam's apple. The giant mouthed a scream but there was no sound: the steel had speared his neck, destroyed the vocal cords and blocked his airway. I grabbed his hair and drove the weapon deeper until the tip buried itself in his cervical vertebrae, preventing it from penetrating further. Mwangi's hands clawed at my back, tearing my shirt and skin, his eyes full of terror. Gradually his strength ebbed away, lips turned blue, and he crashed to the floor, pupils dilating. His chest heaved intermittently as a reflex response to anoxia, but no air flowed in or out of his open mouth. I palpated his muscular neck. Carotid pulse absent. Dead. I yanked the knife from his body and, as the blockage to his windpipe was released, a long sigh emanated from the corpse. Time was short. Surely, Chai would soon send someone to investigate or, if he had finished breakfast, come looking himself.

I grabbed Mwangi's club and wedged it with the handcuffs in the small gap under the toilet block door. Mwangi's body had come to rest on top of the manhole cover. I tugged his arms, heaved him to the door and with difficulty propped him against it. His head flopped forward as if drunk. I checked his pockets. Nothing useful, but then I felt my wedding ring. Beset with rage, I slipped it back on my finger. At the drain, the knife's steel point was ideally suited to lever up one edge of the iron cover, opening a crack that allowed me to slide my fingers underneath. Using all my strength, I lifted the heavy plate but couldn't prevent it from toppling over. Crashing onto the concrete, it rang out as loud as a bell, the sound echoing through the building like an alarm. The reek of human excrement escaped from the sewer and despite my injured nose, I balked at the stench. It reminded me of gangrenous bowel exposed during an emergency laparotomy. I stared into the pit and hesitated. *Was Kamau right? Did the sewer lead to safety or would I drown in the sewage below?* I heard footsteps and then someone trying to force their way in.

'Mr Mwangi, Mr Mwangi, you there?' It was Chai.

I stared at the body, then the hole. There was no choice. I lowered myself into the darkness and heaved the manhole cover back into place above me. Pitch black. Kneeling in the sludge, I groped for the exit. It was narrow. Too narrow for me to crawl through. So I lay down, my face millimetres from the filth, reached forwards with outstretched arms and inched my way into the tube. Pulling with my fingertips and pushing with my toes, I wormed along as slowly as a snail. The drainage pipe must have been less than five metres long, but it felt interminable as I pulled and pushed, my nails scraping the concrete and slime. The effort made me pant and retch as I breathed in the poisonous atmosphere. Two inches forward, one back like a human caterpillar. Chai would, by now, be battering his way into the toilet block. If I didn't drown or asphyxiate first, but was caught as I climbed out then I was dead meat for certain. His gloating image drove me on and the discomfort from torn fingernails was incomparable to the agony that bastard was capable of administering. Suddenly my hands were free, and I slid into a pool of foul-smelling waste. Gasping for oxygen, I blindly stretched up and heaved against the manhole cover above, forcing a gap. Fresh air and tropical sunlight penetrated the gloom. I shoved harder, using every sinew to shift the lid from my murky grave. Head above ground, I looked around: an alleyway, at the end of which the morning traffic crawled past, hooting. As I levered myself out, there was a shout from behind followed by a gunshot. The bullet ricocheted off the iron drain cover, its ring deafening. I ran towards the road, weaving from side to side, oblivious to the pain between my legs. Another shot buried itself in the wall beside me just as I emerged into the street, mingling, head down, with the crowds. If Chai had continued firing, a passer-by might have been hit, but there were no more shots.

As I walked briskly along, a few people stopped to stare, confused by the presence of the stinking, filthy foreigner in their midst. Thankfully most ignored me; busy with their burdens, own thoughts and the new day. Further on, a large crowd waited as matatus pulled off the highway and loaded up with commuters. Packed and overflowing with humanity, each brightly coloured minibus drove off in a cloud of dust accompanied by its own unique soundtrack broadcast from giant speakers affixed inside and out. I shoved through the throng onto the nearest bus, pushing my way to the middle of the aisle, paying little regard to the ensuing shouts of abuse. I passed a fifty shilling note forwards to the driver. If any change had been due, it didn't reach me, but no matter; I was hidden and could rest. A short hunched man with grey curls and wire-rimmed spectacles standing next to me looked me up and down and pinched his nose.

'Mtu, you been in some kind of war?' he asked.

I pretended not to hear and gripped the handrail as the bus pulled out, lurching from pothole to pothole. My leg, groin and face hurt like hell and sweat poured off me, adding to the foul stench that wafted from my clothing. The man poked me with his umbrella.

'English? In trouble?' he mouthed.

My heart raced. Was he a policeman or an informant? The man moved closer and spoke into my ear, his voice just loud enough for me to make out above the music.

'Don't worry friend, have no fear, I'll help you. Follow me when I get off at the next stop.'

What alternative did I have? An hour or so earlier I had killed a member of the Kenyan security services and escaped from their interrogation centre. I was injured, smeared in human excrement, minus a passport or a change of clothes, with only a knife and a few shillings to my name. Without help, I wasn't going far.

With a screech, the matatu shuddered to a stop. The man with the umbrella beckoned to me and elbowed his way to the exit. On the street, despite his years, he walked quickly, and I hobbled after him, always keeping a safe distance between us.

109

Suddenly he dived into a side road, lined with small shops and shanties, then into an alley with an open sewer brimming with plastic and human waste. A stray mangy dog pawed desperately at the rubbish in search of its next meal, ignoring the endless barks that reverberated across the neighbourhood. Finally the man stopped, looked around, then unlocked a padlock on a corrugated iron door and disappeared inside. Catching up, I paused at the entrance to check I hadn't been followed and peered into the gloom.

'Come in,' said the man, 'and close the door.' He stooped over a small cooker, a blackened kettle in hand.

'Please make yourself comfortable. Coffee?' he asked, touching the gas with a match. The light from the yellow flame flickered, supplementing the little sunlight that penetrated a makeshift window made from a dusty polythene sheet. The tiny room was filled with a rickety wooden bed propped up by plastic crates, a table big enough for one and a wide shelf evidently used for cooking and washing. As I went to sit on the only chair my head bumped against a gasoline lamp that hung from the thin roof timbers. The man laughed. 'Sorry,' he said. 'My home wasn't built for people as tall as you. And I apologise but I don't have milk.'

'Anything would be welcome. You're very kind. But tell me, what gave me away?'

The man didn't answer. Instead, he scooped coffee into two cracked mugs. The kettle whistled, and he poured water onto the grounds. 'Sugar?' he asked, holding a spoon over an open bag. 'I expect you need the energy.'

'Thank you, whatever you can spare.'

The man heaped sugar into both mugs, stirring the black hot liquid into a thick syrup. 'Drink this, then we talk and you can wash.'

He handed me a mug, the aroma so strong that even my broken snout was able to appreciate it. Desperate for the fluid and caffeine, I burnt my lips on the chipped enamel. The man sat on the bed and eyed me. 'Take it easy. You're safe for now.'

His voice was calm and reassuring, but I noted the "for now". We couldn't be more than five kilometres from Chai's headquarters. Doubtless all the local Police and security service personnel would have been instructed to search for the reeking Brit. This was at best a temporary reprieve. I blew on my coffee and tried again.

'Thank you. It's the most welcome cup I've had for days.' I said, sipping, the sugar and caffeine finding their mark.

The old man watched as the stimulants worked their magic. 'Better?' he asked.

I nodded, grateful that someone so poor had taken pity on me.

The man took a sip from his own mug and gently placed it on a box at his side.

'Those who work for the Internal Security Service are real bastards,' he began, almost hissing.

I nodded in agreement and continued to drink.

'And I should know. You may wonder why I gathered you were in trouble and decided to help. Let's say it's my way of getting my own back. Are you familiar with my country's history? I see you shake your head, so assume you know little of our turbulent past. In 1982 there was an attempted coup.' He paused and sighed wistfully. 'As a young man, I was full of hope

111

and optimism, keen to rid our land of the corruption that blighted every aspect of our daily lives. But the uprising failed, I had chosen the losing side, and we were crushed within days. Some saw straightaway that the army wasn't with the rebels, halted their protests and escaped abroad. A few stayed on to avenge. The unlucky ones were murdered on Uhuru Highway, shot down by troops loyal to Kenyatta. Others, even less fortunate, were picked up by the ISS, tortured and then executed without trial. There was no mercy.' He pulled up his sleeves to show multiple keloidal scars. 'Look what they did to me; my whole body is covered in burns. I can never forgive them.'

'But you survived.'

His face fell. 'Yes I did, but only because my parents handed over everything they owned. I insisted they didn't bribe my guards because that was exactly the change we were fighting for. But I am an only child and my mother couldn't be persuaded. As soon as payment was made, the abuse stopped and they let me go with one proviso.'

'Which was?' I asked.

'That I work for them: watch my neighbours, report anyone suspected of expressing anti-government sentiments or involved in subversive activity. Naturally, I agreed, otherwise I was dead. But do you think I would really help those bashas screw their fellow citizens?' He sneered. 'No way, quite the opposite. I have grabbed every opportunity to subvert and antagonise the regime and its agencies. Of course, it means I'm forced to live hand to mouth. Without official papers, you can't get a legitimate job and those who do offer employment take advantage of you. But I'm happy here in my small home, safe amongst friends in this shantytown, and especially on a day like today when I can help someone like you.'

'So what convinced you I'd been a guest of the ISS?'

'I wasn't certain, but it was obvious you didn't belong here. Tourists are warned not to visit this suburb; you were clearly hurt, your clothes torn and filthy, and seemed terrified. It was a safe bet. Either you had been beaten during a robbery or the police were involved. So tell me why they are so interested in you? It must be something significant for them to torture a visitor. They know that when a foreigner disappears, there's always an investigation, even if any inquiry is designed only to placate other countries' diplomats. But we mustn't waste time. If we're unlucky, you might have been spotted and they may have followed us here. Please wash quickly and I'll find you clean clothes.' He rummaged under the kitchen shelf, extracted a tatty plastic bowl, half filled it with cold water before topping it up with the kettle. I cupped my hands and splashed the fresh warm water over my face. The man handed me a bar of hard yellow soap and a square of worn grey towel that had once been white.

'I think it might be a good idea if you washed all over,' he suggested, holding his finger to his nose. Then added with a grin, 'Otherwise, if the ISS use dogs, they'll be able to track you right across East Africa. And while you do, tell me what brought you to the attention of the authorities.'

For the second time in less than forty-eight hours, I stripped off in front of a stranger. I laughed inside. It was becoming routine. I moistened the towel and tentatively, through gritted teeth, dabbed my wounds before vigorously wiping away all smears of shit and sludge from the rest of my body. As I

113

washed, I relayed my story, aware that as the man observed my ablutions, he intermittently mumbled and cursed. On seeing the burn on my leg, he blurted out, unable to contain his anger any longer.

'That Cheboi is a mkundu, a real bastard.'

I stopped washing and looked at him. 'What's a mkundu?' I asked with genuine interest. During my short stay with the RAF I had learnt little Swahili. I guessed much of what had been shouted at me was abusive, but it had never troubled me and I hadn't bothered to learn much slang. There were as many Kenyans who welcomed the British forces as resented our presence. The anger in the man's voice faded, and he laughed again.

'Let's just say that if you bent down to touch your toes, I would be able to see yours in all its glory. Let me find some antiseptic cream for your injuries.' He dragged a heavy box from under the bed and tapped on the lid. 'All that is important in my life is in here: family photos, my school certificates and my medicines.' He held up a large tube of ointment and handed it to me. 'It's very good. I think you should use it.' He sighed. 'You know, when I was a child, I always wanted to become a doctor like you, but that dream was crushed long ago.'

I squeezed the tube and coated the wound on my leg liberally. 'I'm sorry,' I said, 'but very grateful you decided to help people in other ways. How can I ever thank you enough?'

He waved the words away. 'Think nothing of it but when you leave my country, please tell the world what really happens here.' He pointed to clothes on the bed. 'They're not going to fit well but it's the best I can do.'

'They'll be fine,' I said as I squeezed into a pair of frayed trousers. 'Please take mine in return. I'm sorry; they could do with a thorough wash.'

He shook his head. 'No. I'd love to keep them, but they must be burnt. There's always a risk someone will recognise the clothes even if the owner has changed.'

'Let me pay you then. I have a few shillings.'

Again he shook his head. 'To succeed, you're going to need everything to be in your favour. In fact...' He stopped talking and knelt over the box again for a few moments before holding up his hand with glee. 'Ah, here it is,' he said, brandishing an old revolver. 'Take it. It's an Enfield; stolen from you British during the Mau Mau uprising. But unfortunately it only has three bullets. I reckon if Kenyatta's security men corner me and they are many, I would shoot two and then myself: they'll never take me alive.'

I pulled on a faded T-shirt advertising adventure safaris. 'Please tell me your name,' I said, smoothing down my wet hair. 'When circumstances improve, I'd love for us to meet again and then I'll be able to repay your kindness.'

'They call me Malaika.'

'Malaika, Malaika what?'

'Simply Malaika, it means the angel. Not my real name of course, but if you return, someone will find me and tell me you're here. I've enjoyed our conversation, but now you must go. Perhaps you should make your way to Eldoret, maybe your nurse is there, after all. If not, it's reasonably close to the border and, for a modest payment, possible to slip across into Uganda.'

'Why don't I simply walk into the British Embassy here in Nairobi?'

He shook his head vigorously. 'You mustn't do that. Those bastards watch every obvious place: the airports, train stations and diplomatic missions. They'll pull you off the street before you can blink. No, take my advice. Get out of Nairobi fast and don't return. In the provinces it's safer. There are fewer Kikuyu, but also many other tribes who hate the government as much as me, all living in hope. Money, corruption and power lies at the centre though all empires fall eventually, however big or small. You British learnt that lesson more than half a century ago.'

In the kitchen he searched for a plastic bag into which he dropped a lump of bread and the revolver and then opened the flimsy corrugated iron door. 'Here, it's only a little food. Good luck, doctor.'

I grabbed his generous gift and slipped out. The late morning sun bore down and clouds of flies rose from the piles of rubbish blocking the open sewers. As I hurried, head bowed, between the rows of shanties back towards the main road, curious faces peered from tin shacks, their eyes following me as I passed. No doubt the jungle telegraph would buzz and it would only take one loose tongue seeking a reward for me to be caught. Time to escape from the city. But how? Malaika had made it very clear – Chai's spies were everywhere. Public transport was definitely not an option, but Eldoret lay more than three hundred kilometres to the north-west; too far to walk. No, better to phone IMS and ask them to help. Perhaps the Foreign Office could be persuaded to assist even if the Kenyans brought the killing of the guard to their attention? I would have to find a computer and search for IMS's number. Surely all that was needed was to send a single message and I would be safe. But should I risk communicating while still in Nairobi? Chai was close. Better flee first, call later.

At the main road, a line of matatus waited on the opposite side of the street, each tooting for business. I hurried past, desperately working through my options. Nanyuki lay close to the Mount Kenya National Park. Could I return to the air force base and lie low there until the immediate threat had passed? I discarded the idea. Kamau had saved me, but admitted that all those years ago his task was to spy on his British visitors. If a single officer was in the pay of the ISS, the game was over. I walked rapidly in a north-westerly direction, but without a clear destination in mind. An internet cafe was what I needed. Perspiration poured from me, saturating the clothes Malaika had so generously donated, my mouth bone dry, lips cracking in the heat, blood in my nose hard and crusty. Ahead, a young boy stood behind a wooden barrow. Delving into a polystyrene cool-box precariously balanced on top, he lifted out a cup of ice shavings then covered them in a bright blue goo before handing the treat to a tall youth with afro hair dyed a similar shade. The buyer, his eyes obscured by oversized sunglasses, confident in fashionably faded jeans, perfectly polished shoes with a heavy gold chain hanging from the neck, casually leant against the barrow. My pace slowed as I neared. Instinctively, I tried to lick my lips but had no saliva. The youth picked up a plastic spoon, shovelled in the cold crystals and between mouthfuls joked with the child vendor. The temptation was too great. I pulled out some money and wandered over.

'How much?' I gasped, proffering a crumpled note.

Both boys stopped laughing. Here was an opportunity for them.

'How much is it worth?' said the youth with the dyed hair as he licked his spoon.

The younger thin boy sniggered. The older youth glared at him.

'I'm asking the boy selling the ice. I need a drink,' I croaked.

'Appears you need more than that. Someone been roughing you up?' He leaned towards me, his face inches from mine as he examined my every feature; so close I could smell his sweet sugary breath. 'Bust nose? Not shaved? In trouble?' He stood back and dipped his spoon into his ice again.

'Listen, I just want a drink and, if you know where there is one, an internet cafe.'

The youth grinned, revealing a row of bright white teeth minus one. He whistled through the gap, glanced at the younger boy and puffed out his chest. 'I can get you anything round here. Ice, computers, drugs, girls. If you've enough cash, nothing's too difficult. Just ask. What they call me, Amana? Tell him.'

The young boy looked down and whispered. 'Djimon,' he muttered.

'Djimon what?' demanded the older boy.

'Djimon, bosi.'

The older youth stepped forward and held out his cup.

'Yes, quite right Amana - "the boss" that's me. Refill, Amana. Top it up and he'll pay,' he said, jabbing his spoon at me.

I decided to take a gamble. 'I'll stand you an ice if I can have one too and you tell me where that internet cafe is. I've some shillings. Fifty for each of you.'

The youth's face crumpled into a grin. 'That's what's great about business. A quick fair deal for everyone. You can use my computer. It's in my office behind us.' He held out his hand.

I unfolded a shilling note and passed it over. He thrust the money into his pocket and showed his palm again. 'Fifty more,' he said. 'Otherwise I might have to call the Police and tell them you've broken our agreement.'

'The other fifty's for him,' I said, indicating the barrow boy who stood silently by, nervously scraping at the ice-block in the cool-box.

The youth sneered. 'Give me the money and he'll give you an ice. I'm in charge around here.' He lifted the side of his T-shirt to reveal the black handle of a small automatic and tapped it with his finger 'Nobody forgets that.'

I handed him the rest of the cash and the youth nodded to the young boy.

'Red or blue? Man U or City?' the young boy asked timidly, as he held two brightly coloured squeezy bottles over a cup of clear crushed ice.

'Who's winning the league?' I asked.

'City.'

'Then I'll have blue, like him.'

The older youth laughed again. 'Good choice, man. If you had chosen red, I'd have blown your head off right here, right now. Only bashas support United. Come with me.'

Gratefully, I spooned in mouthfuls of frozen crystals and followed Djimon into his shop. Inside it was cool and dark, a single light-bulb illuminated a small wooden table surrounded by piles of boxes heaped from floor to ceiling on the garishly patterned lino.

119

'Import, export,' said Djimon proudly, noting my surprise, 'Anything and everything. Here, sit at my desk. The computer's yours.'

I sat down and tapped into Google. Djimon stood behind, watching.

'A bit of privacy, perhaps?' I asked, not wanting him to know who I was or what I was doing.

'You really are in trouble, aren't you? A foreigner in the wrong part of town, bashed up, wearing someone else's clothes.'

It didn't take long to find IMS and a contact number.

'May I borrow your mobile, please? I need to make a quick call.'

Djimon pulled out his phone and held it out. As I reached for it, he snatched it back. 'One hundred shillings,' he said slyly. 'I'm sorry, it's business.'

I slapped another note into his palm and he handed it over. Djimon watched as I tapped the phone's screen. Call dropped. Try again. No luck. I checked the number. It was right though appeared to be unobtainable. One last go. Ringing. At last. I looked to Djimon, gave a thumbs up and waved him away.

'Hello,' said the female voice, 'How can I help you?'

'It's Dr Wright here, I'm in trouble.'

'I'm sorry, who are you? Where are you phoning from?'

'Paul Wright. You know, the Kenyan job. I'm in, well near Nairobi.'

'I'm sorry, this means nothing to me. Who did you want to speak to?'

'Is Sandy there? Sandy Driffield.'

There was a long pause.

'This is IMS isn't it?' I asked fervently.

'Yes, yes. You've got through to IMS but Sandy Driffield? We don't have a Sandy working for us and we haven't any operations in East Africa currently. Sorry to sound vague, but I'm afraid I've never heard of you either.'

'What do you mean?' I said, exasperated.

Despite the poor quality of the call, the other person must have detected the strain in my voice. 'Keep calm, sir. I'm sorry, I can't help you,' she said quietly. The line went dead.

Djimon held out his hand, and I passed him the phone. 'No luck?' he asked.

I shook my head, picked up the paper cup now half filled with sweet blue liquid and gulped it down. 'Fuck,' I muttered, 'what the hell's going on?' I returned to the computer. There was an email contact. Although I didn't know where or when I would have the chance to check for a reply, I typed in a message explaining who I was and requested assistance. As a final thought, I added in Tina's details. If IMS had abandoned me, maybe she would take pity and do some digging at her end.

Djimon watched me closely. 'You're definitely in the shits,' he said.

I stood and made for the exit, accidentally knocking over a box on the way.

'What's in all these then?' I asked, pointing to the piles of goods.

He didn't answer directly. 'I told you. I'm Mr Fixit. Say what you want, anything, and I'll find it.'

'Anything?' I laughed, somewhat in desperation. 'I need to escape from Nairobi and the sooner the better.'

'Don't you like our beautiful city?' Djimon looked upset but had also detected another opportunity.

121

'Not when some of its inhabitants treat its visitors as they did me.'

'I can get you out. Safely and unseen.'

'You can?'

'Oh yes, no problem, but at a price, of course.'

'Of course.'

I had little money left and doubted it was enough. To trust Djimon would be a gamble as he appeared to operate on the fringes of the law. The only hope was that my offer was more generous than the price on my head.

'How much you got?' he asked.

I showed him the remaining shillings and received the anticipated response.

'Not a chance. There are people to be paid and fuel bought. And you'll need food and water.' He stepped forward. 'What about that?' he said, grabbing my wrist. 'The jewellery on your finger.'

'That's my wedding ring,' I protested.

'Yeah, sure. Looks like gold to me. Needs must, bwana. Your choice... Or I could take it anyway.'

He fingered his automatic. I slid my hand into the carrier bag and grasped the revolver.

'I don't care for thieves,' I said, and before he could raise his weapon, I whipped out the gun and pointed it at his head.

Djimon slowly wedged his own weapon back inside his jeans, his confidence dented.

'I was wondering what was in there. Come friend. I won't steal your wedding ring. What would your lady say if you arrived home and weren't wearing it?' He laughed briefly, thought for a moment, before adding, 'I do mean "if". So I'll strike you a deal. Tell me where you want to go and I'll organise everything. In return, when the journey's over, you pay with the gold and the gun. After all, I'm sure you can obtain another ring before you meet your wife again.'

I kept the revolver raised. 'If you get me safely to Eldoret, I'll give you the ring; however I'm keeping this as insurance. Agreed?'

Djimon looked at the revolver. 'Deal. That's a piece of junk, anyway. Probably couldn't hit an elephant at ten paces.'

He slowly reached forward and gently pushed away the barrel. I didn't resist. Djimon was my best hope, and we had reached an understanding. 'When do I go?' I asked.

'Later. It will take me a little while to make the arrangements. I have a shipment of goods for Kitale due to leave this evening. The driver is reliable and will be happy to drop you in Eldoret as he passes through. Where do you want to go exactly?'

'I understand there's a mine nearby...'

Djimon interrupted. 'Oh yeah, I know it. I get regular orders from some of its workers. You can find most things in the town but sometimes they want something different – special girls, other entertainment. I relieve them of their boredom and their cash. Everyone's happy, a win-win situation. Look, you'd better stay here until nightfall. I'll get Amana to buy you food.'

'Can I trust him?'

'Yes, of course. No problem. He's a hardworking boy although still has a lot to learn.'

'Doesn't he go to school? No family?'

'No, neither. Poor mvulana, he's an orphan. Parents died from AIDS and he has grown up the hard way. Unfortunately, he suffers from HIV too. I buy his daily medicines and so far so good.'

'I'm sorry. For him, I mean.'

'Don't be. Most kids in his situation are forced to fend for themselves. Many simply give up and die. Amana and I have an arrangement: I look after him and in return he works for me. He won't cause you any trouble; he's reliable.'

'Could he buy me an antibiotic and painkillers?'

'Yeah. As I said, I can acquire anything though I'll need what's left of your money.'

Djimon led me to the back of his office, opened a door and pointed to a mat on the floor. 'Get some rest. You'll be travelling through the night and it won't be comfortable.' He closed the door behind him, leaving me alone. I lay down, exhausted; the thin reed mat feeling as comfy as a plump mattress. I took off the T-shirt, rolled it into a pillow and tucked the revolver underneath. Like Amana, I was now totally dependent on Djimon. I prayed he really was the Mr Fixit he claimed to be.

Chapter 11

I heard a rustle. Flustered, I fumbled for the gun, but it had vanished. Amana knelt on the floor, pointing the revolver at me.

'Too easy,' he said triumphantly as he handed it back. 'I've brought you the things you asked for. You've been asleep for hours.' He opened a bag lying beside him, then pulled out pots of pills and a tube of cream. 'The boss said you wanted an antibiotic though didn't say which to buy so I got lots of different ones. Even I know you must take the right medicine. And there's fried chicken, a pot of githeri and a bottle of water.' He giggled. 'Hopefully the beans won't make you fart because someone might hear you when you're hidden on the lorry.'

Djimon had clearly told Amana about his plan.

'Thanks very much. Good lad.' I looked at the large portions of food he had brought. 'Would you like some? Join me; you look as if you could do with a good meal.'

Amana's face fell. 'No thanks. I'm not well. When I try to eat it often makes me sick. Sometimes I manage a little rice in the morning; otherwise I live off the sugar I sell.'

'You take medicine, don't you? Djimon told me.'

'Yes. He pays for my treatment, but every day I grow weaker. It's as if it doesn't work. You know this country is swimming in fakes. Who knows what I'm really swallowing?' He pointed to the little boxes scattered beside me. 'Hopefully, your antibiotics are real; however I can't promise.'

'You're right, nothing in this world is certain.'

'That's what Djimon always says. Life like everything else doesn't come with a warranty,' he said quietly, fighting back tears.

I reached out and touched his hand. His slender fingers clasped mine, uncut nails digging into my skin. 'You'll be fine,' I said gently, although we both knew it was a lie. Too often I had held the hands of the dying, uttering words of reassurance as they breathed their last. What else could one do?

Amana pushed on his thighs with his arms and levered himself upright. 'Enjoy your food.'

'Thanks,' I called after him, but he was gone.

I sat in the dark, and slowly, using my fingers, ate the cold meal, washing it and a handful of pills down with the water. Then I squirted half a tube of the Naseptin cream into my nose. If it was a fake, it was a bloody good one; even the smell seemed right. I wondered what the time was, and how long I had to wait. The stifling heat had eased, replaced by a warm breeze that rattled the corrugated roof causing the rafters to creak. Then came the sound of rain. A few delicate spots at first shortly followed by a sudden deluge which hammered down, each bloated drop ricocheting off the iron, gathering to gush into the street.

Djimon burst into the room. 'Get up. You have to go.'

I leapt to my feet and felt my stomach tighten. *Was the building about to be ambushed?* 'Why? What's happening?' I asked.

Djimon saw my face, no doubt a picture of terror, and slapped my back. 'Calm down, mtu, it's OK. It's only the weather. The storm means the truck must leave now. With so much rain the roads will soon be impassable, and both you and

126

my deliveries won't get through. Come on, I'll introduce you to your driver. And don't panic; he's one of my team.' Djimon handed me an umbrella. 'Follow me,' he said, holding the door open just long enough to prevent a river of mud from breaching the parapet.

We strode quickly down the main road. The black sky repeatedly scored by lightning, yielding its vast reservoir of cool fresh water. Vehicles crawled along the highway; those with lights that worked switched to full beam, weaving past puddles that merged into small lakes. Children jumped from the kerb-side, splashing in the muddy garbage strewn flood, shouting and shrieking with delight. Nobody noticed the tall youth with the blue hair accompanied by the European with a broken nose, ill-fitting clothes and an umbrella. Djimon guided me into a scruffy yard and pointed to an old Iveco lorry.

'Your transport,' he said proudly.

I walked towards the cab and started to climb in, but he grabbed my arm and steered me away.

'No, we'll hide you in the back. Wait here.'

He disappeared for a few moments and returned accompanied by a heavily built man. 'This is Mr Otieno, your driver.'

The man held out his hand and grasped mine, his grip incredibly tight. Djimon saw me wince, laughed and patted Mr Otieno on the shoulder.

'This is the perfect fellow for the job. No-one messes with him; at checkpoints, borders, or when he delivers. Even a stubborn flat tyre gives up when faced by Mr Otieno wielding a lever. You'll be in good hands. Nevertheless, we don't want to make life difficult for any of us so we'll hide you amongst the cargo. You will be released when he reaches Eldoret, though with this weather, it's going to take many hours, so be patient. And remember when you arrive, give him your wedding band.'

'OK. I'll do that. Thank you for helping me. And I hope City win the League.'

'No problem and they will. Have a safe journey.'

Mr Otieno dropped the lorry's tailgate, clambered aboard, offered his hand again and pulled me up to join him. He rolled back a tarpaulin and pointed to a small wooden crate, its lid lying to one side.

'Get in and I'll seal you in,' he said. 'Don't worry; there are plenty of holes drilled for ventilation, a piece of foam for your arse and some water.'

'Thanks. A bottle or two of the beer from your stash up front would be better.'

'The Tusker's not for me you will be pleased to hear; I always stay sober. The boss would not be impressed if I crashed his truck and lost the goods. No, it's lubricant for the journey, gifts for the human obstacles we might meet on the way. And rest assured, the lorry's mechanically sound.'

'What are you carrying?'

He held the crate's lid aloft. 'Better you don't know, just as no-one has told me your name or why you're hiding. That way, if asked, neither of us will be forced to answer any awkward questions untruthfully.'

I dropped my carrier bag into the box and climbed in. There was only enough room to sit with my knees bent to my chest. Mr Otieno replaced the lid and hammered it shut. The small beams of light that shone through the air-holes were extinguished as the tarpaulin was dragged back over. It was pitch black and the only noise was the pounding of the constant downpour. For the second time I was incarcerated, although on this occasion the box resembled a coffin. Memories of mock interrogations flooded back; the verbal abuse, threats of violence and stress positions. Held for hours on end, they had been excruciating but survivable. This journey wasn't going to be comfortable, but I knew I could cope. All that mattered was to get to Eldoret and track down Stella and Mr Mbuto. I had many unanswered questions.

The truck's engine growled into life, the vibration resonating through the heavy vehicle. I braced myself as it lurched forwards. Djimon had suggested the road would be vulnerable. I recalled that the route to Nanyuki had been tarmacked, always maintained in a serviceable condition to ensure those at the airbase could, at the government's request, be called to the capital at short notice. Beyond there it had been only rammed earth, susceptible to flash floods. Was the road to Eldoret of a similar construction? If so, at least Otieno knew what we were up against.

It must have been two hours before the lorry stopped for the first time. Water had seeped through the tarpaulin and into my cell, drop by drop seeping into my clothes and the foam beneath. As the engine died, the rain seemed to have abated. Shouts, then laughter. I strained to listen, but it was impossible to discern any words. A checkpoint? Otieno needing a piss? I certainly wanted one. I felt like a dog in a cage not wanting to soil its own territory, but I couldn't hold on much longer. Anyway, the inside of the box couldn't get much wetter and, despite travelling in the tropics, I was getting cold. My mind drifted back to the dummy

129

military interrogations again. Pressed against the wall with extended wrists supporting one's whole body weight caused severe pain, but that was eventually superseded by the agony of a full bladder. Although hooded, you detected when your compatriots were nearby, their presence disclosed by the tell-tale sound of them relieving themselves just as you would soon do too. With that thought I let go and the warm urine pooled around my buttocks. I found myself laughing. In only a couple of days my transport had changed from the extravagance of the executive jet to the dog kennel. *Fuck, life was weird.*

The engine fired up, and we set off again. Soon it was clear we had left the tarmac far behind as the vehicle swerved from side to side, presumably as Otieno endeavoured to avoid ruts and potholes; his attempts only partially successful as my body repeatedly bashed against the walls of my wooden prison. It was as if the lorry had changed into a small freighter tossed mercilessly by the tempest of a violent sea. At last the truck halted again, thank goodness. But my sense of relief was swiftly replaced by alarm as the tailgate dropped and I realised that this time, without doubt, we had stopped at a checkpoint. Whoever manned the blockade seemed determined to carry out a thorough search. I froze as boots clambered over boxes and crates, desperately suppressing the shivers from cold or fear, which made my knees knock against my cage. Wood splintered. Someone with curiosity was using a crowbar to lever open box after box, getting closer. I held my breath. Then I heard Otieno's voice, calm and friendly, speaking in a language that was unfamiliar, certainly not Swahili. Other voices laughed in response, and the search stopped. Whatever Otieno had said or offered as a bribe had worked. The tailgate clanged shut and moments later the lorry moved off, once more swerving to avoid other vehicles and the worst of the road. I chewed a piece of the bread Malaika had given me, partly to pass the time and also in the hope that the calories might warm me. As the highway deteriorated further, I guessed we must have passed Nakuru. A few rays of sunshine penetrated the cracks between the crate's slats. At least the rain had ceased, and I would soon be warmed by the morning sun. A sense of optimism built inside me; it couldn't be much further to Eldoret and the mine, then hopefully all would become clear. Chai had insisted there wasn't a hospital or clinic in the town, but my destination lay somewhere beyond and surely had a first aid post.

Suddenly the lorry rocked violently from one side to the other, accompanied by the crunching of metal on metal. My whole body smashed against the crate's walls as it tumbled before coming to rest on its side. I nursed my limbs and head, rubbing to suppress the pain, and listened. At first silence, then a faint crackling sound followed by the smell of burning, an oily caustic odour that grew stronger by the moment. Fuck, the lorry or its cargo was on fire. I had to get out. I pushed as hard as possible against the crate's lid. During the crash it had been partly torn open but wouldn't budge. Acrid smoke drifted in, choking and poisonous, making me cough and splutter. I heaved again but no luck, my frame bent double, at a disadvantage. The crackle grew louder as the blaze started to cook my prison. I was going to die. I had seen charred corpses in Afghanistan, burnt beyond recognition, the ever present stench unmistakable, so I prayed the toxic vapours would kill me before the heat became unbearable. I banged on the wooden slats and shouted for help, but my calls went unanswered. 'Think, think, you idiot,' I muttered to myself. *The Enfield, of course, find the Enfield.* My fingers searched the confines of the crate until they found the plastic bag. Thank god, the gun was still in it. I pulled it out and wedged the barrel into the crack under the lid and levered. The nails loosened, and the gap widened. I pounded furiously with the butt of the revolver as the smoke thickened and temperature rose. Finally, with my T-shirt over my face, I gave a superhuman heave and the lid gave way. Clutching the gun, I slid out of the upturned crate and fell from the crashed lorry onto the muddy earth. I tucked the weapon into my waistband. The bright sun forced me to squint, but its shimmering disc was intermittently extinguished by the pall of dense smoke billowing from the wreckage. *Where was Otieno? Had he escaped the blaze?*

'Mr Otieno,' I shouted as I stumbled towards the front of the vehicle, mindful of the flames that whipped into the sky turning the base of the swirling black plume orange. Otieno's head hung limply from the smashed cab window, eyes staring straight ahead, motionless. Bottles of beer lay scattered on the ground, most broken.

'Mr Otieno, are you OK?'

I clambered up over a wheel and onto the vehicle's side and it became clear I had asked a stupid question: his tongue dangled from his open bloodied mouth. I waved my hand across his vacant eyes and felt his neck. No reaction or pulse – Djimon's driver was dead. Back on the ground, it was only then I noticed the rear bumper of a small car, the wreck wedged under the weight of the truck. It was impossible to tell how many casualties lay squashed inside or if they were alive.

'Anyone there?' I called in false hope, with the realisation that even if someone had survived, there was little I could do.

As the fire intensified, a tyre smouldered then burst like a grenade. It was too dangerous to stay. But as I backed away, I heard a child, moaning and crying, begging for help. Another tyre exploded, showering me with metal sparks and burning fragments of rubber. I crawled under the cab to see the twisted pulp of the car. A tiny hand clawed at the earth. I reached forward and grabbed it, then gently pulled. The owner screamed and begged me to stop.

'I have to get you out. I have to, I'm sorry.'

I tugged again, this time harder, hoping there would be enough space to pull them to safety. The child shrieked, its agony unbearable, but I had to try. No movement. Above me the heat intensified, burning my back; hotter than the midday African sun. I stopped pulling and stroked the tiny fingers, caressing each digit, desperately considering my options. Finally, knowing I couldn't leave the trapped youngster to be roasted alive; I let go and pulled the Enfield from my trousers. Quivering, I pointed it randomly into the darkness and squeezed the trigger twice. The cries intensified. One bullet left. I aimed again towards the source of the noise, but in that instant, the Afghani father appeared before me, cursing my actions, damning me, and I froze.

'Forgive me,' I said, retching. I slid out from underneath the wreckage, slicing a knee on broken glass and ran, hands over ears to shut out the screams. The blast that followed threw me to the ground. Shards of steel, splinters and debris flew over my head and a black mushroom cloud rose above the remains of the

133

truck into the early morning sky. 'Bloody Hell, Djimon, what were you transporting?' I murmured.

In the distance I spotted red and blue flashing lights racing towards the accident. Someone had called the emergency services, but it wouldn't pay to stay around. Anyway, there was nothing I could do to assist; nobody would have survived. The sirens grew louder. I needed to hide. The bush offered cover, so I slipped into the low dense scrub, pushing the vegetation aside and lay down, no more than thirty metres from the scene of devastation. My knee was bleeding badly with spicules of glass poking through the skin. With clenched teeth, I picked them out, one by one and then bound the wounds using a sock as a temporary dressing.

A police van and fire engine screeched to a halt at the site of the accident. Firemen jumped out, pulled hoses from the appliance and pumped water onto the fiery remains and the blackened vegetation. Clouds of steam rose into the air, white and pure, replacing the evil black smoke that only shortly before had signalled the deaths of all the vehicles' occupants bar one. I watched the scene from my hiding place, shaking and distraught yet fascinated. The lorry had flipped over onto its side, but the dice had rolled in my favour and I had survived. However, there was no elation, quite the reverse. I felt numb, despondent and responsible for the death of another human being; an innocent child who had reached out in desperation and begged for mercy. And I, a doctor, had failed once again in my duty. Trying to be rational didn't help. As I lay hidden, tears mixed with the soot and soil smeared on my cheeks, the ghosts of the Afghani man, his son and an African child choked my thoughts. I wrestled to

134

clear my mind. *Perhaps it was time to admit defeat and face the inevitable consequences.*

Parting the tall grass cautiously, I saw that the fire was out, the firemen returning equipment to the engine and two police officers standing by their vehicle, smoking. But then I heard a crack in the undergrowth as someone approached, and I gently let the green screen slide back. *Had they spotted me? Were they armed? Should I stand and raise my hands in surrender?* Suddenly, the ghastly images disappeared and there was Tina forgiving and encouraging me, telling me to keep fighting, not to give in. I pulled out the Enfield but quickly and quietly put it back again. No more killing. Not today. If they found me, so be it. Life was an endless game of chance. The footsteps stopped and there was a rustling accompanied by the sound of someone taking a crap. From the road came shouts as the others implored the person to hurry, followed by a rebuke and mutual laughter. The performance seemed to take ages, but finally the man tugged up his trousers and re-joined his colleagues. As I lay motionless and focused, I felt the first of many bites as an army of huge ants discovered the welcome supply of human flesh. 'Go, please go,' I hissed, as I squashed one after another between my fingers and thumbs, pulling their vicious jaws from my body.

Finally, the emergency team departed, and I jumped up, brushed myself down, flicking off the remaining shiny black beasts. I watched the rescue vehicles disappear over a distant ridge. It hadn't taken them long to arrive at the crash site so Eldoret couldn't be far, perhaps just over that hill. The occasional vehicle slowed as it passed the wreckage, its occupants intrigued by the devastation and the lone white man before accelerating away again. African roads; accidents all too common a sight. It was tempting to hitch a lift, but inevitably there would be awkward questions and I had encountered enough of those in recent days. No, it would be uncomfortable but better to walk.

I bent down and collected two bottles of beer that had miraculously survived the accident and subsequent blast. Not the ideal refreshment for my trek, but I stuffed them into my pockets anyway. A rubbish strewn footpath followed the road north west; the red mud baked hard and dusty. I picked up a scrap of cloth, wrapped it around my head as a disguise and to protect myself from the scorching sun, then set off, trying to ignore my sore knee. Sweat soaked my makeshift turban as I climbed slowly, wincing with the pain, breathless from the heat and altitude.

Exhausted, I reached the top and collapsed onto the ground. My tongue rasped against the roof of my mouth and head throbbed from dehydration. Time to drink. With the butt of my pistol, I hammered off the cap on a bottle of the beer and raised it to my lips. The amber liquid tasted like nectar as it washed away the dust and dried saliva. I sat looking at the valley below. Eldoret lay as hoped in the distance, a sprawling city surrounded by hills, no more than ten kilometres away. The beer lifted my spirits. A warm wind blew from the south, and it was all downhill from here. I could make it, but during the descent I'd have to think about how to reach the mine. With few resources, it would prove a challenge. And if Stella wasn't there, then what? Perhaps no one would have even heard of IMS and the mysterious Mr Mbuto. My head swirled as the alcohol took effect. I staggered to my feet and set off, swaying gently, but at least it was easier walking downhill and the booze had partly anaesthetised me; the stabbing in my knee now no more than a sporadic prod.

Arriving at the city's outskirts during the late afternoon, I encountered others on the path: women of all ages carrying huge bundles of wood or laden pitchers on their heads, some with babies swaddled to their backs, laughing children in pristine school uniforms, muscular men with wheelbarrows filled with tools and earth. Traditional adobe huts gave way to breeze block and corrugated iron shacks, then rows of two-tiered concrete blocks with shops and bars. The endless chirp of grasshoppers that had accompanied me on my walk was replaced by the babble of humans, all speaking in a local dialect.

Although I had visited Kenya before, the circumstances of my return made it seem as if I had entered a whole new world; one where I felt threatened, suspicious, vulnerable, and confused. Dizzy from hunger and thirst, I desperately hoped for another malaika as I had little money left, only one remaining bottle of beer and an old revolver with a single bullet. And I didn't know how to find the mine and would have to ask. It would be sensible to reach it as soon as possible and certainly before dark. But the further I ventured towards the centre of town, the greater the chance of accidentally bumping into a police officer or being spotted by an ISS crony.

Down the road I noticed a line of white cars topped with yellow roof signs. A taxi rank? The only viable solution came to me. Hire a cab. If Stella was waiting, then she could pay the driver on my arrival. If she had gone, some kind soul at the mine might take pity and loan me the cash. Irrespective, I couldn't walk much further and my nerves were falling apart. I hobbled to the front of the queue where a young man with mirrored sunglasses and a baseball cap sat on the bonnet of a Toyota listening to a transistor radio. He looked up as I approached.

'Need a ride into town,' he asked, seeing me struggle.

'Yes, a lift would be great.'

He grabbed the radio, hopped off the car and climbed in. I opened a rear door and slid inside, grateful for the chance to sit even if the plastic seat cover was torn and the springs broken. The radio sat on the dashboard, African music with a fast beat played at full volume. The driver turned it down.

'Where to, bwana? Which part of town you visiting?'

'The mine, please.'

The driver stared at me in his mirror, clearly disconcerted by my appearance. 'That's a long way from here. The roads are not good and at this time of year, if it rains again, maybe impassable, no go. The journey takes many hours, for certain, and I'm not sure my boss would like me to risk damaging his taxi. You might do better to hire a four wheel drive.'

I held up the last of my money and the bottle of beer. 'Please, this is all I've got,' I begged. 'But you'll get a big tip at the other end if you can get me there tonight.'

The young man looked dubious, then twisted in his seat and took the cash. 'You got business at the mine because you don't look like no businessman?' he asked.

I decided to offer an explanation. 'Yeah, I've urgent work to do. I'm an engineer, but if you're wondering why I look like this, it's because I was held up and robbed on my way here. Band of thugs assaulted me before stealing my car and everything in it. Thought it was a routine police checkpoint, but I suppose they just looked like police officers.'

'Have you reported this to the local force here?'

I hesitated. 'Uh, no, not yet, should I?'

He shook his head vigorously. 'Don't. They may well have been policemen. Even we have to contribute to their pay every time we're stopped. It's all part of the government's economy, another way to collect tax. Look, I won't be long, stay in the car. Back in a minute.' He hopped out and walked into the nearest shop.

What's he up to? Shit. Is he calling the authorities? What to do? I pulled out the Enfield and examined the chamber: one cartridge left. I sat with it hidden on my lap under my head cloth, finger on the trigger, and looked around. The late afternoon crowds swarmed along the pavements, everyone hurrying to complete their tasks before dusk, but no-one seemed to notice me. Behind, other taxis filled with passengers departed, horns blaring. The young man reappeared carrying a large heavy shopping bag. My grip tightened on the gun. He opened the rear door of the taxi and swung it in beside me.

'You OK?' he asked and then pointed at the bag. 'Supplies. Food, drink and cigarettes. I said it will be a long journey, so help yourself. Whatever you take, I'll just add to the bill.' He closed the door, returned to the driver's seat and started the engine. 'We'll make our first stop for fuel at Kaptakat. It's about halfway so if you want to rest, go ahead.' As he steered with one hand, joining the evening traffic, he reached across with the other and turned up the radio. 'I hope you don't mind the music. Say if it's too loud.'

'No, it's fine. What's your name?' I replied, winding up the window to hear him better.

'Daniel. My parents were proud of our past president Daniel Arup Moi so they called me Daniel too. My father worked for his security team.'

I swallowed hard. 'Where do your parents live?'

Daniel swerved and hooted at a cow that had wandered into the middle of the road.

'Ah, they're long gone.'

'I'm sorry.'

'No, it's the government that should apologise. Baba did his duty but was swept up in the corruption which enveloped Moi and his cronies. You can't work closely with these people without becoming contaminated yourself.'

'What happened to him?'

'Prison. You would have imagined that with my father's contacts he would have been out within days, a free man but…'

'But?' I asked

'He was released quickly alright… in a body bag. Mama said he had planned to testify against his boss. She buried him and then was immediately granted an exit visa. I grew up across the border in Uganda. When she died too, I decided to return to my home country. I'm proud to be a Kenyan and Moi can't touch anyone now. That was a long time ago. Anyway, what about you?'

'Me?'

'Yes. What's your name and why are you here?'

I answered with the first name that came into my head. 'Leo. And as I said, I work as an engineer.'

Daniel grinned. 'Leo the bold and daring lion.'

'No, I'm not brave, just an engineer.'

With a skilful flick of his wrist, Daniel swerved again, narrowly avoiding a matatu that had overtaken on a blind bend. He shouted abuse and tweaked the volume control on the radio. 'Crazy driver.'

The tune was fast paced, hypnotic and uniquely East African. It reminded me of my visits to the clubs of Nairobi during my service days. Alcohol and ganja, frenzied dancing, hysterical laughter and more booze-happy times. I relaxed a little, tapped my foot to the rhythm and watched the outside world pass by, hidden from prying eyes by the tinted glass. Daniel seemed straightforward. A young man trying to make his way in a country where jobs for youths were few and far between. He didn't seem like someone who respected authority.

As dusk fell, the conversation between us diminished as Daniel concentrated on avoiding potholes, ruts and wild animals. Despite the roller-coaster ride, I found my eyelids drooping.

A large pothole jolted me awake as the car's suspension bottomed out. In the fading light, I watched Daniel remove his cap and sunglasses. The two items appeared to be joined together. Then, illuminated by the headlights of an oncoming car, I saw why; Daniel's left ear was missing. As a doctor, I was naturally curious. I had seen casualties who had lost part of an ear from an industrial accident or the lobe shredded by a near miss with a high velocity round, but this one had completely gone. No skin or cartilage at all, only a small hole in the side of his head. Even congenital defects tended to be bilateral.

'Daniel, forgive me for asking, but what happened to your ear? I've not seen anyone missing the whole of it before.'

141

Just as I posed the question, my own head hit the roof as the car accelerated slightly and crashed over the rough road. Daniel fixed me in his mirror. 'A punishment,' he said slowly.

'What do you mean?'

He paused, tapping his fingers on the wheel in time with the music. 'Everyone has to eat. In Uganda, mama struggled to feed me and herself despite her profession as a malaya.'

'Malaya? Sounds like a country,' I said, interrupting.

Daniel's voice trembled slightly. 'It's Swahili. It means hooker. Naturally, when I was young, she hid this from me, but eventually it became obvious that all those male visitors couldn't be relatives, especially in Uganda. Inevitably, she contracted the disease and then most of her money went on paying the witch doctor. She didn't understand modern medicine. As her illness developed it became noticeable something serious was wrong, and the so-called uncles unsurprisingly stopped their visits. It was after that I started thieving: to survive and pay for her care. I was good at stealing but not good enough and eventually a policeman caught me in the market. There wasn't really a trial — it was common knowledge that I stole. By the following weekend they had cut off my ear without anaesthetic and in public. It took a long time to heal. And because everyone knew, I had to leave and chose to return to Kenya to make a new life. At night I still hear myself scream.'

'I'm terribly sorry,' I said. 'How old were you when all this happened?'

'Sixteen. It was ten years ago this week.'

'You know there are surgeons who can create a new ear using one of your ribs. The results are fantastic and you can manage fine with one less rib.'

142

The vehicle slowed as Daniel turned to me. 'I thought you work as an engineer?' he said.

'Yes, yes, an engineer,' I replied hurriedly. 'But I've seen a TV program about plastic surgery. Most people think plastic surgeons only deal with boobs and bums. That show demonstrated what other incredible things they can do. It was quite remarkable. Even people with the most terrible injuries can be helped.'

Daniel accelerated again and said nothing more.

Chapter 12

It was pitch black by the time we reached Kaptakat. The taxi turned off the main road into the only petrol station that serviced the small town as well as all traffic travelling between Eldoret and the Kerio Valley. Our food supplies had dwindled to a few biscuits and a single soda.

'I'll fill up and find more provisions. Anything you want?' he asked.

'If they sell bandages, please buy me two. My knee is still oozing.'

'OK, stay here. Let's see what I can get.' He hopped out of the car, filled the tank and then loped across to the garage kiosk. I watched him chat to the attendant who appeared to direct him to a pay phone. With growing anxiety, I saw him make a brief call before walking back. *Who was he calling? Why didn't he use his mobile?*

Daniel climbed in and tossed a paper bag to me. 'Here, the dressings you wanted and some hot samosas. All set?' he said with a grin and turned the ignition key.

I replaced the blood-soaked sock tied around my knee with the bandage and taped it in place.

'No problems at the filling station?' I asked, unable to contain my unease.

'Problem, bwana? What do you mean? There was no problem.'

'It's just you looked worried when you were making that phone-call.'

'I was. The girlfriend had been expecting me home tonight for a little servicing, but I hadn't told her about my journey with you. She was concerned I had run away with another girl. And I needed to tell the boss where his car was.'

It sounded plausible, though something still didn't seem right. 'Why didn't you use your mobile? It's there on the dashboard.'

Daniel reached for the phone and flung it back onto the rear seat beside me.

'You're the engineer. See if you can make it work. I dropped it in a puddle during yesterday's storm.'

I pressed a few keys, but the screen remained blank.

We headed into the hills and the road rose steeply following the rising contours in a series of twists. Daniel barely slowed, driving as if in a rally. I had already been involved in one accident and didn't relish the possibility of another. As we slewed around the tight curves, I found myself shaking not from fear but from disgust. Every squeal of tyres sounded like the screams of that child; unseen and unknown, whose life had been cut short. *Why hadn't I done more? What kind of person had I become?*

'Daniel, slow down a bit please. I don't want to be in another crash,' I urged.

He took his foot off the gas. 'You said you were attacked, not that you were in a car accident.'

Daniel was on the ball. I had to think quickly.

'Yes, assaulted, but I was also involved in a pile-up years ago, and never want to go through that again, thanks.'

145

'OK, I understand, although you did say you were in a hurry to reach the mine.'

As the taxi wound its way through the increasingly dense forest, trees and roots encroached onto the road. The radio hissed as the reception failed. Daniel reached across with his left hand and fiddled with it. It burst back into life with the music replaced by a late evening news bulletin. I listened intently. The president of the republic was lauded for his efforts in dealing with corruption, storms in the northern districts had taken the lives of an, as yet, indeterminate number of local tribes people, and there was a detailed discussion about the Al-Shabaab terrorism attack on the Westgate shopping mall. The atrocity had sparked a number of violent attacks on Somalis living in the capital. The programme ended with a short announcement about a police search for a white British man, who had been injured during an escape from prison in Nairobi and was considered dangerous. Suddenly Daniel slammed on the brakes. In the darkness, I grabbed the revolver.

He pointed to the road ahead. A small animal blocked the way, frozen in the headlights. 'Look. It's a bat-eared fox; I haven't seen one for ages. They are so elusive, secretive and cunning... just like some humans.' In his rear-view mirror, I saw him watch me as I sat passively, my finger still on the trigger. 'Don't worry, bwana, I'll get you to the mine, and nobody will ever know.'

I didn't respond. There was no need to because of the unspoken agreement between us; me the fugitive and him, a victim of rotten justice.

Around midnight the bone-shaking stopped, and the taxi drew to a halt at the gates of the Kenya Fluorspar Company.

Daniel flicked on the car's interior light and grinned broadly. 'Here we are and without incident or accident,' he announced proudly, 'I'll wait until you're safely inside.'

'What about your fare?'

He waved dismissively. 'Don't worry about that. Not all of us are thieves and criminals, well not for our whole lives, anyway. But you could do something for me.'

'Of course. Thank you. What?'

'If you know of one, please write down the details of a British doctor who could build me a new ear. I don't want to be seen as a pariah anymore.' He handed over a scrap of paper and a ballpoint.

I scribbled down my real name and phone number and passed it back. 'If you ever visit Britain, I can find you somewhere to stay and help you in your quest.'

'Thank you,' he said, 'I'll hold on to this carefully.' He pulled out a small wallet, slipped my details inside and reached to shake hands. I grasped his hand firmly, unable to express my gratitude any further, then opened the door of the taxi and stepped out into the cool night air.

Daniel called after me. 'Got your gun?' he asked with a knowing smile.

I nodded.

'Good luck,' he said.

'You too. Maybe see in you in London.'

Daniel waited while I spoke with the guard at the gate who, although surprised by the arrival of someone so late, seemed to have been instructed to allow me in; as if I was expected. I waved goodbye as the taxi drove away and entered the compound. The mine was a hive of activity. The massive breach in the earth's crust floodlit, serviced by dusty tracks along which heaped monster trucks, laden with precious minerals, crawled back to the surface. The quarry so deep that the giant excavators active at the bottom looked like miniscule mechanical insects as they clawed at the rock-face.

The guard showed me to the manager's office, a modest pre-fab that overlooked the loading bays and site entrance. In contrast to the frenetic activity outside, its windows were dark, and the building appeared unoccupied. He climbed the steps to the door and knocked. I didn't follow him, concerned that whoever was inside might prove to be unhelpful or even a threat. *How was it they knew I was coming? Was there a reward for my capture? Were the authorities waiting in the darkness to arrest me?* I considered the Enfield tucked into the back of my trousers and then rejected the notion of fighting my way out should the Police jump me. One round wouldn't save me. Even if I succeeded in escaping, the mine lay hundreds of kilometres from the border and I probably wouldn't get far. The guard took out his club and used it to knock again, so hard the door shook on its hinges. Finally, a single light came on and there was a shout followed by footsteps. A bearded, burly middle-aged white man opened the door.

'Well?' he asked, yawning, clearly irritated.

'This is the British man,' were the guard's only words and with that he returned his club to its holster and marched back towards the gate.

The man standing at the top of the steps looked at me, his face quizzical. 'Who are you?' he demanded, in an accent I recognised yet seemingly out of place.

'Dr Paul Wright. I'm here to collect a Mr Mbuto and also to catch up with my colleague, Stella Atkinson.'

The man's face broke into a grin. 'Come on in,' he said, holding out his hand, 'I've a message for you.'

I climbed the steps, we shook hands, and he welcomed me into a room that evidently doubled as an office and living quarters.

'My name's Christiaan Du Toit, duty night manager; most just call me Du Toit.' He pointed to the camp-bed. 'I was enjoying a nap; I hope you weren't waiting long. If everything is running smoothly, there's no need to miss the opportunity to sleep.' He filled a kettle and held up a jar of coffee. 'Black or white? I'm afraid we have plenty of sugar but only powdered milk.'

'Strong and black please. What was it about a message?'

'Of course, of course. I have it over there on the desk, one important telex in a sea of invoices. I'll find it for you now.' As the kettle built up steam, Du Toit rummaged in the pile of papers, frowning. He paused and scratched his head. 'It was here, I'm sure of it. I read it only yesterday. How very strange. Where has it gone?'

It wasn't a surprise that a single printout had been mislaid. In addition to the stack that Du Toit had searched, further heaps of correspondence and business records seemed to occupy every part of the office. The kettle clicked off. Du Toit interrupted his search and made the coffee.

'Here, take a seat, Mr Wright' he said, and slid a chair across the bare wooden floor in my direction then placed a mug beside me. 'Yours.'

'Thanks.' I took a sip, the coffee strong, sweet and very hot.

'It's Dr Wright, actually. That's why I'm here. I believe you have or had a Mr Mbuto in your care who is very ill. You've probably been told that my nurse Stella and I have been sent to collect this man then escort him back to the UK for specialist treatment.'

Du Toit took a long drink, clearly able to cope with the temperature.

'I'm sorry on two counts,' he said, gently placing his mug on the desk, 'Dr Wright not Mr, how rude of me...'

'No, no, it's not a problem. I find my title sometimes helps things run more efficiently. And the second issue? You said sorry on two counts.'

'I am afraid your journey is not over yet. Neither Stella nor your patient is here, I've not seen either of them. However, I do remember the telex mentioned El Wak.'

'El Wak? Who's that?'

Du Toit suppressed a chuckle.

'Who? No, no. It's a place in the north-east, not far from the Sudanese border. Perhaps they're waiting for you there. I'm sure that was the essence of the message. Oh, and she wished you good luck.'

I was baffled. Du Toit seemed helpful, friendly, though why would IMS involve him in this escapade when he seemed to deny any knowledge of Mr Mbuto and the purpose of our visit. 'Mr Du Toit, I'm confused. Please explain why you were expecting me.'

He hesitated, deciding to refill the kettle before responding. 'I'm an Afrikaner living in a black man's country,' he began.

'I guessed as much, so?'

He waved at me to be quiet. 'My family originally came from South Africa, yet I've never lived there. I was born in Eldoret and have always lived in these parts. Once many Afrikaners had homes in the town and the English too, though few remain. The decline started during the Mau Mau rebellion. My respect for the British faded somewhat after you lot failed to secure the land and our future. Until then, life had been very good. Afterwards, everything changed; intimidation and corruption rife. Empires, even yours, can be better than independence.' He collected my coffee cup and moved over to the sink. 'More?' he asked.

'Yes please. However, you haven't explained how you know about me and why you're helping.'

Du Toit spooned granules into the two cups and filled them with the freshly boiled water. 'School friend loyalties.'

'Meaning?'

'You do favours for those you relate to, people with whom you share a common history.'

'So you're Stella's friend then?'

'No, I've never met or heard of your nurse. I'm referring to Alex. We grew up on opposite sides of the street here in Eldoret and played together even though he was English and me Afrikaans. That's how our two cultures existed; divided by the main road that ran through the town but united in our opposition to the threat posed by the uprising. I would always help Alex and I am certain he would likewise look after me and my family. He lives in London now. Works for a security firm. Quite successful. One day I'd like to visit although I'm concerned if I travel abroad the government might make it difficult for me to re-enter the country.' Du Toit returned to his search for the telex.

I sat contemplating his words. *Alex. Short for Alexander? Sandy? Another abbreviation. Could he be referring to the man I had met?*

Du Toit thumped his cup on the table, spilling coffee over the piles of documents. 'Vervloek dit, damn it, what's happened to it?' he muttered.

'Don't worry. You've told me where I have to go so the telex isn't important.'

He fixed me with a stare. 'Worry? You do need to worry. We both do. The whole point of a telex is it's secure. That's why companies and governments still use the old technology. However, if you lose the paper printouts then... What concerns me is who might have taken it? We'd better get going. El Wak is nearly a day's drive from here and that assumes the roads are passable.' He sat there frowning then an idea popped into his head. 'If we take the company's Cessna, I could deliver you within a few hours. The only problem is we have to wait until dawn.'

'Because?'

'Visual flight rules. I'm not trained or experienced in night flying.' He relaxed a little and laughed. 'In the air, I navigate with a road map. If you keep below the clouds, and know the lay of the land, it's really straightforward.' Du Toit checked his watch – his demeanour changed again. 'Daylight is still five hours away. Let's hope the telex has been lost rather than stolen and ended up in the wrong hands. Otherwise we may find there's an unwelcome reception for us at El Wak.'

'But why are the authorities so interested in me and Mr Mbuto, this whole thing?'

He paused before answering. 'I've no idea, though if Alex has been in touch it must be important. He might be living in England, but his heart remains here in Africa. We both want the situation to improve, revert to how it was, although realistically our hopes exceed our expectations. We are just biding our time, waiting for the moment.' He didn't elaborate further.

'So what do we do now?' I asked, desperately tired despite the infusion of caffeine.

'Right,' he said, 'I'll need to check and refuel the plane. The strip is at the far side of the mine. It will take me about an hour. Do you know how to use a gun?'

I pulled out the Enfield and showed it to him. 'Unfortunately, yes. It's not something I ever considered I would have to do as a doctor.' I didn't mention the child crushed under the lorry.

Du Toit looked at the weapon and raised his eyebrows. 'Good and not so good. Good you can shoot but, huh, that...' he pointed at the old pistol, 'that's a museum piece. Little better than a pea-shooter though keep it handy whilst I'm gone; you never know who might visit.' He grabbed two radios from a shelf behind the desk and handed me one. 'I'll tell the guys that I'm away from the office and then hopefully nobody will disturb you. Any trouble, call me. And please try not to shoot anyone with that thing. You might even kill them and then I'd have a lot of explaining to do.' He clumped out of the room.

153

I sat back down, rested my feet on the edge of the desk, the Enfield and radio on my lap. *He was an enigma. A man willing to help a stranger because of lifelong loyalty to a friend who he never sees, yet shares the vision of a future based on a rose-tinted past. Prepared to put his career and maybe his life on the line for something undefined or someone unknown.* My thoughts turned to Sandy Driffield and Mr Mbuto. *Mbuto must be an important player in this strange game if so many risks were being taken to secure his extraction.* Sandy, Alex, or whoever he was, hadn't been totally straight with me, still somehow I wasn't surprised. I just hoped Du Toit was indeed refuelling a plane rather than gathering a posse to re-arrest me. I discarded the notion and relaxed a little. *He would only have had to call security and I would be a prisoner again.* I closed my eyes and dozed, unable to fight the exhaustion, adrenaline spent.

Chapter 13

I rubbed my eyes, trying to focus. Du Toit towered over me, his face etched with anxiety. 'Quick. Come on, get up, we have to go.'

'What now? It's still dark.'

'Yes, now.'

'You said we leave at dawn. Your flying experience...'

'Yes, yes. It's OK, there's a full moon. Anyway, it will soon be light and it's not safe to stay any longer: the police are on their way.'

I jumped to my feet. 'How do you know?'

'I have a contact at Kaptakat, works at the fuel station. He's always on the lookout for trouble. He just called me.'

'So that's how you knew I was coming. Sorry to be the trouble.'

'Hey, don't worry about it. A friend of Alex's is a friend of mine. Loyalty is a special attribute. Are you ready? Jump into the pickup while I'll grab a few things.'

Moments later Du Toit reappeared, lugging a large black holdall. He slung it into the back of the truck, climbed into the driver's seat and started the engine. As he set off, the radio burst into life. He picked it up with one hand, negotiating the winding track with the other. It was the security officer, guarding the main entrance, with bad news. 'Fuck,' he shouted, 'the police are at the gate. The guys can stall the bastards for a while but can't stop them entering. Hold tight.' He dropped the radio and accelerated, causing a plume of dust to rise as the wheels spun.

The vehicle rolled sickeningly as Du Toit wrestled to keep it on the road. 'Always wanted to be a racing driver,' he yelled above the din.

I grasped the grab-handle above the door. For a moment, I was back in my crate, tumbling around.

The pickup screeched to a halt at the far side of the mine beside the Cessna, parked at one end of the grass airstrip. Du Toit jumped out. I looked back across the chasm in the earth to the office block. Flashing lights. The police had entered the compound and were heading in our direction.

'Hurry. Load up, jump aboard and strap yourself in.' shouted Du Toit, pointing to the holdall.

I lifted his heavy bag out of the pickup, swung open the plane's right-hand door and heaved the baggage onto the rear seat which was already occupied by three jerry cans, then climbed into the front. The smell of fuel was almost overpowering.

Outside, Du Toit ran to pull away the chocks and then clambered into the pilot seat. He tightened his own harness and pushed the start button. 'Ready?' he asked.

'My door won't shut properly,' I replied anxiously.

'Don't worry, it doesn't,' he shouted, his eyes wide with excitement, as the engine fired and the propeller rotated faster and faster, making the whole airframe vibrate and rattle. 'Hold tight.'

He swung the aircraft around, switched on the headlights and opened the throttle. The ancient machine trundled onto the runway, gathered speed, its small wheels seemingly finding every imperfection in the grass surface, shaking every loose panel and rivet. I looked behind. Two police vehicles cornered the pickup; men jumped out and pointed their weapons at us.

'Rotate,' called Du Toit as he pulled back on the stick, and the Cessna lumbered into the air. He patted the instrument panel. 'She never fails me,' he said with a satisfied grin.

Suddenly there was a loud bang and the sound of tearing metal, followed by further metallic thuds.

'Fuck, what's that?' shouted Du Toit. To me the noise was instantly recognisable. Instinctively I tightened my harness, gripped the seat, and clenched my jaw. I could have been in Afghanistan. 'They're shooting,' I yelled, praying their next shots wouldn't hit us, the plane's control systems or the spare fuel.

Du Toit threw the Cessna about the sky, laughing maniacally. Finally, out of range, the plane levelled off, and he stuck his left hand out into the slipstream, raising his middle finger in defiance. 'Op joune, you bastards,' he roared at full volume. He closed the window, although that didn't quell the gale that howled inside due to the damaged aircraft skin and the partly open door. Du Toit checked his bearings. 'We need to fly northeast. Keep an eye on the compass for me as I concentrate on avoiding the hills. Fortunately the moon's bright and it will be dawn soon. I'll stay high until it's safe for us to descend and follow the roads.'

I sat with my eyes alternately flitting between the compass, the altimeter and the outside world. Du Toit clearly hadn't been joking when he advised me that his navigational skills were limited. It wasn't reassuring. 'How long do you expect the journey to take?' I asked.

'Not more than three hours, assuming we don't make any mistakes. El Wak in time for breakfast.'

'What if the police are waiting there? After all, someone told them that I had arrived at the mine and you couldn't find the telex. Surely, we've been compromised?'

By the light of the instrument panel, I saw Du Toit raise a wry smile. 'Do you think the telex actually mentioned El Wak? Geen, far too dangerous. The message was in code.'

In code, why? I was baffled. *What was he up to?*

'Anyway,' he continued, 'If there's a reception party, we will be able to give as good as we get.' He briefly let go of the control column, reached into the rear of the aircraft and unzipped the holdall. 'Take a peek? I'm sure you'll know what to do.'

I loosened my harness, pulled the bag towards me and glanced inside. 'Bloody hell. Where did you get them?'

He didn't answer my question, instead he posed his own. 'You've fired a sub-machine gun before, haven't you?'

'No, never,' I lied.

Du Toit looked surprised. 'Well, there's always a first time. Let's hope it won't be necessary. El Wak is so near to Somalia; trouble often flares up in the town or from across the border. It's bandit country.'

Bandit country. The words reverberated in my head. I despaired; it felt like the Middle East all over again — I thought I had left that traumatic and tragic phase of my life behind. Now here I was, a fugitive, sat beside someone whose agenda I didn't quite understand, who nevertheless appeared willing to risk everything for what? And there we were flying, in a wreck of an aircraft, towards a place in the desert where, if unlucky, we might have to fight. To say it was disconcerting would be a major understatement.

Just as the sun rose above the horizon the engine spluttered. Du Toit tapped the fuel gauge. 'Bugger,' he mumbled, 'didn't expect that. I filled it to the brim.' He tapped it again, harder. 'We'll have to find somewhere to land. Who knows what's happened? Thank God for daylight.' He dipped the aircraft's nose and donned a pair of sunglasses. 'I'll fly at three hundred or so. Keep your eyes skinned for a potential landing site or pray for a road. I reckon we've less than five minutes before this girl turns into a glider.'

I scanned the ground below to the horizon. Scrub everywhere, interspersed with animal tracks; a few gazelles and impala leaping into cover as our aircraft buzzed overhead. As we skimmed over a small village of traditional houses constructed from timber, reeds and adobe, a lone farmer corralling spooked cattle into a pen shook his stick at us.

'There, there, almost directly ahead. Isn't that tarmac?' I shouted with relief, shielding my eyes from the glare.

Du Toit leant forward and slapped the dash. 'You're right. Well done. Must be the main highway. Perfect. Who needs navigator training!'

The aircraft limped along, dropping and rising a few feet as the engine repeatedly coughed before bursting into life again.

'Do you think we'll make it?' I asked.

He shrugged his shoulders and pointed skywards. 'It's all in his hands,' he said, any trace of a smile gone, face now tense. 'Potholes are bad enough when driving, but if we hit a big crater with this baby, we could flip. Try to secure the jerry cans with the rear belts and then brace yourself.'

Du Toit used the last drops of fuel to circle the empty road below before lining up with the tarmac. The engine hiccupped one final time before the prop stalled. Near silence. Neither of us spoke as the wind whistled through the battered airframe. Du Toit gripped the joystick, totally focused as the ground rushed up to meet us. 'Gently does it, come on my beauty,' he whispered, his voice barely audible above the airflow. The Cessna's wheels squealed, and the aircraft bounced along the road. Du Toit kicked the rudder first one way then the other as he wrestled to avoid the potholes that randomly appeared, desperately fighting to keep the plane on firm ground. The machine shuddered to a halt; Du Toit lifted his hands from the controls and raised them to the heavens. 'Fuck me, that was close!' he said, beaming. 'Thank you, God.'

It took me a little longer to relax my grip, my clothes soaked in sweat from fear.

Du Toit removed his sunglasses, grinned and slapped my thigh. 'Hey, you look like you've died though I can assure you that you haven't, not yet anyway.'

Ignoring his comment, I forgave him for not knowing my past. 'Terra firma,' I said. 'Well done. Let's see what the damage is.' I thumped the buckle, released myself and climbed down, legs like jelly.

Outside the air was still, and it was already hot. So hot, the Cessna's wheels had torn ruts into the molten tarmac. We walked slowly around the aircraft. Three bullet holes in the left

160

wing and two more in the fuselage. One shot had passed all the way through, a few centimetres behind our seats.

'That was close too,' I said.

Du Toit stroked the plane's old oxidised aluminium skin. He poked a finger in the hole, withdrew it and held it up for me to see. 'Inch as good as a mile, isn't that the expression? They missed us and the spare fuel. Someone was definitely smiling down on us.'

'Maybe, though it's a pity their benevolence didn't stretch to the fuel tank. Seen that?' I said, pointing to a rupture in the wing and the small puddle of fuel below. 'The fuel gauge was clearly working. Any idea where we are and what we do now?'

'We'll sort it. Have faith. Help me lift out the jerry cans and the bag with the weapons. Under the rear seat there's a small tool kit and a roll of sticky tape. You'll also find water and beer. Don't know about you, but before I do anything else, I'm having a drink.'

'You want some water?' I asked.

'Fuck no. Never know what you might catch from that stuff.' He patted the Cessna's engine cowling. 'The water's for her. Pass me a beer.'

If anyone had driven past at that moment, they would have been mystified by the sight of two men sitting on jerry cans beside a light aircraft parked on the highway, miles from anywhere, drinking from brown bottles, laughing and joking. Du Toit opened a second bottle, put it to his lips and then pointed into the distance. 'Right. See that road sign? There must be a junction ahead. Go and check it out while I mend the fuel tank.'

'You think you can?'

161

'Hey, anyone who lives in this part of the world has to be able fix things, look after themselves. Talking of which; take a machine gun with you. Who knows who or what might appear.'

I pulled out the Enfield.

'This will do. Somewhat more discreet and it kills.'

'Really?' He raised his eyebrows. 'Well suit yourself. Looks like a toy to me. Let's hope you don't meet an elephant or a pack of hyenas. They'll definitely laugh if you threaten them with that piece of shit.'

The road sign lay about a kilometre away. Bleached by the sun, bent and dented where someone had crashed into it; Wajir to the right, Nairobi left. In the time it took me to walk there and back, Du Toit had sealed the hole in the fuel tank, refuelled the plane, and was sheltering under a wing, enjoying his third beer.

'Well?' he asked. 'Any luck? Have we been flying in the right direction?'

'Says Wajir right, Nairobi the other way. I'll get the map.'

'Don't bother. One of us lives in this country. Wajir's on the route to El Wak, though we need to take care as we're very close to the Somali border.' He guzzled the rest of his beer and threw the empties into the bush to join the other trash that littered the road.

'Would the Somalis intercept us if we stray into their airspace?' I asked, not relishing the idea of being held in that country.

Du Toit detected the anxiety in my voice. 'No, don't think they have the resources to do that, but...' he patted the

162

Cessna, 'if the old girl misbehaves, we could end up grounded and be taken hostage. Even with our weapons, I wouldn't fancy our chances. The whole nation is armed to the teeth, and we would be a valuable prize. Come on; let's go before some drunk drives his truck into our transport.'

Some drunk. 'Talk about black pots and kettles,' I said to myself as I clambered back into the plane and strapped in. 'No bottle to throttle rule for amateur pilots here then?' I teased.

Du Toit adjusted his sunglasses, checked his straps. 'Bottle to throttle? What's that?' he asked, smirking. 'Never heard of it.' He pushed the starter, and the engine spluttered into life. 'I'll follow the highway all the way to El Wak. Should be there in an hour.'

The noise in the cockpit grew to a crescendo as the poor plane shook violently. Every loose bolt rattled as the fragile machine trundled down the makeshift runway before lifting into the air. Moments later, with the road junction below, Du Toit banked sharply right to follow the black ribbon that stretched to the horizon, the aircraft swaying gently from side to side. *Makes drink-driving seem an innocent activity,* I mused.

'Is the airstrip at El Wak by the town?' I asked, shouting above the incessant din.

He glanced across. 'There is a strip that services the local population, however we won't land there. If we use the main airfield, I wouldn't be at all surprised if there was a welcoming party waiting. And it's not the sort of bash either of us would enjoy. I'm aiming for another smaller place further north.'

'If there's alternative airstrip, surely the authorities are aware of that too?'

'Who says we're going to land at an airfield? Roads, as you have seen, aren't only for vehicles.'

'And when we arrive, what do we do next? How do I find my nurse?'

He didn't answer immediately but tapped the fuel gauge and the compass, checking he was happy with both. 'If she's anywhere, I know exactly where she'll be,' he said. There was an air of confidence in Du Toit's voice. It was reassuring, although I had learnt that for him, nothing seemed too difficult. What I couldn't fathom, though, was how he knew where a British nurse and a French aircrew might be holed up? To me, it appeared he was better informed about IMS than he was prepared to admit.

Du Toit's estimate was about right. Just under an hour later, the little plane flew over the settlement of El Wak; thin lines of corrugate covered shanties all leading to the centre with its few substantial brick buildings. Some locals paused to watch the aircraft as it passed low over their heads; the occupants of the Cessna unaware that not all observers of their arrival were innocent bystanders. With the threat of Somali insurgents, the Kenyan armed forces and security services maintained a major presence in the town. On this day, they had been instructed not only to watch for terrorists, but to be vigilant in case two fugitives tried to escape the country.

Du Toit followed a minor road north of El Wak, heading out into the desert. After a further fifteen minutes of flying he leant forward, searching for something. 'See the long straight section ahead? Look out for a group of large sheds. They're farm buildings and should be visible just before the road makes a sharp bend. If I'm correct, we'll be on the ground shortly.'

'OK. Farm buildings,' you said. 'Can anything grow here? It's all sand and scrub.'

'You'd be surprised. It might not be cattle and wheat, but there's a market for camels and aloe vera. And if the drought is really bad, there are always other ways to make ends meet. Remember, we are near Somalia.' He didn't elaborate.

As predicted, after a few minutes, a compound composed of a collection of barns surrounded by a high fence appeared to one side of the road. Du Toit circled the area, picked up his radio and called repeatedly. 'Fluorspar calling, fluorspar calling, come in please.' As he made his third circuit, the radio crackled into life.

'We can see you, Fluorspar. It's safe to land. We'll open the gates and you can taxi right inside.'

'Cheers. Any cold beer available?'

'We assumed you were bringing supplies.'

'Sorry, you're out of luck although I've a special cargo.'

'That's good news. Don't worry, we have refreshments.'

'Dankie tog. Otherwise I would be turning this baby around and going straight back home, special cargo or not.'

Moments later the Cessna bounced along the dusty road, taxied slowly through the farm entrance and came to a stop. As soon as the machine was safely inside, a giant of a man wearing white overalls and a large floppy hat pulled the mesh gates closed. He signalled to Du Toit, indicating a large shed with huge sliding doors. Du Toit manoeuvred the plane to a point just outside and cut the engine. The man with the hat followed and then stood patiently waiting for the propeller to cease rotating before stepping forward to greet the visitors. He climbed up on the aircraft's step and opened the door.

165

'Welcome to the farm,' he said. He shook Du Toit's hand, then looked to me and beamed. 'You must be Dr Wright.'

I nodded, noting his thick African accent.

'I'm Alamini. There's someone here who will be very pleased to see you. Follow me.'

Still feeling nervous, I hid the Enfield in a small bag and climbed down from the aircraft.

Du Toit patted the Cessna on the nose. 'Well done, old girl,' he said.

'Well done, Du Toit,' said Alamini. He glanced at me. 'I hope this man didn't frighten you; his flying skills are legendary.'

At the far end of the makeshift hangar, Alamini ushered us from the heat into an office cooled by a large ceiling fan. 'Wait here a moment. I'll be back shortly. There are drinks in the fridge. Help yourselves.'

Du Toit walked over and opened the fridge door. 'Want one?' he asked, holding up two bottles.

'Is there anything non-alcoholic? I'm thirsty, but would prefer to keep my wits about me.' I replied, clutching the bag.

'Suit yourself.' He rummaged inside, threw a can in my direction, popped the crown cap from a bottle with his teeth and flopped into a chair. I remained standing, coke in one hand, the bag with the gun in the other.

Du Toit beckoned to another seat. 'Take it easy. You don't need the pistol. You're amongst friends here. The only danger lies beyond the wire and Alamini is very observant. If there's trouble, he'll spot it a mile off.'

As I pulled the ring on the can, Alamini returned. 'Dr Wright. Your patient awaits. Come with me.'

166

Confused, I looked across to Du Toit who simply raised his eyebrows 'Go ahead, Paul. It's OK,' he said, putting the beer to his lips.

Alamini held open a heavy metal door and waved me through. The door clanged shut behind and I followed the African along an air-conditioned corridor; white, gleaming, clinically clean, as cold as a freezer compared to the harsh heat outside. This wasn't a typical farm, more a hospital, the characteristic smell of disinfectant all pervading. Alamini didn't speak until we reached the far end when he opened another door and called out. 'The doctor's here. I'll leave you now.'

I stepped from the bright corridor into a hushed cramped dimly lit room.

'Hello Paul,' said Stella quietly, 'It's good to see you again.' She sat beside the only bed, pen in hand, her unconscious patient connected to a ventilator and wired to an array of monitors. The breathing machine pumped gas rhythmically into the man's chest and each beat of the body's heart resulted in a soft bleep from the ECG. It was like a scene from any intensive care unit anywhere, though this was bizarre. A single incumbent in a tiny ward hidden within a so-called 'farm' on the Kenyan-Somali border.

'This is Mr Mbuto,' announced Stella. 'He's doing very well.'

For a moment I was dumbstruck. 'Stella. I'm delighted to see you too, though tell me, what the fuck is going on?'

Stella held a finger to her lips then checked the monitors, laid down her paperwork and glanced at her watch. 'I'll check if Adimu is awake. If she takes over, we can chat. It's almost time

167

for her shift, anyway.' She pointed to the immobile form on the bed, covered in a single white sheet. 'It's better we speak out of earshot. Be so kind as to keep an eye on things while I find Adimu. As you see, the kit is all standard stuff, and he's quite stable. Back in a minute or two.' She stood up, waited until I was settled beside the patient then walked from the room.

The ventilator and physiological monitors were state-of-the art. Resuscitation equipment including a defibrillator placed at the end of the bed, to one side a work surface with boxes of gloves, spare syringes and other customary sundries. Everything neat and spotlessly clean. I could have been in Bastion, although this peaceful scene lacked the blood and guts of the war zone. I systematically checked all the patient's parameters: Heart rate steady, blood pressure perhaps slightly low yet oxygen levels normal, ventilator settings unremarkable, no increase in oxygen requirements. Sedation was being provided by drugs derived from a column of infusion pumps, flowing through tubes and linked together before they joined a single cannula in the forearm. I examined the labels: all proprietary names with their generic alternatives printed below: propofol, midazolam and atracurium. A typical cocktail to render someone immobile and insensate. I turned my attention to the nursing charts: except for normal diurnal variation, almost straight lines and no high temperature. It seemed Mr Mbuto had recovered from his malaria. I scratched my head. *Why keep him asleep?*

The door opened and Stella entered accompanied by a pretty young African woman with traditional tribal facial scars dressed in a smart clean tunic and trousers.

'Adimu, meet Dr Wright. He's an intensive therapy specialist. Now he's here, we will be moving Mr Mbuto as soon as transport is arranged. Would you mind taking over while I brief the doctor? Nothing much has changed. There's more propofol drawn up and ready in the fridge and I've turned our patient within the last hour. I was just about to change his urine drainage bag and carry out mouth and eye care when the cavalry arrived. Sorry to leave you with those tasks. I'll be in the office with our knight in shining armour.'

Stella was throwing out compliments left, right and centre leaving me wondering what her game was. I had many questions and wasn't convinced she was going to be completely straight with her answers. Adimu smiled at me, settled into her chair and picked up the observations chart without a word.

'Come to the office,' said Stella. 'I'll make some tea. Fancy a cup?'

I followed her back down the corridor. She opened the door to another room and ushered me inside. It was windowless and bare apart from two beds, a shower cubicle and a kitchenette lit by a single fluorescent strip light. Stella's personal bag lay open beside one immaculately made bed, clothes scattered over and around the other.

'I'm sorry about the mess,' began Stella, pointing to the chaos. 'Adimu is an excellent nurse and yet hopelessly untidy once she steps out of the clinical environment. She would benefit from a stint in an old fashioned hospital with a traditional matron – alas, those times are long gone. She seems to spend an inordinate length of time doing her make-up. I don't know if it's to hide the scars on her face or not. Perhaps they bring back memories of being cut as a child. It can't have been pleasant, though it is traditional amongst many tribes-people even today. Do you find them attractive?'

169

I had noticed the symmetrical lines of pimple-like scars that formed swirls on her cheeks, although it had been her shy smile that I had found most appealing.

'Talking about messes, what's wrong with your nose?' she asked, leaning forward and gently twisting my face to the side. 'What happened? Let me clean it for you. Do you have any other injuries?'

'Only my knee, you could check that.' I wasn't going to ask her to examine my groin. *Strange, what made her wonder whether I had other wounds?* And she hadn't seemed surprised to see me or shocked by my appearance.

'OK. Can you make the tea while I collect some things from the stores? Everything's in the cupboard above the sink. Won't be long,' she said, and disappeared from the room.

I don't know why I did it, but as soon as the door was closed, I knelt at the foot of Stella's bed and started to rummage in her bag, unsure what I was really looking for or what I might find. It felt perverse to be searching through a middle-aged woman's belongings: underwear, wash-bag, a change of uniform, the book she had been reading on the flight out and two in reserve. At the bottom, I found a small black diary. Opening it at a random page, I discovered a list of dates beside the names of countries, most though not all Middle-Eastern or East African. Each entry appeared to be associated with a pair of capital letters and a short word; some decipherable, others in Arabic or another foreign script. *Codes or people?* I was intrigued. *Had I not seen similar information on the whiteboards in Croydon?*

The kettle whistled, disrupting my search and just as I slipped the slim tome into my trouser back pocket, Stella returned clutching pads and dressings. At the sink, I poured boiling water over a spoonful of leaves lying in each of two mugs.

'Sorry, couldn't find a strainer,' I said, holding up the tea.

Stella laughed. 'Standards, Dr Wright, standards. We use the cafetiere from the cupboard. It's not a proper teapot. Still, at least you can enjoy a drink without roughage. Now sit down and I'll wash your face unless you want a shower?'

A soaking would have been welcome, yet I wanted answers urgently. 'Thank you. That would be kind. I've tried to pack my nose, though it might need a thorough clean. You must remember, I'm a doctor not a proficient nurse like you.'

'Flattery, Paul, will get you everywhere.'

'You've been everywhere,' Stella, I thought, feeling the little book tucked into my trousers. I was itching to examine it further. A visit to the toilet would provide the opportunity and then I had to return it surreptitiously.

'Move that chair over to the sink and sit down, Paul. Promise to be as gentle as possible.'

Stella dabbed my swollen nose with damp cotton wool, wiping bloody crusts from my tender nostrils.

'Come on, explain the real purpose of our endeavours,' I demanded as she dropped the contaminated swab into a bin and reached for the next clean piece. 'Why aren't we at Eldoret and what makes our Mr Mbuto so important that the Kenyans were prepared to torture me for information I didn't have? I think, after all I've been through, I deserve some answers.'

Stella squeezed excess sterile water from a swab and dabbed my face again. 'I'm sorry you've had such a rough time. We were so unlucky with the storm. The weather really threw a spanner into the works.' She paused. 'As soon as you were

171

arrested at the New Stanley, there were people working all hours to find you, aiming to secure your release.'

'Nevertheless they didn't, did they?'

Stella tugged at the dressing in my nose making me wince then cry out. 'Hey, that's bloody sore.'

'Sorry again,' she said, ignoring my question and discomfort. She tugged harder and the slimy pus-coated pack popped out.

'Stop, stop a moment,' I whimpered, wiping away tears and grabbing her arm.

'No-one cared where I was or what was happening to me. Fortunately I escaped, even without assistance. I was lucky, very lucky. A few more hours, and no doubt, I would have become another statistic: Body found in a ditch somewhere; an innocent traveller murdered for his cash and credit cards.'

'You're wrong, Paul,' she said softly, freeing herself from my grip. 'I'm sorry you were beaten up yet didn't someone help you abscond?' A knowing smile flitted across her face. 'A man who showed you the way…'

My thoughts returned to the interrogation centre and Okeyo Kamau.

'It is impossible to do this vital work alone,' continued Stella. 'It's no different to running a hospital. Everyone acknowledges the roles of the doctors and nurses, the cleaners and the kitchen staff, yet they forget about all the others who contribute to the success of the organisation. No operation can succeed without the technicians and quartermasters doing their bit in the background.'

'So what's your role in this global game, Stella? Are you just a nurse and is Mr Mbuto simply your patient or is there more?' I asked, noting the military reference.

Stella squirted antiseptic cream onto her gloved finger and gently wiped it around my nostrils. 'I'm a nurse, Paul, cleansing the world of germs as and when I can. It's my responsibility and yours too. You've been involved in this fight before, although as part of the military. There are good reasons why Sandy Driffield offered you the post and don't forget the generous reward waiting for you at the end.'

I decided to change tack. 'Where are the French aircrew?'

'Gone. Another job in the pipeline. They couldn't wait; it's too expensive to keep aircraft idle: money's only made when the undercarriage is raised.'

'So where's our kit and how do we get out?'

Stella detected the anxiety in my voice. 'Relax, everything is safe including the duty-free although we might need to give something to Christiaan; oil the wheels or should I say propeller. He's always so helpful.'

'You've met him before then?' I replied, thinking, 'Du Toit you liar.'

Stella paused. 'Let's just say, he's an important link in this patient transfer service with opinions and objectives that dovetail with our own.'

'And what might those objectives be?'

Stella wiped my face one final time. 'There, your nose looks nothing like as swollen with the pack removed. You appear almost human again. Now drop your kegs, Paul. Let's check that knee.'

173

I wriggled out of my trousers and rested my leg on another chair. 'You didn't answer my question, Stella,' I said as she pulled on a fresh pair of gloves and began to unwrap the bandage.

'Nice legs,' she said, delaying any response further. She sighed. 'In summary, my task, no ours, is to transfer Mr Mbuto safely back to the UK, nothing more.'

'Stella, you and I both recognise he's not ill, not now anyway, if he ever was. The physiological parameters don't fit. So explain to me why the sedation? It doesn't seem right.'

Instead of replying straightaway, Stella dabbed the gashes in my knee with a cleansing solution, causing them to sting like hell. 'First do no harm,' she said as she took a syringe and whooshed cleansing agent into the wound. 'Perhaps the corollary is to try to do some good. Not all patients appreciate what will help them and sometimes, out of necessity, one is required to act in a rather more paternalistic manner than usual.'

I butted in. 'Or maternalistic in your case.'

Stella failed to laugh at my quip. 'Yes, I suppose you're right.'

'So cut the ethical waffle and tell me how this helps Mr Mbuto.'

Stella bent forward and examined my knee carefully, unaware of how I had received the injury. 'See what the authorities did to you? And you're a British subject, a foreigner. How do you think they treat their own? All I know is we need to extract Mr Mbuto as soon as possible. And now you're here, there's no reason to delay.'

'Extract'. The word stuck in my head. She hadn't said transfer or accompany but 'extract'. This wasn't a standard

medical evacuation in any sense, more something secretive and sinister.

'What if I decide that I no longer wish to be involved, I want out?'

Stella took a padded dressing and wrapped it around my knee. 'No-one can stop you yet neither could they prevent the Kenyans from finding you and…'

'That sounds like a veiled threat,' I said curtly.

'It's how it is, Paul. The world is a nasty place. So much happens that shouldn't. However it doesn't mean we should rest on our backsides and idly watch events unfold. There's always something useful to be done. You, with your background, are ideally suited to act. In a day or so we will be home having discharged our duty. I will wait for my next deployment and you, if you wish, can return to the NHS. It will be your choice, though for now I suggest you help me transport our patient to safety and let others decide on the morality of our actions.'

'So the file I read in Croydon was all nonsense. Eldoret, malaria, head of the mine's security – all lies?'

Stella flicked her gloves into the bin and washed her hands again. 'Who knows what the truth is? Still, I believe Sandy when he says Mr Mbuto is in danger and needs rescuing. I've no idea if he's good or bad, though he is a human being, and surely it's wrong for his life to be threatened if we can prevent it. Isn't that also a part of our raison d'être? Hasn't your role always been to save not kill?'

I thought back to Afghanistan and my dishonourable discharge then to the two shots I had fired into the blackness of the crushed car. Stella's philosophy was black and white, too simple. My life and work was more nuanced; decisions often tainted by more than just clinical need. I envied her apparent simplistic approach.

'Come,' said Stella, 'let me help you with your trousers.'

I reached down to pull them up, aware of the item stowed in the back pocket but her hands were already tugging them past my ankles.

'There that's better,' she said. 'And I'll take this, if that's OK with you?' she added, waving the stolen book in front of my face. 'Don't dig, Paul. It will end in tears. Now, I must catch up with Christiaan. Do you want to join us or perhaps you should rest? We're going to be very busy shortly.'

'You go ahead. I'll shower and change into clean clothes – that's if my bag is here. I left it at the New Stanley.'

'I rescued it before the authorities had a chance to search your room. The hotel receptionist was most helpful; a smile and a modest pecuniary gift opens most doors.'

'You knew I had been arrested?'

She nodded.

'Yet you didn't say anything or ask questions about where I'd been taken and why?'

'There's a limit to what I, a humble nurse, can do. As I said earlier, others were better placed to assist. Your things are under my bed and a clean towel in the bathroom. When you're washed and refreshed, join us and we will brief you on what happens next.'

'Humble nurse, my arse,' I thought. 'You are as tough as any of my old Afghan team.'

Stella left the room, and I pulled out my holdall. It didn't seem as if anyone had interfered with it: Everything was still inside including the screwdriver. Before taking a shower though,

I wanted to speak to Adimu. Perhaps she could throw more light on events. *Don't dig advised Stella. Huh, that was definitely a red rag to a bull.*

As I entered the mini intensive therapy unit, Adimu was loading a new syringe of propofol into a pump. 'I hope, doctor, I'm doing the right thing,' she said as I picked up the obs chart again.

'I'm sure you are,' I replied encouragingly. 'How's he doing, any problems?'

'No. He's been very stable throughout. Much better than the others. As you know after a few days of sedation immobility often starts to take its toll. Chest infections, pressure sores and more despite our best efforts. With Mr Mbuto, we've been fortunate.'

'How long has he been asleep?'

'This is day ten. Let's hope you and Stella can move him soon. To be honest, I'm exhausted having worked twelve-hour shifts ever since he arrived. The delay was unexpected.'

'Twelve hours. Who else helped before Stella came?'

'There's always a small team who delivers the patient and one person kindly stayed until your plane landed in Nairobi, then he left.'

'Who was in the team?' I asked, butting in.

'After that, until Stella arrived, I worked non-stop,' she continued, totally ignoring my question. 'It was a relief that nothing untoward happened to my patient during that time.' She pointed to the figure in the bed. 'Thank god, he's so slender and light, otherwise I couldn't have turned him on my own.'

She was right. Covered in a sheet, Mbuto's build had passed me by. He was tall and wiry, totally unlike the security officer I had imagined.

'Adimu, what tribe do you think he belongs to? He doesn't look like a Kikuyu to me.'

Adimu looked at me in surprise. 'Kikuyu? Of course not. Possibly a Turkana or Luo. Certainly from near here, anyway.'

'Did anyone say where the team went to collect him?'

She hesitated, then shook her head. 'My job is to ensure everything is prepared for an arrival and to keep each patient safe until they're moved elsewhere. Usually it's only for a few days. This case has been unusual, though I don't ask questions: I'm paid well and thrilled to use the skills I learnt in Nairobi.'

'Unusual? In what way?'

'Simply in the time it has taken to collect him. The organisation doesn't normally take as long to arrange things. Generally, the team arrives within a day or two. Recently it's been Stella and Dr Sam Everton. Do you know what happened to him? He was always very nice; sometimes brought me little gifts and medicines I struggle to obtain here. I hope he's OK. When I asked Stella and Christiaan, nobody seemed to want to talk about him.'

'Sorry, I've never heard of him,' I replied truthfully. I thought about my own circumstances. *Perhaps the other doctor had worked with the same aims as me. Top up the bank balance and move on, no questions asked.* I changed tack. 'What brought you here if you were working in the capital? After all, it's somewhat remote.'

'Oh, I don't live here permanently. When there aren't patients requiring care, this clinic, like the others, is mothballed.'

'Others?'

'Yes. Didn't they tell you? There's a network of facilities, all equipped to the highest standards. A group of mini private hospitals.'

'Really? That's fascinating. However, you haven't answered my question. Why travel so far for only a few days' work?'

She eyed me knowingly, her smile revealing perfect gleaming white teeth.

'The same as you, I guess, Dr Wright. For the money. It solves many problems.'

'And creates them,' I muttered.

Adimu wrinkled her nose then waved her syringe at the pump stack.

'I don't wish to sound rude Doctor, but are you going to wash? Mr Mbuto hasn't acquired an infection yet, and I'd hate to be held responsible if he does. Anyway, I need to reload the infusers, otherwise he'll wake.'

'What about your pink earrings? In the UK, when on duty, nobody is allowed jewellery except their wedding band. Though yours are beautiful and unusual. Are they coral?'

She nodded.

Adimu was right, of course. I stank. Time to spruce up and time to think. *Mr Mbuto didn't have malaria or any other illness, conceivably no disease at all.*

The shower was cool and refreshing. Dirt mixed with blood streamed down my legs, disappearing with a gurgle into the drain-hole in the corner. I scrubbed my body with soap wondering whether my life was following the filth into the sewer. *A hunted man, a killer maybe three times over, embroiled in an organisation with objectives and methods as murky as the muddy water that slopped around my feet. And yet did I have any other choice than to work alongside Stella, Du Toit and Adimu? Should I flee using guile alone or continue to participate in this strange game, playing the innocent physician?* The water stopped draining, and I wiggled my big toe in the plughole in an attempt to unclog it. *Was it me who had choked it or was there another fugitive hidden in the pipework?* I shivered; not from cold but from fear. Chai's sadistic face surfaced in my mind. There was no choice: Work with the others to escape from Kenya — mission completion; a secondary consideration.

Clean and dressed in fresh clothes, I found Stella and Du Toit in the kitchen engrossed in conversation. Stella looked at me and raised a smile. 'That's better, you look like yourself again,' she said. 'We're discussing how to move Mr Mbuto. It might prove challenging.'

'Because?' I asked.

'Christiaan has just explained the near miss you had at the mine. It seems the Kenyans will use any means to halt this operation.'

'Operation? This sounds increasingly like a military affair.'

Stella, ignoring my comment, glanced at Du Toit. 'Look Paul, it's only a matter of time before we're tracked down. We can't stay here long. Christiaan's suggested we move today. He's willing to fly us all to Ethiopia where we can rendezvous with another aircraft capable of transporting us home.'

'The Cessna's tiny; it will be a challenge for three as it is. Are you suggesting we squeeze in a stretchered patient too?

This is madness. Why not wake Mr Mbuto and let the authorities question him or put him on trial or whatever they intend to do?'

'No can do, Paul. I've strict instructions: Bring him out, come hell or high water. And if that proves impossible…' She hesitated.

'Continue,' I said. 'If we can't, then what?'

Stella glanced again to Du Toit as if seeking his support.

'The Hotel California option. We go, but he never leaves,' she whispered. 'You appreciate as well as anybody circumstances can arise when it becomes necessary to assist someone to go to a better place, depart this world.'

Stella referred to Mr Mbuto as if he was terminally ill. That was bullshit though it wasn't necessary to probe further. Unless I went along with their plan, Mr Mbuto was going to die. Either from the contents of a syringe administered by a so-called health professional, shot by a gun-toting Kenyan Afrikaner or, worse still, tortured to death by his own government.

'OK, what do we have to do?' I asked.

'Help Christiaan refuel the aircraft and remove the rear seats to make space for a scoop stretcher and vacuum mattress. It will be tight, although it's a short hop to Ethiopia so we shouldn't need to do much for our patient during the journey. I'll squat on the floor with him and you sit up front in the co-pilot's seat. Have something to eat while I tell Adimu that we're leaving. She'll be disappointed and relieved. It's been an exhausting stint for her yet despite her dedication, she can't go on forever without a break.'

'Why disappointed?' I asked, baffled.

'It seems unlikely that she will be offered more work anytime soon. London's hinted this might be the final transfer. It's getting too hot here and I don't mean the weather.'

'Isn't she at risk too? What happens to her if she's left behind?'

It was Du Toit who answered. 'I'm sorry. The aircraft can't take more. It will be loaded to the limit as it is. Don't worry about Adimu. Providing she leaves at the same time as us, she should have a head start on the Police and Security Service. She simply has to be herself.'

'So Adimu is not her real name then?'

'What do you think, Paul? Anyway, does it matter? Right, I'm going to sort out the Cessna. Join me when you're ready. Let's aim to leave within the hour.'

Stella turned to me. 'I'll pack my bag and we must make sure everything is organised for the transfer: drugs, oxygen, spare batteries etc. – you know the routine. Adimu can get started. You should check you are happy with all the equipment. Once we depart, there's no turning back.'

'OK. I'll tidy my few things before I help her.'

Just as I reached the door, it burst open and Du Toit returned, looking agitated. 'Fok, fok, fok,' he shouted, 'Someone's messed with the plane. It's been sabotaged.'

Stella's cool demeanour crumpled. 'What do you mean? There's nobody anywhere near who could have known about the aircraft. What's happened to it?'

He held up his hands, both black and oily. 'The cooling system pipes have been cut and the engine sump holed. If I hadn't noticed oil dripping onto the ground, we might have managed to take off although it would have been a short flight.'

'So where was Alamini? He's meant to guard the gate at all times.'

Du Toit wiped his forehead on his sleeve exchanging sweat for grease. 'That little bastard, it must have been him.'

'Why? He has always been reliable.'

'Why? Because the kont's left. Disappeared. I've searched for him everywhere.' Du Toit laughed ironically. 'Do you know the meaning of Alamini, Paul, its literal translation?'

'No, tell me.'

'Trustworthy. What a poepol! Or Arsehole to you.' He twisted his huge hands together as if coiling a rope. 'If I lay my hands on him...'

Stella checked her watch. 'How long do you think he's been gone? It's at least an hour to town and then assuming he's informed the authorities it will take them a similar time to get here. Two hours max in total. We'd better get a move on. Go for Plan B?'

'Yep,' said Du Toit. 'There's no choice. Prepare the patient and be ready for a rough ride. It's going to be a long hard drive. Paul, help me unload the plane and transfer everything to our Defender. Let's hope whoever fucked with the Cessna didn't do the same to the Landrover.'

I followed him outside to the disabled aircraft. Oil dripped from the engine cowling forming a black glistening puddle below. Du Toit spat at it.

'See what the bastard did? Better make sure you know how to use the machine guns. If, I mean when, they return, it will be to kill or capture us, and I have no intention of letting either happen.' Du Toit climbed up onto the fuselage step and was about to open the door when he suddenly stopped.

'What is it?' I asked.

He held up his hand, shielding his eyes from the sun and scanned the road in the distance. 'Dust,' he said, 'lots of it. There's a column of vehicles heading this way. Come on, hurry.' He yanked open the door, climbed inside and tossed out the jerry cans and then heaved the black bag containing the weapons in my direction.

'Careful,' he said. 'There are other potentially useful items beneath the guns. Don't want the pins to fall out unexpectedly, do we?' He climbed back down, patting the aircraft on the nose as he went. 'Sorry old girl, there's no time to fix you. You've been a loyal servant however your time has come.' He knelt beside the black bag, unzipped it, rummaged inside and then held up two grenades. 'If we can't fly her, nor will anyone else. Whoever tries to interfere with her can expect to enjoy a little surprise.' He scrambled back up and secured a grenade under each front seat, tying the firing pins with short lengths of string to the door handles. Booby-traps in place, he gently closed the doors and climbed down. 'There, job done. Right, let's load the Defender. Grab a couple of jerry cans and refill them with diesel. There's a fifty-gallon drum and a hand pump around the side of that shed. We won't make it without refuelling on the way and there are no filling stations.'

It seemed to take ages to fill the cans, the sweat once more pouring off me as I pumped furiously. Now and then I paused to catch breath and scanned the road. Du Toit was right. Someone was coming, and they weren't wasting time. Three vehicles raced towards us, perhaps less than ten minutes away. Diesel spilled onto my shoes as I accidentally overfilled the last twenty litre container. Quickly I snapped on the lids and heaved the cans to the Landrover.

Du Toit had stopped loading the Defender. Instead, he crouched on the ground deftly packing cartridges into magazines scattered at his feet. 'We won't manage to load your patient and get away before whoever is paying us a visit arrives. Help me with these while I work out the best way to defend ourselves. If my suspicions prove correct then there are probably at least two men in each vehicle, possibly four, so we could be facing a dozen. And only three of us.'

'This is madness Du Toit. How do you know whoever they are signal trouble and what do you mean by three?'

He stopped loading rounds and fixed me with a stare. 'If you want to survive Paul, you have to trust me. I can smell danger. You, me and Stella must be prepared. Adimu needs to look after Mr Mbuto.'

'Stella! You have to be joking Du Toit? A nurse who is barely able to walk, let alone run. What about her leg?'

'You're right. She's lame and can't move quickly, though never underestimate her. Like you she's meant to be a healer, yet when your lives are threatened you're allowed to protect yourselves, surely? Let loose with an automatic she is as dangerous as any gun-toting maniac. Though perhaps, with our limited resources, it's better if you are armed with a machine gun and she defends herself with your feeble Enfield and a couple of grenades. Stella always says she loves cricket. This might be her chance to demonstrate her bowling skills.' He laughed nervously as he glanced to the road. 'Bliksem, don't think there's time! Best Stella stays inside. Quick Paul, climb the water tower. From there, you can cover me. I'll greet them at the entrance and find

185

out what they want. If you see me sprint to the small wooden shed to the left of the gate, you'll know we're in trouble. I'll hide my weapon in there. Let's hope I'm wrong. Ideally, everyone leaves here quietly and in one piece.'

I slung the machine gun over my shoulder and climbed the steel ladder to the top of the tower, scalding my hands on the sun-baked rungs. A narrow service platform, ten metres up, guarded by a hand-rail circled the dome of the elevated reservoir. I lay down on it, almost hidden from view though still able to watch the main entrance. Du Toit disappeared into the low-key guardroom, emerged moments later and raced to the gate, securing it with a padlock just as the little convoy skidded to a stop outside: the lead vehicle readily identifiable as a police car, the other two unmarked. A police officer leapt from the passenger side of the first car and strode quickly across to Du Toit. The other vehicles disgorged uniformed men: two, three, five in total; all armed with handguns. The driver of each car remained at the wheel. Du Toit appeared to hold a vigorous conversation with the policeman, and from the way he rattled the locked gate it was clear the officer was becoming agitated.

Suddenly, he drew a pistol and pointed it through the mesh at Du Toit who sprinted away, diving inside the shed as a shot rang out. I aimed at the officer then froze, unable at that moment to let loose the hail of bullets that would have definitely killed him. *No more killing. Perhaps I should give myself up. After all,* I reasoned, *that might save the others.* The policeman stepped back as the lead car reversed a short distance and its driver revved the engine before, with a squeal of rubber, he accelerated forwards. Initially, the chain and padlock held, and the car rammed three times before finally forcing an opening as the gate toppled from its hinges. The vehicles surged through the gap followed by the men. Three headed for the outbuilding where Du Toit was hiding, firing intermittently as they darted across the yard. The others split; one dashed to the Cessna while another ran door to door, trying to enter the barn. Du Toit didn't allow anyone to get near: once they were less than twenty metres from his lair, he squeezed the trigger and fired a brief burst at his assailants. All tumbled to the ground though to begin with, from my vantage point, it was impossible to tell whether they had been hit or were frantically seeking cover. Two bodies writhed briefly before lying motionless while the third desperately scuttled back towards the vehicles, one useless leg dragging in the dirt. A second spit from the machine gun stopped him. 'Oh fuck, Du Toit. There's no way back now,' I muttered to myself and aimed at the man kicking the door that led to the clinic. If he got inside, god knows what would happen to Stella or Adimu let alone the oblivious Mr Mbuto.

I was about to shoot when I heard a single shot and the man fell backwards clutching his stomach. Stella appeared from behind the door, crouched, the Enfield clasped in both hands. I watched in horror as she advanced towards her victim and then kicked the lifeless contorted body before retreating back into the building. Meanwhile, the officer who had approached the Cessna had disappeared from view. I crawled around the metal staging, sporadically glancing over the edge. *Where was he?* Suddenly, as I peered over the parapet, I spotted him sheltering under the Cessna's wing. He stared straight at me. As I ducked down, there was a burst of gunfire; bullets ricocheted off the steel structure and ripped into the huge vessel. I felt warm water gush over me, showering down onto the parched earth far below. Another salvo, closer, perforated the platform I lay on, no more than a few feet away. There was no choice. I waited until the man paused to reload, then knelt, steadied the automatic on the rail, took aim and emptied the whole clip at him. There was a short pause as my shots peppered the aircraft, punching neat holes right through its thin skin, before a massive explosion erupted as one of Du Toit's grenades detonated, igniting the plane's ruptured fuel tanks, creating an intense fireball. Debris flew over my position and screaming shards of red hot metal rained down. I dived for cover, grateful for the water that continued to cascade onto me. Black smoke billowed skywards. I glanced once more at the wreckage. A figure, engulfed in flames, staggered randomly close to the inferno. *The poor bastard.* Briefly, I was mesmerised before I grabbed a second magazine, rammed it into the machine gun and lined up the sights, but again my finger was paralyzed. Flashbacks of Afghanistan and the road leading to Eldoret overwhelmed me. I struggled to hold the weapon, vertiginous and sick, blinded by the dreadful images. The man below screamed as fire tore the clothes from his body and the heat cooked his flesh. 'For Christ's sake, do it Paul. Do it now,' I shouted to myself as the man's scream turned into a high-pitched whistling screech and his skin crackled like a pig on a spit. Smoke wafted past, dense and choking; a mixture of burnt hydrocarbons and protein. I wiped tears from my stinging eyes and ordered myself to take aim again.

Did I fire? I don't know. I've no recollection of the second explosion. When I came to, Du Toit was standing over me, his expression wild.

'You OK, Paul? Good shooting.'

I nodded, soaked and exhausted, my head hurting like hell. Blood from my scalp, mixed with water from the tank, ran down my face. Du Toit helped me to my feet. He took a rag from his pocket and wiped the gash on my forehead.

'You'll live,' he said. 'We've two excellent nurses who will patch you up. Let me help you down.'

'Did I kill him?' I asked, pointing to the charred twisted form lying a few metres from the smoking tangle that was once Du Toit's pride and joy.

It was Du Toit's turn to nod. 'The fucker deserved it,' he grunted. 'You think you can climb down OK?'

I nodded again and descended the ladder, my hands burning once more as I grasped each rung, now heated not just by the sun but by the ferocious blaze too. Despite this, I forced myself to clasp tight partly because I was unsteady but also because I welcomed the pain; a token penance for what I had done.

In the yard, we paused in front of the contorted charcoal mass that no longer seemed human but had taken the form of a ghastly modern sculpture. The sight and stench of burnt flesh forced me to step back.

Du Toit kicked sand at it. 'That Damien Hirst fella would sell that to the highest bidder. And some sick bliksem would pay good money for it.'

'That poor guy certainly paid the ultimate price,' I whispered, fighting a surge of horror induced by my actions. All the dead men had just been doing their job. How many had families or friends waiting for them to come home at the end of this dreadful day, unaware that their loved ones had made the ultimate sacrifice? Guilt started to overwhelm me. *Had we killed them all?* 'What about the drivers?' I asked quietly.

'Two got away. I tried to shoot out their tyres though only managed to stop the police car.' He sounded disappointed.

'And the policeman driving. The one who didn't escape. What happened to him?'

He didn't answer. Instead he shrugged his shoulders and pointed his gun at the black column rising high, obscuring the sun. 'Come, let's go. That smoke will be visible for miles around and I reckon we have less than an hour's head start before the bastards who escaped call for reinforcements. We need to cross the border as soon as possible.'

'Where? Into Somalia?'

'You're joking. That's where they'll be expecting us to hide. No, we must reach Ethiopia. There's only one highway so we'll head north and cross off-road at night. Blessed be the British Landrover. If any vehicle is built to undertake the journey, it will be that one. Go and help the nurses get Mr Mbuto ready. I'll drive around to the entrance and then, together, we can stretcher him out.'

'How far is it to the border?'

'About a hundred clicks. My aim is to reach the outskirts of Malka Mari by dusk. It's a tiny place which lies at the edge of Kenya's least known yet most beautiful national park. You should book a holiday there one day. We just have to hope the Kenyans don't have any assets that are capable of catching us on or off the road before we reach Ethiopia.'

'And once there, what's the plan?'

Du Toit grinned and made a circular motion in the air with his finger. 'Hey, drop the worried face, Paul. As soon as we are out of Kenya, the flying cavalry will come to our rescue and then we'll have nothing more to worry about.'

I didn't share his unbridled confidence.

Chapter 14

In the tiny ITU, the nurses were making the final preparations for our departure. Mr Mbuto had been transferred to a portable ventilator and the sedative infusions continued by the pumps secured to a short drip stand. Stella and Adimu barely looked up as they busied themselves; both working efficiently and precisely, their experience and teamwork self-evident.

'Looks like you have everything under control,' I said. 'Anything I can do?'

Stella pointed to the small pile of medical cases and spare oxygen cylinders. 'Carry those to our transport and then come back to help lift our man. Tell Christiaan, we'll be ready in five minutes.'

It appeared to be more an order than a request; Stella in control. With a rucksack on my back, I grabbed two other bags and headed out. Du Toit had moved the Landrover to the clinic's entrance. He sat on its roof, scanning the horizon with binoculars, a machine gun lying ready by his side.

'Anyone or anything?' I asked.

He shook his head. 'We're OK at the moment. Tell the girls to hurry though, we must move.'

'We'll be ready to load Mr Mbuto within the next few minutes. Everything's packed,' I said.

After three further trips, Du Toit abandoned his position and together we returned to the sanctuary of the secret clinic for the last time, thankful for the air-conditioning that cooled our sweat-soaked clothes.

'Right,' said Stella, her tone more relaxed, 'If you two gentlemen each take an end of the scoop, Adimu and I will make sure nothing gets tangled. Don't rush; it's vital our patient's endotracheal tube isn't dislodged and his drip doesn't fall out.'

On a count of three, we lifted the stretcher with ease. Mr Mbuto was light; definitely built for distance events rather than sprints. Images of Ethiopian athletes winning marathons passed through my mind. *Was Mbuto a good runner, escaping justice in Kenya, like me?* I had yet to be given a plausible explanation for his evacuation. At the first opportunity, I intended to corner Stella and delve into her background and role. A nurse capable of using a handgun without hesitation to deadly effect wasn't a typical health-care worker.

With the patient loaded and secured, Adimu brought out our personal bags and stood waiting to wave us off. Du Toit clambered onto the roof to cover the luggage and spare fuel with a cargo net.

'Paul, watch our man while I say goodbye to Adimu,' said Stella.

Through the rear window of the Landrover, I saw Du Toit shake Adimu's hand before Stella stepped forward and hugged her. The young nurse's shoulders shuddered as she wept. Stella mouthed some words and gave Adimu a small package. Adimu shook her head but took it anyway. Stella joined me in the back of the vehicle while Du Toit climbed into the driver's seat.

'Is Adimu OK?' I asked, concerned.

'She'll be fine,' replied Stella. 'I've made sure she's received her pay and suggested she keep a small memento of her final job.'

'What was it?'

'A Patek Phillipe watch. Gold. Unfortunately, it's designed for a man, although she can sell it someday if necessary. It will be worth a small fortune.'

'Where the devil did you get that from?'

Stella raised her eyebrows. 'You know you shouldn't leave anything on an unconscious patient that might cause problems if their limbs swell.'

I looked at her in astonishment. 'That's theft.'

'Huh! It's a small contribution towards the cost of this operation. Anyway, he won't be needing it.'

He wouldn't be needing it? That didn't sound good.

The Landrover's engine roared into life, and Du Toit stamped on the accelerator. The tyres kicked up sand and grit as our makeshift ambulance swerved around a corpse lying in a pool of blood, the shot-up police car and exited through the gap where the farm gates had once stood.

I glanced back at the scene. Adimu stood motionless, head bowed, surrounded by devastation: police vehicles riddled with bullet holes, fly-ridden corpses amongst the wreckage of the still smouldering Cessna, and beside it the grotesque twisted charred form looking like a burnt bush from a forest fire. A wave of nausea swept over me, not helped by the Landrover's motion as Du Toit wrestled it onto the main road and accelerated hard, ignoring all potholes and fissures in the patchy tarmac.

'Easy Christiaan,' shouted Stella above the din created by the vehicle's panels as they rattled and shook like cymbals. 'We need our precious cargo and us to arrive in one piece!'

Du Toit eased back momentarily before gathering speed again. The highway was quiet with only the occasional lorry rushing past in the opposite direction precariously laden, tilting loads restrained with ropes and straps. If Du Toit encountered a slower vehicle, he ignored any oncoming traffic and overtook, laughing like a lunatic as horrified drivers leant on their horns. As the Landrover bumped and bounced over the deteriorating road, Stella repeatedly checked and tightened the belts which secured patient, stretcher and kit to the vehicle's floor. Outside, despite the sun's slide towards the horizon, the residual heat from the scorched earth cooked the air that blasted through the open windows, offering little relief from the almost unbearable temperature. Stella loosened the sweaty sheet that covered Mr Mbuto and dabbed his face with a damp cloth, trying to provide the best care and attention under the conditions, her charge as vulnerable as an infant.

'Can I help?' I asked, wiping sweat from my own forehead onto a grubby sleeve.

Stella nodded. 'Inside the large cool-box you'll find propofol and chilled drinks. His sedation infusion needs replenishing and I'm dying of thirst; my tongue is desert dry and my head's throbbing.'

It was only then I realised we hadn't eaten or drunk anything since long before the firefight at the farm. However, even with the heat, I found myself shivering. Yet again I imagined I was back in Afghan. This time lying in a shallow ditch during the roaster of a summer's day, caring for a squaddie who was missing his right arm and his Mum. My job to control the haemorrhage from ragged torn arteries, stem the flow of blood that trickled into the dust, calm the screams until the lead stopped flying and we could run to the MERT chopper. Still you never feel so alone when over the radio, and above the din of battle, someone shouts in your ear that the Chinook is U/S, fucked. Then you get scared, really scared. Who's going to win? How much longer can the team hold out as the Taleban reinforce their numbers with motorbike riding, AK toting fighters swarming in from neighbouring villages? It felt like General Custer's last stand, though I knew that if we were overrun then for us, there would be no lasting epitaph. I gave my remaining water to the lad, only nineteen and one limb down, barely able to speak as his life ebbed away. And above, bearded vultures circled, seemingly oblivious to the noise of combat, waiting patiently for their next meal.

Stella nudged me. 'Hey dozy, it's there,' she said, pointing to the white box.

As I stretched for the polystyrene container, the vehicle leapt from the tarmac then lurched violently causing me to smash my head hard against the drip pole, throwing me onto Mr Mbuto. In my dazed state I heard an alarm sound and Stella shouting. She banged on the partition between her and the driver's cab.

'For fucks sake, Christiaan, stop, pull over now! Paul, his tube's out!'

The Landrover slewed to a halt as the ventilator that had kept Mr Mbuto alive pumped life-giving gas through a hose that now lay uselessly on his pillow. Stella grabbed a resus bag and placed the mask over Mr Mbuto's face. 'Squeeze this Paul while I find you a laryngoscope; his oxygen sats are sagging already.'

The light shining through Mr Mbuto's finger, detecting the oxygen depletion in his arteries, prompted the pulse oximeter to alarm as his oxygen levels fell critically low. I frantically squeezed oxygen into his lungs, halting the decline, sustaining him with the invisible gas. Stella passed me the laryngoscope.

'Ready?' I asked. 'Pass me the tube when I say.' I flicked open the scope, activating the intense light at its steel tip. I opened his mouth and slid the shiny blade alongside his tongue deep into his throat, searching for those familiar vocal cords. But his airway brimmed with white liquid – regurgitated naso-gastric feed.

'Suction, Stella, now!' I held out my right hand impatiently as the oximeter shrilled. I heard the electric unit suck air as she switched it on. A rigid tube was placed into my palm and as I thrust it into the goo, the view cleared. Bugger, Mbuto's vocal cords had reflexively clamped shut.

'Sats 50% and falling fast,' called Stella, 'Do something Paul, we're losing him.' It was the first time I recognised fear, bordering on panic, in her voice.

'Give him some sux,' I demanded. 'And pass me the tube.'

Stella fed the narrow plastic tube into my right palm. I waited and watched, laryngoscope held in place in one hand and endotracheal tube poised ready above his larynx in the other. It would be nearly a minute before the drug paralysed his muscles and the throat spasm subsided. The oximeter's tone deepened. Seconds inched past. There wasn't much time left before he would arrest. With relief I saw the thin bands of tissue guarding his airway twitch and part. Swiftly, I slid the simple length of plastic through his cords into the trachea.

'Cuff up, Stella. We're in.'

Using a syringe, Stella inflated the little balloon at the tube's tip, sealing it in place. She re-attached the ventilator, secured the endotracheal tube at Mr Mbuto's mouth and checked the monitors. The oximeter's tone rose as Mr Mbuto's oxygen levels steadily recovered.

'Good work, Paul. I thought we had lost him.'

'No worries. Done it a thousand times.' Though I noticed my hands were shaking.

Stella smiled. 'That's exactly why you're here,' she said.

The door at the rear of the Landrover swung open. Du Toit stood there looking perplexed. 'Is there a problem?' he asked.

Stella shook her head in disbelief. 'Problem, Christiaan? It would be good if you stopped driving as if you were practicing for the bloody Paris-Dakar rally!'

'Sorry,' muttered Du Toit, 'However we have to reach Malka Mari before dusk.'

'Sorry?' retorted Stella. 'Better to arrive late than never.'

'If we don't hurry, we'll be dead anyway,' countered Du Toit and slammed the door shut. A few moments later, the Landrover's engine burst into life once more and with a screech of tyres we set off again. I passed Stella a bottle of water.

'Here, drink this,' I said. 'Ladies first.'

She glared. 'After you. You look like you need it more than me. I'm not a feminist Paul, yet neither am I for this "Ladies first" crap.'

I unscrewed the cap and gulped down half the water before handing it to her. There was no doubt in my mind, if there ever had been any, Stella was tough. Forget the lady bit, she was more of a lad than a lassie. Perhaps the childhood Polio had nurtured her survival instincts.

'So explain,' I yelled above the racket and roar as the Landrover raced on, 'if a helicopter is coming to the rescue why doesn't it fly the extra few miles and collect us from near here? It would be a hell of a lot more comfortable than this.'

'UN,' shouted Stella before taking a swig of water and passing the bottle back to me, 'Can't cross into Kenyan airspace. No-one wants a diplomatic incident, not least us.'

'What did you say? A United Nations chopper? Where from and who gave permission for that?'

Stella leant towards me so I could hear better. 'There are helicopters based at the Kobe Refugee camp and we have a contact there. Christiaan radioed not long before we departed the farm, although apparently our man was in Addis, off-duty. Knowing how he likes the high life, we have to hope he got the call, has had his fill of ganja and girls, and is heading back south.'

I didn't relish the idea of a ride in a helicopter captained by a doped-up, hallucinating pilot. Du Toit clearly disregarded the eight hour bottle to throttle rule, yet choppers and drugs were on a different scale. The Americans had learnt that to their cost in Vietnam. 'You say you know the guy, so who is he?' I asked.

Stella didn't seem to hear, or ignored my question, busying herself with cleaning and tidying away the tools we had just used to save Mr Mbuto's life.

United Nations aircrew coming to rescue a bunch of fugitives carrying an anonymous though clearly invaluable cargo in the form of Mr Mbuto? Another piece of the enigmatic jigsaw? I determined to discover the true purpose of this adventure, fill in the gaps and complete the picture. I had put my life on the line for queen and country too often and always without question. Yet that was as a serving officer years ago. Now, in civilian life, it wasn't unreasonable to expect answers when one's existence was repeatedly being threatened by this mad escapade.

The infuser pushing propofol into Mr Mbuto's veins beeped to indicate it was nearly empty. I took a fresh syringe of the milky fluid, expelled an air bubble from its tip and inserted the next dose into the pump. Mr Mbuto sedated, unconscious, his thin frame quivering with every jolt, totally oblivious to the dramas of the day. For a moment I felt quite envious until I realised that if Stella and I didn't make it then our Mr Mbuto, lying there completely dependent on us, would die too.

Chapter 15

As the sun dropped below the horizon, I sensed the Landrover leave the road, bump along for a few minutes before gently rolling to a stop in a small clearing. Du Toit pulled open the rear doors.

'Anyone need a piss?' he asked. 'We'll wait here until dusk and then drive over the border in the dark.'

'I'm OK, Paul. You go and I'll stay with Mbuto,' said Stella.

I climbed out of the Landrover and stretched; every limb stiff and aching. All around birds flitted amongst the scrub, singing their evening melodies, settling for the night. A warm breeze rustled the tall grass and foliage, and the sky above had turned a crystal-clear deep blue; devoid of clouds and vapour trails. The beauty and tranquillity a complete contrast to the earlier carnage and gore. The battle at the farm seemed a million miles away. Du Toit stood on one foot, performing contortions.

'Tai Chi,' he said. 'Thoroughly recommend it. Good for body and soul. Guarantees a long and healthy life.' After a few more twists and turns, he produced a cigarette.

'Want one?' he asked, offering the open packet. 'Don't usually smoke. However, when it gets rough, I find fags helpful. You wouldn't approve of me downing more beer while I drive. Alcohol, which you will have guessed, is my other vice.'

'No thanks. I have my own ways of dealing with stress and danger,' I replied, amused by his contradictory behaviour.

Du Toit lent against the hot metal of the Landrover and puffed away at his cigarette. 'Like betting?' he asked, probing.

His words stunned me for a moment. *How did he know about that? Who had told him, and what else had he learnt about my past?* It was my turn to ignore the question.

Du Toit took a long drag and ground the fag-end into the rust-red dust with his boot. A series of smoke rings rose into the air as he exhaled.

'Thought you didn't want us to be spotted, issuing Red-Indian signals as you are?' I said.

He chortled. 'We should be OK here though when we drive through the game park you'll need to sit up front with me, armed and alert.'

'Because?'

'Poachers, rangers, cross-border Somali bandits and of course wild animals. Is that enough?'

'Of course, silly me, just a few more hurdles then we're home and dry.'

Du Toit scuffed the dust at his feet. 'You're a sarcastic bastard, Paul. Listen, what we're doing is crucially important. I don't want to fuck up when success is within our grasp. There are only three things I desire: Deliver the patient safely from this place, money and to live — in reverse order of importance, naturally. Now, grab a machine gun and check it's loaded. When we set off, I will concentrate on the driving, steering us out of trouble should it occur. I'll let Stella know the plan.' He disappeared into the rear of the Landrover, leaving me to mull over his words. *"What we are doing is crucially important." So vital that torture and death were tolerated?* It was tempting to wake Mr Mbuto and find out.

Du Toit reappeared carrying duct-tape. He knelt in the sand in front of the vehicle's headlamps.

'Didn't know you were a religious man, Du Toit, praying to St Christopher for a safe passage,' I teased.

'Bugger off,' he retorted and covered each lens with tape, leaving only a narrow horizontal slit.

With darkness falling fast, the Landrover reversed from its hiding place and headed north through the nature reserve, following dusty tracks. Du Toit drove uncharacteristically slowly, weaving a path through endless obstacles: boulders, large enough to rip wheels from axles, ruts as deep as trenches, the headlamps barely lighting the way. Even termite hills tried to block our route; each colony, taller than a man, erect like abstract tombstones casting long grey shadows as the dim lamps picked them out. With the sun gone, I expected some respite from the heat but hot air, as if from a furnace, rose from the parched earth and filtered into the Landrover. I leant out of the window, sub-machine gun on my lap, and looked up. A cascade of stars, a lone planet and no moon. In better times, it would have been a perfect night to camp. I felt Du Toit nudge my arm.

'Paul, check our location. There are some taller trees up front. We should be nearing the Daua River.'

I lifted the portable GPS unit from its cradle and scrutinised the map. 'Yeah, you're right. Looks like it flows north-west to south-east directly in front of us. Should be straight ahead.'

'Good. Hopefully, the water level is low and we can cross, mud and crocodiles permitting.'

'Crocs? I didn't know they lived in such arid places.'

'Wherever there's water in this country, beasts congregate, desperate for a meal. Though they're not the animals we really have to worry about.' He slammed on the brakes, switched off the engine and pointed to a cackle of hyenas. Startled by the Landrover's lights, they blocked the route, their devil-red eyes glowing like rubies. 'Those little fellas are far more dangerous. Most foreigners fear lions and snakes, yet it's those guys who cause trouble for the Gurreh and their stock. All wildlife struggles to survive in in this semi-desert land, so those hunters have to snatch any calories on offer. At least they've an endless supply of termites in reserve.' The hyenas, no longer interested in the strange creature that was the Landrover, padded away into the bush. 'Beautiful, aren't they?' whispered Du Toit, turning the ignition key. 'We'll have to be careful crossing the river. They may be heading that way to drink.'

'Thanks for the warning,' I replied, noting the addition of yet another danger to our journey. 'Anyway, who or what are the Gurreh?'

'Nomads; a unique tribe who live in the park and roam beyond into Ethiopia and Somalia. Borders don't mean anything to them. It's believed they have occupied this territory since long before the concept of nations ever existed, moving freely, where and when they wish.'

'Are they friendly?'

Du Toit screwed up his face. 'The occasional tourist visits this area and I'm not aware of anyone being harassed, but then there isn't usually the offer of such rich pickings.'

'Meaning?'

'Us, of course. Without doubt, there will be a price on our heads and a high one at that. Nobody could blame anyone for seizing the chance to make a few extra shillings. Life's harsh here; the Gurreh must exploit every opportunity.'

The Landrover wended its way through the increasingly dense bush, passing trees and shrubs with impenetrable foliage. I ran my fingers over my weapon, checking. Hyenas, crocs and the indigenous peoples of this remote land all potentially dangerous. 'There's been enough blood-letting for one day,' I thought. All we desired was to pass through quietly, without a stir. Gradually the forest thinned, and the ground changed from hard packed earth to a viscid gloop in which a blanket of reeds grew, so tall they obscured the view. Du Toit drove on slowly, scything a path through the thicket. At any moment the Landrover could be wrecked by a fallen log or slide into one of the many deep channels that fed the river during the sporadic rains. Despite Du Toit's efforts and the four wheel drive, I sensed the tyres slip more and more until finally they lost traction completely. With a final brief spin of the wheels we stopped, stuck up to the axles in thick mud.

'What's happened?' shouted Stella from behind.

'Bliksem, the girl can't cope with this muck,' grunted Du Toit, switching off the engine. He reached under the dash and retrieved a flashlight and a small automatic pistol. 'Here take these,' he said to me. 'Find a tree or rock to use as an anchor for the winch.'

I took the torch and gun, though was reluctant to venture out. Inside there was the continuous hiss of Mbuto's ventilator as it cycled from inspiration to exhalation and back again; a strangely soothing sound. In contrast, through the open window, the outside world seemed alien and menacing. Frogs croaked, crickets chirped amongst the towering grasses, although these friendly conversations were almost drowned out by the incessant whine of a million mosquitoes. I swatted away the first few that ventured in whilst winding the window shut.

'You're not serious Du Toit?' Shining the torch through the windscreen at the wall of green, it was easy to imagine how one could get lost.

'You've got a better idea?' he retorted. 'The longer we wait the greater the chance this machine will sink further and then we're definitely in the shit. Grab a long rope from the back while I pay out the winch and you secure it to the cable. There's a machete amongst the tools. Use that to cut a path as you go but don't drop the rope. You could tie it around your waist to pull on in case you fall into water or deep mud.'

'What about the crocs?' I asked, increasingly nervous.

He patted my shoulder. 'Hey, don't worry. If they get you, it will be quick and we'll know what's happened when we wind in the winch. We might find the brute still hooked on the line. It won't have been my most favourite fishing trip, although at least the catch would make a magnificent trophy or more than a dozen handbags and a great story.'

'OK, OK. That's enough Du Toit. Here, you look after the machine gun.' I wrapped a cloth around my face, tucked the automatic into the belt of my trousers and stepped outside. Immediately swarms of insects attacked, attracted by the torchlight, each creature determined to have the first meal. I slithered to the rear of the Landrover and opened the back, inviting a cloud of insects to swarm inside.

'What are you doing?' demanded Stella, clearly irritated.

'Won't be long. Need a rope and machete. Shift yourself. They're in the toolbox you're sitting on.'

'Well hurry,' she replied, swatting, 'Or both Mr Mbuto and me will need transfusions to replace all the blood being sucked from us.'

With Stella sealed in once again, I attached one end of the rope to the winch cable's hook and set off into the bush with the torch and machete. Paying out the rope, I sliced my way through the undergrowth, mindful of the hidden threats. The cut stems, as sharp as daggers, pierced my trousers, stabbing the skin of my shins. The light from the torch barely penetrated the green curtain in front, its powerful beam attracting hordes of flying creatures; moths, beetles and ever more mosquitoes. I ducked as a bat swooped past my ear with a squeak, making the most of the dense airborne menu. The air, hot, humid and close, caused sweat to pour from me with the exertion. Slow progress. I edged forward warily. My foot caught on something, making me leap. The light focused on a slender black curve. *A snake? The spine of a crocodile?* No, I laughed at my misinterpretation. It was the branch of a tree, fallen long ago, probably swept down-river during a rare flood and still joined to the main trunk, nearly half a metre in diameter. That would do. I tied the rope securely around it, picked up the machete and trod carefully back to the vehicle.

'Think it should hold,' I said to Du Toit, as I climbed inside and slapped at my bare flesh, squashing the biters against my skin.

'Good work,' he said. 'I'll try the winch and gently deliver power to the wheels though we will need all the help we can get so you'd better push as well.'

'You're kidding?' I snapped, 'I've been eaten alive and my legs torn to shreds. How about I drive?'

He shook his head. 'She's my baby. I know exactly how to do this. We'll probably only have one chance. Go on. Hop out before your extra weight makes us sink even deeper.'

To say I was unenthusiastic would be an understatement, although there was no alternative. I covered myself the best I could and stepped outside again. On Du Toit's signal, I heaved my shoulder against the rear of the Landrover. At first the wheels spun, throwing out slime and vegetation then the vehicle began to move, inching forwards out of its muddy trap. I jumped back in, relieved, and handed back the pistol.

'Thank god that worked,' I said.

Du Toit stopped the Landrover and sat there grinning. 'Well done, Paul. Let's hope we don't get bogged down again otherwise you know the score. Now all you have to do is untie the rope.'

'Oh piss,' I muttered as I opened the door yet again.

The Landrover plunged into the river, creating a wave in front that flowed over the bonnet.

'Does it get much deeper?' I asked, eager to avoid a swim as black water swirled around the wheel arches.

Du Toit leaned forward, his face almost against the windscreen. 'Can't see yet. There's not a lot of vegetation so reckon we're probably in the middle.'

He was right. Within a short distance the waters ebbed and the Landrover, washed clean, climbed out at the far side; the bank steeper and not marshy. Soon the vehicle's wheels found an old track, and we started to make better progress.

'We did it,' he said, patting the dashboard as the Landrover gripped firm ground. 'That's my girl.'

'We?' I countered incredulously. 'Don't you think I deserve most of the praise?'

Du Toit snorted. 'Listen. If you hadn't fucked up in Nairobi, we wouldn't have had all this hassle. We could have taken the road straight to the border and would have been safe by now. Look at you — unshaven, covered in dirt and insect bites. Not the picture of the archetypal medic.'

'I'm not convinced it was my fault. I didn't choose to be arrested or interrogated for that matter.'

'True, but I'm sure the man who helped you escape had expected you to incapacitate your guard not kill him.'

How did Du Toit know about Kamau? I flipped down the sun visor and checked my reflection in the vanity mirror. Tired, unshaven and smeared in filth. He was right, of course. My whole professional life had been unconventional, almost anarchic. An ex-military medic who should have been pursuing a noble career within the Health Service, saving lives in the sterile environment of a reputable hospital. Instead I was roaming barren lands as a fugitive and a killer; escorting one vulnerable, comatose man for cash.

Du Toit appeared to read my mind. 'So why did you do it, Paul? What made you join IMS? For the geld or the cause?'

It was the first occasion Du Toit hinted there was a hidden agenda. Could he be persuaded to reveal more?

'It's embarrassing, but I needed the dough. Time is running out to repay a big debt owed to some rather unpleasant people, and I value my health. And you? How about a straight answer? You told me you're a friend of Alex and both of you want to turn back the clock here in Kenya. Is that the only reason? What really made you join IMS?'

209

Du Toit wasn't playing. He ignored my probing and continued. 'If you get home safely Paul, my advice is get help with the gambling. Betting with money is bad enough though to wager with your life is utter madness.'

'I don't like the "if", Du Toit. "When" is better, somewhat more optimistic.'

'Sorry, when. It's just this has been the most challenging delivery to date. I'm wondering if this spells the end of this game. I can't see how the mechanism can work again, given we've left a trail of corpses in our wake.'

So there it was. An admission of sorts. The surreptitious movement of so-called patients had occurred before, but why? Mr Mbuto, an apparently healthy man on his way to the UK, oblivious to our conversation and his journey. The last of many?

'So tell me Du Toit, what has the guy in the back done to deserve this special treatment? What makes him worth so much to the Brits and Kenyans that both are willing to expend lives to have him?'

'I don't know Paul, I really don't. Sometimes it's best not to ask; you may not like the answer. My advice is just take the money and move on.' He glanced at the GPS unit and tapped its blank screen. 'Vervloek dit! The bloody thing seems to have died. Probably got water in the electrics. See what you can do.'

Three times I pressed the on/off button and still the little device failed to respond. 'We'll have to navigate using the stars,' I said. 'Anyway, we should be close to the border by now.'

'Or we could ask them the way,' said Du Toit quietly, bringing the Landrover gently to a halt. 'They must have heard the engine as we crossed the river.'

I looked up. A group of five or six men dressed in white robes and caps, carrying spears and automatic weapons, stood blocking the trail.

'Let's hope they're hunting animals, not humans,' he added.

Du Toit rummaged under his seat, retrieved a bottle, opened the door and stepped out. He waved and called out in a language that, though totally incomprehensible to me, seemed to reassure the group who lowered their weapons as he approached. I heard Stella tapping from behind.

'Paul, what's happened? Why have we stopped?'

'Tribesmen. Du Toit's speaking to them. Think he's asking them whether we're going the right way. All OK in the back?'

'Yes, our patient's stable. No change. Hope we arrive at our destination soon; my body's had it with the thumps and bumps. Feels like I've gone a dozen rounds with Mike Tyson.'

'Yeah, nonetheless, I would bet on you to win that match.'

Du Toit returned to the Landrover and opened the passenger door. 'Move over Paul, this is Awale. He's going to guide us to the border. Says it's not far, only a couple of hours on foot so we should make it long before dawn.' In the headlights, the others passed the bottle between them, swigging the clear liquor and laughing, any possibility of hunting put on hold for the night. Awale grinned as he slid in beside me accompanied by the strong smell of an unwashed man, his friendly smile revealing a mouth full of brown broken teeth. In contrast, his robes were pure white, immaculate, untouched by the dust and grime of the bush. His smile paled as he spotted the sub-machine gun, his face a mixture of fear and envy. In an attempt to reassure him, I unclipped the magazine and handed him the firearm. His expression changed immediately and eyes sparkled with delight as he stroked the gun with one hand, believing it to be a gift. The other clutched the bone handle of a large knife, its blade hidden in a scabbard in a belt at his waist. Awale reached over me and nudged Du Toit who nodded.

'If he gets us safely to the border, he can have it. Once we're across, we will have no more need for weapons.'

Awale's grin broadened. He pointed forwards, spoke a few words in the strange language and Du Toit restarted the Landrover's engine. As the vehicle rolled towards Awale's companions, they waved and stood aside, one of the group acknowledging us with the near-empty bottle.

Sat in the middle, I turned to Du Toit. 'What did you offer to persuade him to act as our guide?'

'Only a ride to Malka Mari and a little cash. We'll drive as close as it is safe for us to go before letting him out. He wants to buy a camel and drink beer. The border lies just north of the settlement so we will skirt around it and then follow the compass.'

'How do you know he won't shop us in return for a bigger reward?'

'He'll have to walk the rest of the way into town and by the time he arrives, we should be celebrating in Addis.'

'That assumes the helicopter comes as expected, or should I say as hoped,' I muttered

'Sometimes Paul, you are such a pessimist. Let me reassure you; Awale won't betray us and our airborne transport will arrive. Sit back and relax, it's nearly over.' He reached across behind me and patted Awale's shoulder.

'Glad you're so confident. After-all, it is not as if anything has gone wrong so far, has it?!' I slumped into the seat, mental and physical exhaustion taking their toll. Still, we had no choice; our lives depended on one man who owed us no favours, and the reliability of a piece of ancient four-wheeled British engineering.

Chapter 16

With dawn breaking, the Landrover bumped onto an empty road and Awale indicated for us to stop. Du Toit applied the brakes and everyone, including Stella, climbed out, desperate for cool fresh air. In the East, a few lights shone, no more than five kilometres away, marking the isolated settlement of Malka Mari. Du Toit gave Awale a few notes and then turned to me.

'Give him the magazine,' he said. 'Empty,' he added.

Reluctantly I handed it over, feeling vulnerable, certain it was a mistake. Just as Awale started his walk towards town, the silence of the dawn was broken by the distant sound of a helicopter approaching.

'Ours?' I asked.

Du Toit, flummoxed, strained to identify the machine that grew rapidly from a far-off speck to something resembling a giant flying black bug silhouetted against the early morning sky, its rotor rhythmically beating the air.

'Is it?' I demanded anxiously, all too aware we had yet to cross the border.

There was no time for an answer. Bright flashes from the helicopter were rapidly followed by ear-splitting explosions as rockets rammed into the earth either side of the road before detonating, throwing dust and dirt high into the air. I threw myself to the ground, shouting to the others to do the same, anticipating more incoming ordnance. Du Toit stood in the middle of the highway, pointing his gun at Awale who was running as fast as he could.

'Get down,' I yelled, covering my head and shaking with fear.

A single shot rang out, and the white-robed figure fell to the ground.

'Paul, grab the gun off the fucker and load it,' ordered Du Toit, 'We have to take out the chopper.' I froze. It was as if I was back on the frontline; lying in a ditch, behind a wall, cowering from the Taleban's RPGs, hearing the bullets from their AKs ricochet off the stones, shattered fragments piercing exposed skin.

'Paul, did you hear me?' he bellowed.

Raising my head, I looked around. The Landrover posed an easy target in the open, its sole occupant immobile and utterly defenceless. A strange sense of envy overwhelmed me: Mr Mbuto drugged, oblivious and about to die without terror or pain. For a moment I would have given anything to change places with him, but then I spotted Stella kneeling to one side, pointing the other sub-machine gun skywards.

'Paul,' she shouted. 'Get off your arse and help.'

The thump of the helicopter grew louder. Moments later, its machine gun rattled, spitting a hundred rounds in our direction. I heard Stella's weapon respond as the grey-green monster circled, poised to attack again. Stella fired another volley, emptying the clip. Almost at once black smoke began to swirl in the aircraft's downdraft. Seconds after, it flipped over in the air and, inverted, crashed to the ground in a burst of flames not more than fifty metres away, spilt fuel igniting the bush. Screams emanated from the inferno. Frozen to the spot, I covered my ears, as the shrieks faded in the fierce blaze. Images of the blackened corpse at the farm and a child's hand under the crushed car vivid in my mind. Someone touched my arm.

'You OK, maat?' said Du Toit, kneeling over me. 'Go and check Awale. If he's still breathing, you know what to do. Stella's already had a look at your patient. He's alive, although his left leg's in a mess. Looks like a few rounds hit the Landrover and he caught some shrapnel. She's busy with a bandage though says his life's not in danger. Come on, we need to shift before they send another chopper.'

Aided by Du Toit, I staggered to my feet and walked down the road.

Awale lay lifeless, face up. Eyes wide, corneas dull and dry, flies already exploring his nostrils, his white robes spattered with blood, a large stain at his chest. A hand still clutched the handle of his knife at the waist, the other a mobile phone. The sub-machine gun rested a few feet from the body, flung away when the bullet met its target. I collected the weapon and the phone and then walked back briskly.

'Dead?' called Du Toit as I climbed into the Landrover.

'As a dodo,' I replied, showing him the mobile.

'Kak, we forgot to tell him to switch it off,' muttered Du Toit, cursing himself.

'I don't remember him making a call,' I responded, confused.

'No, perhaps not, although his friends may have and then it would have been easy for the bastards to track us using Awale's signal.'

'You didn't have to shoot him, Du Toit,' I said quietly.

'No? You might have trusted him, but I certainly wasn't going to let him reach town. We can't afford to take chances.'

'So you intended to kill him all along?'

Du Toit shrugged his shoulders, looked away and turned the ignition key.

'You'd better join your nurse. She could do with some help to patch up your patient. Tell me when you're ready to go.'

In the Landrover I found Stella hanging a litre bag of intravenous fluid.

'He has lost a quite a lot of blood so I'm topping him up,' she said. 'Wounds aren't critical though; most of the bleeding has stopped. Hopefully they won't become infected.'

'What do you want me to do?'

'Another drip would be good. Reckon if we fill him up a bit his blood pressure should improve and as he's a fit man, he'll cope with the haemodilution. Anyway, obviously we haven't any blood to give him so this is the best we can do.' She handed me gloves and a Venflon. 'Veins still look OK at his elbows.'

So she had admitted it at last. Mbuto had not suffered from a deadly tropical disease or multiple trauma, and was definitely not critically ill. A healthy individual placed in peril by his medical attendants; vulnerable to the hazards associated with intensive care and threatened by his injuries. And for what reason? Was it worth the risks?

I popped the sharp needle through his skin and slid the narrow plastic tube into a vein. 'Pass me the line,' I said, and connected him to the bag of clear liquid. I banged on the aluminium partition. 'OK Du Toit, let's go.'

The Landrover sped off, leaping over bumps and boulders. Du Toit had decided we must cross the border before

217

the Kenyans sent reinforcements. Stella tightened Mr Mbuto's straps, and we braced ourselves.

Within half an hour we reached Ethiopia. The boundary between the two nations marked by a single flimsy strand of rusty barbed wire proved no obstacle to the speeding Landrover. Du Toit crashed through the fence and drove further north for ten minutes before stopping under the shade of a tree. A few moments later he appeared at the open rear door.

'We made it,' he announced triumphantly. 'You can get out now. We're safe.'

Stella and I clambered out and rubbed our bruised bodies. The sun had risen, and the air shimmered as it cooked the bare red earth.

'Wow, it's scorching already,' I said taking in a deep dry hot breath. 'How long do we stay here?'

'Not long,' replied Du Toit, exuding confidence. 'Gus, our United Nations contact, should be on his way. I'll switch on my mobile so he can find us.'

'There can't be a phone mast for miles. How are you going to call him?'

Du Toit pressed a few buttons on his hand-held device and raised an eyebrow. 'You only transmit with this kit when you need someone to locate you. Must I say more?'

Stella offered me a bottle taken from the Landrover. 'Drink as much as you want. Fresh supplies are on their way.'

I rested against the trunk of the tree, grateful for the leafy canopy. The water was lukewarm, yet it tasted delicious as the first sip unstuck my tongue. I swirled the second around my mouth, in a vain attempt to cleanse my slime-coated teeth before draining most of the liquid. With the last drops, I splashed my face; enjoying fleeting respite from the heat as the fluid evaporated before the sweltering arid atmosphere resumed its slow cook. The sun continued its relentless climb, foreshortening the shadows. Exhausted yet relieved, I found my eyelids drooping. However, as soon as my eyes closed the horrors of recent days flashed through my mind. The surprise arrest at the hotel, the agony of Chai's interrogation and the fear during my escape from detention. Mwangi skewered, the innocent trapped child, the policemen at the farm killed just doing their duty and young Awale the nomad, shot down purely for carrying a mobile phone. Every episode stained by death and destruction. What would happen next? Who could I trust? My old friend Kamau, an agent of the Kenyan state, had saved me, though why did he risk his position, his life for me? What did he want in return? And then there was Du Toit and Stella, unlikely companions with a common goal; the safe transfer of a certain Mr Mbuto, an objective still vague. And here we were, pursued in one country, now illegals in another, waiting for a United Nations helicopter to whisk us to safety. At least that was the hope.

A repetitive sound, delicate and musical, interrupted my attempt to sleep. I glanced up. A lone tiny brightly coloured bird flitted past, its emerald green plumage a jewel amongst the brown drought-riven branches, its urgent song beautiful yet sorrowful. I wondered what it sought — maybe a lost mate? My thoughts turned to Tina. She was probably laughing with friends, building a new life. Perhaps out with a different man. Did she ever think about me? Did she care? The bird disappeared from view, its melody replaced by the rustle of leaves as a hot wind rose from the north. Suddenly I felt so alone and full of guilt. A doctor who

219

sought adventure, but at great cost. Yes, I had saved lives yet also taken too many. And the strain of it all had inflicted untold damage, creating a self-centred, unforgiving husband and an addict whose gambling habit had brought financial ruin. Tina deserved better, that I couldn't deny, though I missed her so much. If only I could start off over again. Yes, life had played out like a game of snakes and ladders, but the ladder's rungs too often seemed rotten or missing and the snakes venomous and deadly.

'Here he comes!' shouted Du Toit with elation, his outburst disrupting my thoughts.

'Are you sure?' I said, jumping to my feet. Our last airborne visitor had not been so welcome.

'Yes, yes, look for yourself. Approaching from the north, a white chopper.'

He handed me a small pair of binoculars. I adjusted the focus. And he was right; a large single-rotor helicopter with 'UN' stencilled on its cabin. Du Toit leapt into the Landrover and manoeuvred it into a clearing just big enough for a landing zone.

'Gus will be able to spot us here,' he yelled, jumping out of the vehicle and waving. The scream of the aircraft's turbines and the steady thump of its rotor grew louder. A flock of black and white hornbills, startled by the disturbance, flew from their hiding places in the bush, their terrified caws drowned out by the thunder. As the helicopter gently descended, the force of its down-draught created a whirlwind that stripped brittle leaves from trees and spawned a dense choking brown dust-cloud. With the engines shut down, the pulse of the blades slicing through the air slowed and near-silence returned. The aircraft was a Russian Mi-8. I had seen many carcasses of these workhorses in Afghanistan, their empty shells littered the countryside where they fell, scavenged bare until they resembled the carapaces of giant beetles. A figure clad in navy-blue overalls clambered from the machine and waved to Du Toit who, brushing himself off, ran forwards to greet the man.

'Come, Paul,' he shouted, 'Meet Gus, the best chopper pilot this side of anywhere.'

I walked over and shook his hand; his grip was reassuringly firm. The unshaven face suggested life had been hard: skin burnt and leathery, bags below eyes and when he spoke you could see both front teeth were missing.

'Hi, I'm Paul, Great you made it here.' I said, relieved our departure from the border zone was imminent.

'How goes it?' he asked, in a broad Glaswegian accent. 'Is your patient alive and ready to fly? I hear you've had a rough time so the sooner we're airborne the better.'

I nodded enthusiastically, desperate to leave.

'Patient's in there with my nurse,' I said, pointing to the Landrover.

'Yes, how is Stella? Back yet again. She's a tough one, that woman; always a reliable volunteer for the cause.'

'*Back yet again?*' The phrase echoed in my mind. *Yes, Stella was robust. More resilient than many others I worked with in war. She was in a class of her own and I knew this wasn't her first visit. How many so-called patients had she shipped across this border?*

Du Toit interrupted. 'She's fine — we all are, though I expect after this, we may not be needing your services again. We've burnt our bridges here, almost literally. It would be foolish to return.'

'Yeah, the message I received emphasised the urgency. Sounds as if you had a close shave.'

'More than one. It was only a matter of time before our luck ran out. That's the nature of this work. They'll have to find another way to solve their problems.'

I listened intently. *Who were they? What were their problems?* Half of me wanted to probe, the other advocated restraint. Sometimes it was best to just follow orders.

Stella emerged from behind the Landrover. 'Hi Gus,' she called, 'Now will you buggers stop nattering and give me a hand with this stretcher. We're all set to go.'

Within minutes Mr Mbuto, snug in his vacuum mattress and attached to his life support, was strapped securely to the floor of the ageing Soviet-era machine.

Du Toit went over, checked the Landrover and returned. 'You've got everything?' he asked.

'Think so,' I replied.

'Apart from this,' he said, passing me the Enfield. I'll keep the other weapons if it's OK with you.

'You're not coming with us?' I said, surprised.

'No, I prefer to take my chances in the land that I love. With time, and a change of government, my tribe might regain its rightful position.'

He shook my hand warmly. 'Wish you luck, Paul. If I had been a betting man, I wouldn't have wagered on you making it this far. The game is over for me and I'm out. You play it to the end and win. They are all relying on you to succeed.'

He turned to Stella and hugged her tight. 'It's been fun and an honour to work with you, my meisie. We did OK, didn't we? Look me up if you're ever passing.'

'Of course, Christiaan. I could never have managed without you. So where will you go? How will I find you?'

Du Toit gave her a single tender kiss and turned away without another word. As he walked over to the Landrover, he waved over his shoulder. She watched him climb into it, waited while he started the engine and raised a hand as her friend drove off into the bush. For a minute she stood impassively, appearing to wipe her eyes. I hadn't seen her so emotional before and wondered if they had enjoyed more than a simple working relationship.

Chapter 17

'All aboard,' announced Gus, 'We'd best make a start. Your onward transport will be arriving at Addis within the hour.' As we climbed in he handed over three pairs of headphones.

'Better put one set on your guy there if you don't want to deafen him. This old bird's reliable, but the Russians were never interested in creature comforts. The turbines, coupled with the shuddering of the airframe, create a horrendous din. Belt up for take-off. Once we're on our way, help yourselves to the cool box strapped in the rear. Mine's a large beer.' With that, he disappeared into the cockpit.

Stella saw my anxious expression. 'Don't fret Paul, Gus flies best tanked up. Only worry when his alcohol level drops too far; then the shakes begin. I can tell from bitter experience there's nothing worse than our Gus wrestling with the controls when he's sweating and trembling, his mind consumed by his craving.'

With a large puff of black exhaust, the twin turbines kicked into life. The aircraft's old frame shuddered, the vibration magnified by the onset of the rotor's motion. Over the headphones Gus asked if we were ready yet before either of us had time to respond the chopper lifted from the ground, gaining altitude and speed by the second. I gazed down from one of the portholes to see a trail of dust leading south. At its head, a lone vehicle weaved between the scrub. Du Toit was nearly at the border.

Ahead, a ridge of barren hills forced Gus to climb, causing the helicopter to be battered by strong thermals. It all felt strangely comforting. I had experienced similar sensations every time the RAF boys scooped us up in their Chinooks, whisking the team away from the fear and fight of battle. I glanced at a placid Mr Mbuto and saw instead the young squaddie with his arm gone, calmed by morphine. Back then I had smiled gently in an effort to reassure the lad. His war over and short career at an end but at least, unlike so many others, he might have lived. We levelled out, and Gus came over the comms.

'You can unbuckle now. Don't forget my refreshment. It's bloody hot up front.'

I disconnected my headphones and moved to the rear of the chopper while Stella busied herself adjusting Mr Mbuto's restraints.

'Want something?' I mouthed, raising my hand as if drinking.

She nodded. I peered inside the cool box to discover it contained beer and only beer. As I passed Stella, I handed her a can and made my way to the cockpit. Gus, looking the part in his aviator's sunglasses, patted the worn co-pilot's seat indicating I should sit. Strapped in and wired up, I pulled the rings on the two cans and gave him one.

'Cheers,' said Gus, raising the tin to his lips, 'Aye, that tastes good.' And indeed it did. Within moments of drinking the cool golden liquid my head began to swim and the pressures of the past few days slipped away, like Kenya, far behind.

'So Dr Wright, how's it feel to be a member of the team, serving queen and country again?' asked Gus, stuffing his empty can under his seat.

'Do you want to elaborate, Gus?' I replied.

'Come, come, Du Toit filled me in on much of your background even if he sensibly omitted many personal details. I'm sure you understand that in our business, it is always safer to know less. It's a shame about your premature discharge from the Air Force. Tough luck. Still, at least other doors such as this have opened.'

Gus's commentary irritated me; the elation that had accompanied the lift-off replaced by anger and frustration.

'Well, you all seem to know a lot about me. Tell me about yourself – without revealing too much, of course?' I countered. 'I'm sure I know you from somewhere,' I added, aware of a distinct sense of déjà vu.

'Been employed by the UN for nearly a decade. Mainly humanitarian stuff and the occasional shipping of dignitaries and politicians. Spent over a decade in these parts. Would almost call it home. Can't see the UN leaving anytime soon. Too many refugee camps, an endless demand for peacekeepers. Despite the efforts of the international community, the whole region permanently sits on the brink of disaster. Sudan, Ethiopia, Somalia, even Kenya; all suffer from internal power struggles, ideological conflict and cross-border terrorism. None of the problems are soluble unless you eradicate the endemic corruption.'

'So what did you do before?'

'Same game as you though in the Army Air Corps. That's where I learnt my trade and to drink. Took both skills with me when I left – one good, the other less respectable. I'm not trained to do anything else. What about you? What was your legacy from the RAF?'

226

Watching the verdant hills of Southern Ethiopia scoot past below, I contemplated his question. *What were the consequences of my service? Indoctrinated in the ways of military thought, brainwashed to ignore ethical principles, trained to save lives but also to kill. Then when I fucked up, chucked out with all the shit that might cause embarrassment. Dumped alone in the mental gutter to fight my demons in my own way. Result: no money or wife.* I suspected Gus didn't need me to confess about my gambling habit.

Before I could answer, he butted in. 'Well, if anyone has reservations about our mission's ethics, which I don't, remember the pay's excellent and the adventure, though not a patch on a good war, is better than nothing.'

I was struggling to warm to Gus. *A necessary conflict possibly, but a good war? Never.* I had seen pointless death and devastation, so much desolation.

'Nothing like a good war? Is that your honest opinion?' I snapped. 'For Christ's sake, didn't you see the mayhem and misery? Don't know where you fought, though doesn't sound as if you faced the same challenges as me.'

Gus sat quietly for a moment, checking the map strapped to his thigh. 'No,' he said finally. 'War's fucking awful. However, when you're immersed in it, sometimes there's this exhilaration that's difficult to explain. Like simultaneously driving a Formula One car and having an orgasm. And when it stops, you are sapped of emotion and drive, lacking enthusiasm for the mundane. What I do now is my way to reignite the fire and to add to the bargain helps stop conflict. Yeah, war is shit, but those who experience it know how hard it is to let go. Often

227

us veterans find it's easier to replace one addiction with another and mine, I've been told, is steadily destroying my liver.'

'So where and when did you fight?' I asked, mellowing slightly.

'Same place as you,' he said quietly. 'You don't remember me, do you? I was part of the team that hauled you out that time Terry tied you down. We were lucky not to lose more. Airborne and out of danger, I recall seeing you hold that young trooper's remaining hand. The only one on-board wounded rather than dead: the rest, all five of them laid out on the blood-soaked floor — it was left to me to mop out all the congealed blood. It had been one hell of a fucking awful day.'

'Bloody hell, Gus, I'm sorry, I didn't know. I've never forgotten that episode; it comes back to haunt me too often. I was so focused on the task, my mind ignored everything else and I was desperate for that lad to survive. Is it too late to thank you?'

'No apology or thanks needed or expected, mate. We were all doing our job weren't we, as now.' He paused. 'So did he make it, that young soldier?'

I hesitated. 'Yes, I'm sure he did,' I lied. In reality, I wasn't certain. The teenager had lost a lot of blood and was pulseless when I handed him over to the triage guys at Bastion. I had seen them shake their heads and push his trolley into a corner, alone. With resources stretched, others, with better numbers, improved chances, took priority.

'Thank God for that,' replied Gus, 'At least that poor fucker survived.'

'Yes,' I said, 'it was all worth it to save the one.'

Gus stuck his thumb over his shoulder. 'Yeah, it's always worth it, even for him back there.'

He licked his lips. 'Hey, Paul, nip back and find me another beer, would you? Can't run on empty.'

I took off my headphones, unbuckled and made my way to the rear of the aircraft, stopping to check on Stella. 'All OK?' I asked, noting her frown.

'Think so. Though our man's heart rate has risen quite a lot. Up to one hundred and thirty now. Not sure why.'

'He's not losing blood from his wounds, is he?' I continued, concerned.

'No, nothing's seeped through his bandages.'

'That's good. Could be his body's reaction to the vibration of the helicopter, despite the sedation. Does strange things to your physiology. Gus has requested another beer. Can I get you one too?'

She shook her head. 'No thanks. Someone needs to stay in control,'

'Don't worry, I'm not partaking either. Hey, found out Gus worked the same patch as me in Afghan, yet something tells me you knew that already?'

Stella didn't answer. Instead she busied herself writing Mr Mbuto's observations on a chart.

Beer in hand, I returned to the cockpit. 'How long to go?' I asked as I handed it to Gus.

'Forty-five minutes, more or less. The plane's arrived and has been refuelled. We'll park alongside, making it easy to transfer your patient discretely without the assistance of any ground crew. With luck and a fair wind you should be home in time for dinner.'

'What about the Ethiopian authorities? Won't they want to see passports? I lost mine in Nairobi.'

'Oh, I nearly forgot.' He reached for a small black leather case and passed it to me. 'Have a rummage. You should find a replacement.'

I opened the bag and withdrew a slightly tatty red British passport, similar although not identical to the one I had left at the New Stanley Hotel. I flicked through the pages: Stamps and visas from all over the world, including one for Ethiopia. On the first page; definitely my photo, but not my name.

'Who is Dr Nightingale?' I asked, confused.

'You, of course,' retorted Gus. 'A doctor travelling on a British passport with a valid Ethiopian visa, carrying out a vital humanitarian mission. Don't look so worried: The embassy's sorted everything. It should be plain sailing now.'

'And what about you? What's your name in this game?'

'Oh, I'm me, Angus MacCafferty, United Nations employee with all the advantages of a diplomat. You'll find two other passports. One for Stella, aka Anna Templar and the other for a Gathii Chelule, your patient. They'll all pass muster though note the irony of the choice of names. Stella should be Ms Nightingale and you Mr Templar, and I wouldn't have chosen to name the guy on the stretcher after the famous Kenyan long-distance runner, David Chelule. After-all, look at him, he isn't going anywhere fast, is he? Surely, his race is over.'

Clutching the replacement documents, I moved to the back of the aircraft. 'Here Anna, for you and Mr Mbuto,' I said to Stella, as I gave her the new passports. 'From now on, I'm Dr Paul Nightingale and you are the female alter ego of Simon Templar, the Saint. Those Foreign Office folk certainly have a sense of humour. Doubt you read Charteris's boys' stories. As a child, I adored them. The good guys always won and isn't that how it's meant to be?'

She nodded and scrutinised the documents. 'Yes, Dr Nightingale, that's exactly how it should end.'

In the cockpit, Gus worked the radio, negotiating with air traffic control his path to Bole International Airport. Below, the A1 highway from the south merged with the capital's ring road, choked like every other city artery.

'Always glad to be up here when I see those poor buggers stuck in their vehicles,' he said as the Mi8 dropped height. 'Touch down in five.'

I buckled in beside Stella and held up five fingers.

The helicopter swooped over the airport's outlying buildings and landed next to a line of aircraft evenly spaced across the apron. The odd one was shiny and new, yet most were decrepit, dusty and of questionable airworthiness. As Gus shut down the engines, I removed my headphones and turned to Stella.

'Well Ms Templar, let's hope that one there is ours rather than any of those wrecks,' I said, pointing at the anonymous white business jet parked alongside, its stairs deployed. Two faces appeared in the doorway, looking very much like the French crew we last saw at Wilson airport.

Gus joined us at the back. 'When you're sorted, I'll help you with the stretcher and all your kit,' he said. 'However first, I'd better go across and speak to your pilots to make sure they're all set.'

'OK', said Stella, 'we'll be ready after I've swapped his oxygen supply from the concentrator to a cylinder.' She disconnected Mr Mbuto's ventilator and quickly reattached it to the portable gas.

Through the small window I watched Gus greet the two smartly dressed pilots on the steps of the Learjet. They slapped each other's backs, chatted and laughed, and it was obvious they had met many times before. One of them handed Gus an envelope which he stuffed into his pocket before returning to the helicopter.

'Right,' said Gus, 'the jet's been refuelled and flight-plan filed. They are ready; just waiting for you and the authorities, who should arrive soon. Can't move until the immigration officials are happy and sometimes they can be awkward.' He pulled out the envelope and counted out a few banknotes. 'This usually speeds things up a bit.'

'Usually?!' I blurted out.

'Hey Paul, don't pretend you've no idea what's going on. It's a well-oiled machine we've been running.'

He gesticulated towards Mr Mbuto. 'Just a pity that's the final consignment.' He flicked the cash in his hand; hundred-dollar bills, more than a centimetre thick. 'Some for the locals as the reward for carrying out their job, the rest mine; severance pay.'

A small dented yellow van, its paint bleached and peeling, appeared from behind the line of planes and stopped beside the helicopter. Both front doors creaked open, and two officials wearing peaked caps, dark sunglasses and leather gun holsters stepped out.

'Give me your passports and leave this to me,' ordered Gus, before strolling over to meet them.

232

Again it was evident, that for Gus, the process was routine. He shook hands, handed over the documents and a wad of cash. After a cursory examination of each passport, they counted the money before shaking Gus's hand again and returning to their vehicle. The little van screeched away in a dense puff of grey exhaust.

'All sorted,' said Gus, beaming. 'Local dues paid. We can go. Those guys are going to miss their regular bonus.'

'I'll check everything's in order before we lug the stretcher across to the jet,' I said.

'Good idea,' said Stella. 'Say "bonjour" from me.'

So I was right. It was Captain Montpellier and First Officer Delaroux; waiting to whisk us home.

With Mr Mbuto safely transferred, I checked the helicopter one final time for any forgotten kit. Back at the aircraft I found Gus at the foot of the steps hugging Stella, a holdall at his feet.

'Must say goodbye properly,' he said, looking up.

Stella pulled away and wiped her eyes. 'I'd better check my patient,' she muttered hurriedly, and disappeared inside the cabin.

'So what's your plan?' I asked. 'Will you return to the UK?'

'Nae. My life is here in Africa. I love this country, its people and anyway it's always pissing with rain in Glasgow. Expect I'll stay a few more days in Addis, drink too much honey wine and Bedele beer and then fly back to the camp. The UN's task will last for decades, so I won't be out of work.'

I shook his hand. 'Thanks for saving us,' I said.

233

'Hey, drop the melodrama. It was no problem; a simple hop to the border. Always feels good to serve and earn some cash into the bargain.'

'No, in Helmand. Thanks for pulling us out of the shit.'

'Oh that. I was just doing my job, we all were. Look after yourself and if you ever return, I'll stand you a bottle or two of Tej. It's a local speciality, not too strong though delicious.'

'Take care too. And don't abuse that liver,' I said, patting his stomach. 'You only get one.'

Gus grunted. 'Bloody quacks, best ignored,' he said before picking up his bag and walking away towards the terminal.

'Sorry we had to leave you in Nairobi,' said the Captain as I climbed aboard the jet. 'We couldn't risk having the aircraft impounded. Had to fly all the way back to Paris before changing aircraft.' He looked at my appearance in disdain. 'You seem like you've had a rough few days. Still, a successful mission?' he asked, indicating the figure on the stretcher.

I rocked my hand from side to side, recalling the trials of the journey.

'I mean, despite everything, you got your man?' he continued.

'Yes, we did, but we aren't home yet. So let's go.'

'Sure, let's do it.'

Chapter 18

Captain Montpellier pushed the throttles forward and the million dollar jet rose gracefully into the clear evening sky. In the cabin, the dying sun cast a warm red glow. It felt strangely reassuring to be insulated from harm within the confines of this metal tube; safe as if in the womb. While Stella busied herself in her nursing role, I watched the sprawl of Ethiopia's capital fade as the aircraft climbed and sped north. *We had done it. In less than eight hours the plane would land at Biggin Hill followed by a short ambulance trip to the Princess Royal Hospital. Once delivered, Mr Mbuto could be left in safe hands to have his wounds treated. By tomorrow, it would all be over. Pay day and no debts. I might try to contact Tina; see if she would be willing to forgive and forget.*

'Paul, look,' said Stella, tapping her pen against the screen of Mbuto's monitor. 'His pulse has risen further and blood pressure is falling. Do you think we should take a peek at his leg to check the wounds are OK? Perhaps he's becoming septic.'

I glanced at the numbers. 'You're right. Something's amiss and if we don't intervene, then the next few hours might prove critical. Let's remove his dressings.'

Thousands of miles from definitive care, if suffering from an infection, Mr Mbuto could deteriorate so fast there would be no saving him. I didn't want the responsibility of delivering a corpse to the morgue rather than a man with modest injuries to the accident department.

Wearing sterile gloves, Stella peeled away the layers of crepe exposing bloodied swabs; the stench repulsive. With a pair of forceps, she gently removed the sodden dressings.

'No doubt about it, the wound is infected,' I concluded 'Do we have any antibiotics?'

She shook her head. 'No, afraid not. Nearly everything was left at the farm. I grabbed only the drugs I thought we'd need for the journey. Sorry. Though I'm sure we have a bottle of gentian violet — the African "cure-all".

'That should help. Let me find it while you remove all the slough. If we flood the wounds with the lotion, it might buy us enough time.' I had just opened the first bag when Stella called me back.

'Paul, see this. It's disgusting.' She held up her forceps, the tip clasping a tiny white wriggling worm-like creature. 'There are dozens of them,' she said, pointing to the writhing mass in the pus.

'That's impressive,' I replied, much to her disdain.

'What is? They're horrible, like something out of the movie "Alien". I'll get rid of them.'

'No, no, leave them. Haven't you seen maggots before? Left alone, they'll gobble all the bugs and crud, and help clean his wounds. It's remarkable they've appeared so quickly. Back in Afghanistan, flies laid their eggs on corpses within the day, yet I don't recall seeing maggots until the flesh started to rot.'

'But they're so small.'

'Not for long! There's plenty of food.'

'Surely they'll eat into healthy tissues too?'

'No, that's their beauty. They only like the dead stuff. Back home, plastic surgeons still use them to remove dead tissue,

236

although those are specially bred for the task. Let's paste gentian violet on the skin around his wounds and redress them with fresh bandages. I'll mix some adrenaline to stabilise his blood pressure during the few hours left to run.'

With clean dressings in place and the drug infusion in progress, Mr Mbuto's physiology improved. Stella relaxed. 'Want coffee?' she asked. 'I'll make a pot for all of us.'

While she bustled around in the galley, I gazed down to the desert far below. Barren and, from this altitude, seemingly uninhabited. However, I knew the reality was different: a tough environment, home to resilient peoples whose cultures and beliefs developed over centuries sustained them. And we, the West, seemed bent on interfering, meddling in their ways and their wars, ever determined to impose our values.

Stella handed me a mug of coffee and took a sip from her own. 'Captain Montpellier says we're making good progress,' she said. 'Soon we'll cross the Med and he's not expecting any delays with ATC across Europe.'

I think she noticed I wasn't paying her much attention.

'So what's on your mind, Paul?'

I thought for a moment. *Was this the right time to persuade her to reveal everything about herself and this mission or would it be better to keep stumm, take the money and disappear? It might be best to never know.* But something inside niggled. I had risked my life, everyone had, and for what? It wasn't unreasonable to expect answers.

'Look at the desert; it seems so beautiful,' I said, placing my coffee on the table. 'Makes me recall the landscapes I saw from the air in Afghan and Iraq. From up high, it's impossible to believe that down there every human activity and endeavour takes place, good and bad. I convinced myself then that the wars were justified, even honourable, however now I'm not so sure. Why risk everything for a country whose people probably, on balance, don't want you to interfere? Our foreign policies have caused so much misery and destruction. And during this mission to save just one man we have taken lives and destroyed livelihoods. Tell me, why? For what purpose?'

Stella lifted her mug to drink but hesitated. 'Paul, what is it with you? There's something about flying that brings out the philosopher in you. Nevertheless, to answer your question, I suppose you have to decide whether our culture is worth defending. Do our values justify intervention in territories where groups of individuals plot to destroy us? Is our way of life better than theirs? In my opinion, the answer is definitely yes. The ends do justify the means.'

'So, who is he? Isn't it about time you told me the truth?' I asked, pointing to the lone unconscious figure, nestled in his mattress, harnessed to a stretcher.

'Don't force me to tell you, Paul. Remember when I said we had lost our last doctor. He was also inquisitive, made enquiries and eventually found out too much.' She paused. 'When he failed to keep in touch, his ex-wife sounded the alarm. His body was discovered in a London flat — not his own. He had been tortured then strangled with a length of wire weeks earlier. The garrotte had almost separated his head from the torso and being high summer, the corpse had decomposed making immediate identification impossible. The murderer has never been caught.'

'Oh shit, that's awful. Did he have kids?'

'As you might imagine, we were all devastated; he was an excellent physician. And as for a family? Three very young children who will most likely never remember their father. I'm telling you all this, Paul, so that you avoid the same fate.'

'Thanks for the warning. But then again, I'm in this up to my elbows anyway, so whoever killed your last man might equally consider me a target.'

'True, we're all vulnerable, though surely it's better to keep the odds in your favour. Especially you, with your background Paul, should appreciate that.'

'I don't gamble with my life or relationships,' I snapped, angry that she had intimated my problems, although we both knew she was right.

Stella sighed. 'Are you sure?' She reached for my hand and squeezed it. 'Best not dig — unless you want to risk digging your own grave.'

Irritated, I turned away and closed my eyes. I must have fallen asleep because when I opened them again the Alps had appeared, their snow-capped summits, lit by a full moon, poking through dense grey cloud, beneath which, I guessed, it was quite likely raining or snowing. Under this cushion, I imagined the valleys' residents sheltering from a late wintry downpour, embroiled in their everyday existence: farmers and woodsmen, builders and plumbers, teachers and doctors. All walks of life, all able to hear but not see the tiny jet as it slid across the sky, totally ignorant of its precious cargo. Men and women with infinitely different opinions and outlooks, though all human. The division between us merely a fluffy vapour barrier which could quickly dissipate with the wind. So perhaps it was luck rather than providence that set each person on their path. Me, the doctor/airman, Captain Montpellier and his first officer, Stella the nurse and Du Toit the fixer.

And Mr Mbuto, an exceptionally valuable African of unknown origin, having done something so serious, so dramatic, that the Kenyans had risked lives to try to capture him. Instead he had been snatched by IMS and extracted at great expense; the intensive care provided purely a convenient way of preventing him from discovering where he was going and who had abducted him. I scanned the equipment that was keeping him alive. The ventilator's valve cycled with a regular clunk and hiss as it released exhaled gas. The infusion pumps administered life-sustaining fluids, drop by drop, into his body via his naso-gastric tube and veins; each dose represented by a flash of a green LED. Disconnected from the breathing system, he would die in seconds, from the adrenaline after just minutes or hours, and deprived of water or food lifeless within days. Vulnerable as a new-born although manifestly not so innocent.

Stella was right, of course. Employed as one tiny, though vital, cog in the machine, it was still often best to leave the big decisions to the commanders in charge — the bigger picture only revealed on a need-to-know basis. The journey was nearly over, mission soon to be accomplished. I closed my eyes, hoping to catch a few moments more rest before the final road transfer. However every time sleep encroached disturbing images randomly flooded my mind: the sadistic Mr Chai with breakfast dribbling from his curled lips, the burning car and screaming child, bodies lying in blood on the floor of the Chinook, the stench of the blackened twisted corpse at the farm. And each time I fought the horrors, I recalled the sharp pain of a screwdriver being thrust into my thigh. Checking, I rubbed my leg, but no lump or tenderness at the site of injury remained. Had it all been in my imagination? I opened my eyes, unbuckled and stood.

'You OK? Can't sleep?' asked Stella, looking up.

'I'm fine. Just need to check something.'

In the rear of the plane I found my holdall buried under the medical kit. I tugged it from the stack, unzipped it and rummaged inside. My fingers touched a hard object. Yes, the screwdriver was still there, so I pulled it out and examined it closely. There was no doubt. Dried blood smeared into the grooves of its tip. I dropped it back in and closed the bag. Now I was sure — the whole fucking thing was true.

As I returned to my seat Captain Montpellier announced that the aircraft had crossed the channel and commenced its descent. Far below I spotted the welcome sight of Brighton Pier, twinkling like a bejewelled finger as it stretched out into the dark waters towards France.

'Can't be more than twenty minutes to Biggin Hill,' I said to Stella as we busied ourselves checking Mr Mbuto's straps and life support.

The aircraft dipped its port wing and swung west. Stella stopped. 'Paul, the plane's not going to Biggin Hill,' she said quietly, her face impassive.

'No? Why not? Weather? Air traffic?'

'You'll know the chosen airfield very well. We're due to land at your old stomping ground, Lyneham.'

'But the base closed more than five years ago and it's miles from anywhere?'

'Precisely,' mumbled Stella and returned to her duties.

'Everything secure?' came the call from the flight-deck.

'Yes, ready,' answered Stella as the aircraft lost height rapidly.

'Paul, be prepared for a bumpy landing, the runway hasn't been repaired for a while despite our requests.'

'Our requests?'

'The organisation's. If they believe our work is important then it seems reasonable to invest in the base's infrastructure. Maybe they think the sight of heavy machinery might attract unwanted attention.'

'You're very well-informed about the place.'

As ever, she ignored me. I looked forward towards the cockpit. Captain Montpellier was donning night vision goggles.

'Extinguishing all lights now,' announced co-pilot Delaroux.

Through the canopy I saw the M4 motorway snake away to the horizon. I expected to see the runway lights of Lyneham to its south, but the only illumination came from the scattered villages on the Wiltshire plain. No visible cues — so that was why our pilot was using NVGs. I just prayed he had landed there before.

Stella and I sat in darkness as the Learjet made its final approach. In the gloom, her face, calm and composed, almost serene, eerily lit by the faint green glow from the monitors, as enigmatic as the mission itself.

With the lightest of bumps, we touched down. Guided only by the magnified light of a pale moon, Captain Montpellier taxied the plane off the unlit runway towards one of the colossal reinforced concrete hangars that previously housed the RAF's transport fleet. As the aircraft neared the giant grey structure, its massive hangar doors slowly opened and the tiny Learjet rolled inside before gently coming to a halt. Montpellier cut the engines and as the hangar doors closed, the cabin darkened further and near silence ensued. The only sounds within were derived from the regular inflation of Mr Mbuto's lungs and the beeps of his heart monitor. I glanced at Stella to see her smiling with a grin as broad as the cat that had got all the cream.

'Yes?' I said. 'And what now?'

Just as I posed the question, the whole hangar lit up as banks of floodlights were activated. Blinding light penetrated the cabin, forcing me to shield my eyes. When I removed my hands, I saw Montpellier had switched on the cabin's interior lights and Stella already at the aircraft's door deploying the stairs. Just as I rose to join her, a familiar figure stuck his head around the corner.

'Welcome home team,' said Sandy Driffield. He bounded into the cabin, hugged Stella, and then took a long look at Mr Mbuto. 'Yeah, that's him. Well done.' He turned to me, eyes sparkling, arm outstretched. 'Congratulations Dr Wright. A great success.'

I shook his hand without enthusiasm. Sandy gave a wry smile. I was certain he sensed I wanted answers.

'Sorry you had such a rough time during your maiden mission,' he said. 'Hopefully I can offer an explanation, although let's get this guy off the plane first and send him on his way.'

'Is the road ambulance here, I don't see one?' I asked, concerned.

'No. Your task is complete, but your cargo hasn't finished its journey. If you're ready, all you need to do is transfer him to our colleagues waiting over there.' He pointed to a sleek black executive jet, significantly larger than the Learjet and lacking registration marks.

243

'No Sandy. This is my patient, and he needs urgent medical attention for sepsis. Unless his wounds are cleaned, and he's given the right antibiotics, he could be dead within hours. I insist he goes to hospital.'

Sandy slapped me on the back. 'Hey, don't worry. That machine is a flying hospital,' he replied, thumbing at the other jet. 'They carry almost every kind of medicine and can even operate in there. Rest assured, he'll probably receive better and swifter care than if we took him to the local NHS unit.'

I looked across to the other aircraft. Two men dressed in dark blue overalls stood on the steps.

'Problems Sandy? Can we help?' one shouted, his American accent obvious.

'No, all's good,' replied Sandy, 'We'll be over in a minute.'

I turned to Stella for support. 'Our man needs urgent specialist treatment. His pulse is up and blood pressure only OK because of the adrenaline. We have to say no. Once he leaves the ground, he's vulnerable again and will most likely die.'

Stella shrugged her shoulders. 'Sorry Paul. He has to go. I'm sure the Americans will care for him very well. After all, it's in their interest. Once recovered, they'll want to ask him a few questions.'

'So that's it. I guessed right, and you've told me at last — I've been duped into a fucking rendition. And there's me assuming us Brits had abandoned that policy years ago. No, I can't be party to this even if our transatlantic friends request our assistance. It's not right. I won't allow it. He must be admitted to a British hospital.'

Stella bent down and pulled something from her bag. She stood upright and pointed the Enfield at my chest. 'Sorry Paul, out of the aircraft. Mr Mbuto is leaving the UK with or without your help.'

'For fucks sake, Stella. What's that for? Drop the bloody weapon.'

I stepped forward a pace but her hand was steady, finger curled on the trigger.

'Don't make me shoot,' she said. 'Because I will. And it's not worth it. There's been enough killing, and our goal is to prevent more. You may feel you've been deceived; however IMS's ultimate objective is a noble one. Mr Mbuto is responsible for the slaughter of countless innocent people. He's a merchant of death and destruction, a peddler of hatred and misery.'

I didn't believe the revolver was loaded. *Surely Stella had used the last shot at the farm, or had she?* I no longer cared.

'Fuck it. Go on, pull the trigger. You're a really bitter and twisted bitch, aren't you? Full of bullshit.'

'Not bitter,' she replied softly.

'Everything she says is true, Paul.' Sandy had sat in one of the luxurious leather chairs behind me, silently watching the unfolding drama. He indicated for me to join him. 'Come Paul, sit down, you deserve an explanation.'

I sank into the seat. Stella remained standing, gun poised while he began.

'You've heard of al Qaeda, of course. Although that organisation's activities have been superseded by those of ISIS, there remains a core residual group that continues to plan and plot. They are responsible for low-level terrorism funded by extortion, crime and money laundering, though have much bigger aims. Another atrocity on the scale of the twin towers would attract a whole new generation of recruits and reassert their influence. So we have to stop this hydra before its re-birth.'

I butted in. 'You said "we". Who are "we"?'

Sandy leant forward, rested his chin on his interlocked thumbs and stroked his lips with an index finger. 'I'm the head of IMS, a patriotic outfit that provides professional services to our government — for a fee. We deliver success quietly and anonymously.'

I was incredulous. 'Quietly! Hasn't been so peaceful this time, has it?'

Sandy's face hardened. 'No. This mission was exceptionally challenging. I am sorry it had to be your first. I didn't intend for you to return to a war-zone, although we knew you would cope. It was the main reason you were selected. I always back winners.'

'Well that's good to hear,' I retorted.

Sandy ignored my sarcasm and changed tack. 'I've decided to double your pay. It should be enough to fund a break from the NHS unless...' He trailed off.

'Unless?'

'Well, providing you don't take up your old habits and blast the cash in places where you can't win. Consider what happened to your advance.'

My face reddened. I felt exposed and angry. This man knew me inside out. He had a nerve. 'What I do when I walk out of here is entirely my business.'

Sandy gave another wry smile. 'Almost,' he said.

'Meaning?' I demanded.

'Nobody can stop you throwing your money away but you have to consider your responsibilities. May I remind you of your obligations under the Official Secrets Act and I don't wish to sound sentimental, but there are those who love you.'

He had me cornered. Stella nodded in agreement and lowered the weapon.

'Help us, Paul,' she said gently. 'The sooner we handover Mr Mbuto to the Americans, the quicker he receives specialist care. What happens next is not our responsibility.'

'OK. Nevertheless it would be great to know who this guy is for whom we've risked our lives.'

'That's fair,' said Sandy. 'So let me tell you. Our friend here is a Somali and a pirate. One of the most successful. The intelligence agencies believe he masterminded the capture of at least five ships and only released the crews after the payment of huge ransoms. Yet unlike his contemporaries who spend their ill-gotten gains on fast cars and other luxuries, he invested in regional cross-border smuggling, especially weapons. So his wealth and power grew. And all the time he was bankrolling a resurgent al Qaeda.'

'So that's why the Kenyans wanted to get hold of him: to suppress the anarchy within their northern territories.'

Sandy Driffield roared with laughter. 'Come on Paul, this is Africa. Never give credit where it's not due. No, many in the Kenyan government turn a blind eye when to do otherwise would erode their bank balances. They maintain an agreement with these bastards: pay a regular dividend, don't terrorise our people and we will let you operate with impunity. Of course, we couldn't allow such an arrangement to continue.'

247

'But hasn't al Qaeda shown its face in Kenya many times with devastating effect?'

'Yes, true, the system isn't perfect. Sometimes a low-level Kenyan official detains someone without knowing which group they belong to. On other occasions, demands for payment are excessive. Then the terrorists flex their muscles, and if they can hit Western targets at the same time, all the better. Remember the American diplomats killed during the bombing of their embassy in Nairobi or the UK tourists kidnapped while sunning themselves on the white sands of Mombasa. All such events offer ideal propaganda for their bloody cause.'

I stared at the unconscious, defenceless Mr Mbuto. One human in a global population of many billions. Seventy percent water with a sprinkling of minerals and organic carbon whose anomalous brain chemistry filled him with hatred and greed.

'Alright, let's shift the bugger,' I said, standing.

I grabbed a small oxygen cylinder then disconnected his ventilator from the gas concentrator that had dutifully and unceasingly sieved life-sustaining gas from the ambient air. His lungs deflated with an audible sigh. With the cylinder's connector in my palm, I watched his pulse oximeter readings start to fall. Soon the reassuring beep was replaced by an increasing stringent shrill similar in tone to the burning policeman at the farm. Mbuto had caused so much misery; it was tempting to let him die.

'Paul.' Stella nudged me. 'Don't do it.' She tugged the equipment from my hand and thrust the connection into the ventilator. Mbuto's chest steadily rose and fell once more. 'Come,' she said. 'We've done our duty.'

248

As we laid Mr Mbuto's stretcher on the floor of the hangar at the bottom of the black jet's steps the two burly Americans reappeared at their doorway.

'Hey, Wright, fancy meeting you here!' called one.

'Fuck,' I said, jumping to my feet. 'What the devil! Joe Cally. You in this game too? You were at Bastion the last time I saw you, determined to hang up your army boots and grow pineapples; leave medicine forever.'

He held up his hand to high-five. 'Hey, we all need a cover story. And anyway, this isn't routine doctoring, it's far more important.' He pointed to the figure on the stretcher. 'Your guy OK?'

I outlined Mr Mbuto's injuries and explained his deterioration before Stella handed over the notes and observation charts.

'Don't worry Wright, he'll be fine. Once we get airborne, we'll operate to clean and fix his wounds. It will be interesting to see how big the maggots have grown since you last changed his dressings.'

A few minutes later the stretcher with its precious load disappeared inside the black jet. Joe Cally waved from the aircraft's doorway.

'Look after yourself, bud. There are a lot of bad dudes out there. Don't let them get you.'

And with that, the plane's steps retracted into its fuselage and the door slammed shut.

Stella and I stood in silence, our kit littering the floor. 'Let's tidy,' she said at last. 'And then I could do with a bloody stiff drink.'

'I'm buying,' called Sandy from behind. 'However first, I need to borrow Paul.'

I followed him to the far end of the hangar where he opened a door to a maintenance store and waved me inside. 'After you,' he said as he flicked on the lights. Shelves covered the walls: most laden with aircraft spares, others occupied by ammunition boxes and crates of explosives with an armoury bolted to the ground, secured by padlocks. Sandy walked across to a table and two chairs. He gestured for me to sit before occupying the other.

'OK,' he said, 'it's better we deal with the formalities alone.'

'Because?' I replied.

'Well, everything you've heard is true and must be kept secret, yet there are aspects to your mission that are only relevant to you.' He paused. 'First the good bit,' he said withdrawing a fat envelope from his jacket and pushing it across the table towards me. 'Pay as promised — with a bonus.'

'And the not so good bit?' I asked, resting my fingers on the envelope.

Sandy's face gave nothing away. 'Do you still have that screwdriver? I'd like to return it to those hardworking tradesmen.'

'You little shit,' I muttered, barely able to contain my fury. 'You arranged to have me roughed up; it was your guys who were sent to collect my advance.'

Sandy sat back in his chair. 'I couldn't let you run off with five thousand quid without being confident you would deliver. A pity they caught you after your visit to the bookies.

250

Left me with a hell of a lot of explaining to do. It's only because of me that those who were chasing you for their money decided not to pursue you further.'

'Because of you!' I was incredulous. 'It is because of you that I got involved in this crazy caper.'

'Yes. Though you were the right choice, despite your failings. An experienced medic, a war veteran, someone in need of adventure and financial help. A person who, when you consider their record, is fundamentally a patriot. That element was crucial. That's where our last man fell down: far too greedy.'

'What do you mean?'

'Meaning, you can't sell the country's secrets to the highest bidder and not expect to pay a heavy price.'

I stared at him; his eyes cold, face expressionless.

'IMS, whoever they are, was responsible for his death?'

Sandy sat for a moment, slowly tapping each of his fingers in turn on the formica.

'Let's just say, it would be nice if you returned the screwdriver. And there's one other matter to be considered.'

'And that is?' I murmured, my jaws clenched.

Sandy Driffield pulled a scrap of paper from his pocket and held it out. 'Go on, it's yours, take it,' he said, nodding.

I didn't need to. I recognised it from the heading at the top — 'The Thorn Tree Cafe' Below my scribble, my message to Tina. *How had the bastard obtained it?*

'You wouldn't dare!' I shouted, spittle flying from my lips.

Sandy pulled out a handkerchief and wiped his face. 'Calm down, we've no intention of hurting her. I'm just reminding you of your responsibilities.'

251

His answer was ambiguous, yet gave me no choice. I snatched the note, thrust the envelope inside my pocket and pushed away the chair.

'Hang on Paul, sit down, you can't leave quite yet. We haven't had our celebratory drink and there's someone else who's keen to meet you. I'll find Stella, a bottle and some glasses.' He stood, walked to the door, opened it and disappeared.

I held my head in my hands, confused and angry. Driffield had seduced me with his money and threatened me as well. People had died, most innocent, others with blood on their hands. My predecessor had been murdered and if I didn't toe the line, the same fate awaited me. I was up to my neck in this pile of shit and could drown at any moment.

The door opened again, and instead of Sandy Driffield, I looked up to see Stella enter carrying a tray with a bottle of champagne and three flutes, accompanied by a stout middle-aged man wearing a dull suit, his vivid striped tie a bright beacon in an otherwise grey demeanour.

'It's time for that drink?' she said, placing the tray on the table 'Allow me to introduce Mr Somerville from the Foreign Office.'

The grey-haired individual, whose appearance suggested a career about as dramatic as an insurance salesman, stepped forward and held out his hand, his convivial smile stretching his slack jowls.

'Dr Wright, we meet at last. Sandy has spoken highly of you. On behalf of Her Majesty's Government, and our French and American colleagues, allow me to offer my congratulations on a job well done. Glad you got out safely. I've been told that you've had one hell of a week. You must be exhausted. I'm going to offer you the chance to enjoy a few days rest at a delightful rural retreat in Yorkshire. It's a large private house owned by a retired major who understands our work. He'll look after you until you feel better. And we have contacts in a nearby clinic should you wish to receive help for your psychological difficulties. Sandy can make all the arrangements. Unlike other services, we really try to look after our own. Despite deploying all our local assets, I'm sorry we weren't able to trace you after that unfortunate business in Nairobi. We had hoped the note you left might have given us a clue as to your whereabouts. Anyway, all's well that ends well. Please enjoy the champagne. I'm sorry not to join you: have an urgent report to write for an impatient minister.' And without another word, he was gone too.

'Drink?' asked Stella, untying the wire. 'Courtesy of the boss.'

'Which one?' I said. 'Sandy or Mr Somerville. Who was really behind all this?'

'Huh, not Sandy!' scoffed Stella. 'Mr Somerville's always in charge.'

'Is that his real name and does he really work for the Foreign Office or is there another twist to this tale?'

Stella began to lever the cork from the bottle.

'He's usually better known by his formal work title.'

'Which is?'

'Control.'

'Sounds like an Ian Fleming character. I assume he owns a white cat?'

'Control operates on the right side, Paul. He's the head of one of our more secretive branches of the Civil Service.'

Just as the cork popped, the sound of jet engines shook the air. Stella filled two trembling glasses, passed me one and then clinked hers against mine.

'You're a good guy, Paul.'

'Thanks for the flattery, but tell me one thing.'

'And that is?' she replied, sipping her champagne.

'Would you have killed me?'

Stella paused with the glass held to her lips before bursting into laughter. 'Don't forget, I'm just a nurse, a health professional.'

'Professional certainly,' I countered, recognising the futility of pursuing the question.

'I would have liked to have thanked the crew,' I shouted above the din.

'You'll have the opportunity to do that on a future mission,' she said, raising her glass.

Prologue

'A lie that is half-truth is the darkest of all lies.'

Alfred Tennyson

'Accident or...?' The police inspector glanced up from his notebook and interrupted the tall middle-aged man standing in front of him. 'I'm sorry sir; I didn't catch your name. Your ID please.'
Mater withdrew a card from his wallet and held it up.

The officer raised his eyebrows, noting the service shown. 'Did she work for you?' enquired the policeman.

Mater ignored the inappropriate question. 'If you don't mind, inspector, there is little time. I need to see the body.'

'Of course, sir, but I warn you the vehicle that hit her must have been travelling very fast.' He pointed to a small table beside a large blue and white tent emblazoned with 'Police'. 'Your PPE. Please wear the full kit. Forensics have yet to complete their work.'

Mater donned a barrier suit, facemask and a pair of nitrile gloves. For an early spring day in Essex, it was surprisingly warm and immediately sweat started to pool inside the impervious material. He stepped over the boundary tape and into the tent that protected the incident scene, preparing himself for the sight within. He was used to grim viewing but despite this, the task he faced was never easy and had grown more challenging as he aged.

Her head had been squashed against the kerb like a mashed rotten pumpkin. Bloody brains, flesh and matted hair; face distorted as the image created by a comic mirror. The mouth, lipstick smeared, lay open with a bloody hole where there were once perfect teeth. One leg, bent in the wrong direction with a fractured bone protruding through ripped jeans, revealed an obvious tyre mark rising up the thigh, at the top of which was a tattoo; unusual in design and location, disrupted by a red wound, almost a scar, but it told Mater what he needed to know. Although surprised that her mangled body failed to shock him, he felt an overwhelming sense of despair and depression. Unlike many, he never thought her attractive but now her basic humanity was gone and, more importantly to him, as an asset she was no longer effective. Intellect and experience spread on the cold tarmac of a minor road in the English Home Counties. His work taught him to be hard; there could be no other way. He turned and stepped from the tent with the picture of her exposed brain burning into his memory. Normally, he would have visited her grieving relatives straightaway to explain, but the current crisis prevented him from doing this or even attending her funeral. At some point, however, he would need to meet her family. Then, he wanted to be sure that what was said, what he added to their understanding, would be, for once, accurate and truthful. Everything else about him or his organisation could be a lie, one big white lie but in death others had to be told the truth; recognising their loss had not been in vain.

As Mater removed his protective clothing, the policeman approached.

'Seen all you need to see, sir?' he enquired, wondering if the man undressing in front of him might divulge the body's identity or why he was interested in her.

He tried to be courteous. 'Thank you, Inspector, plenty. Please ask the investigating officer to send me a copy of their report as soon as possible.' He handed a card to the policeman with a name and London address. 'And you're right; the vehicle must have been travelling fast.'

Mater strode back to his car, retrieved his mobile from his pocket and speed dialled as he walked. His call answered, he tapped in further digits and spoke clearly and briefly. Within seconds the speech recognition security system put him through.

'Your conclusion or at least supposition M please,' requested the voice.

Mater knew better than to conclude but had little doubt. 'I think targeted likely, an unfortunate accident most improbable, sir. We'll see what the CID come up with, but it was a sunny, dry day, a straight road and the speed limit low. She didn't have a chance. You should receive the formal Police report within days. I'll travel back North straightaway.'

Call over. Another life ended. Time to act. He needed Control's agreement and assistance, but couldn't afford to delay much longer. The score didn't look good.

Printed in Great Britain
by Amazon

51298313R00158